# YOUNG RHIANNON IN THE TEMPLE OF ISIS

## WINGS IN THE NIGHT
### BOOK TWENTY-FOUR

## MAGGIE SHAYNE

OLIVERHEBERBOOKS

Created with Vellum

# A Note from Maggie

Dear Reader,

This is Rhiannon's origin story! It covers her life from age 5 to 20 There is a lot more to tell, but there are some crucial things here, and I'm dying to know if you pick up on the big clue I dropped about Pandora.

I love Rhiannon. I will continue her stories for as long as I live. Promise. She's lived thousands of years, so there are lots more to tell.

A couple of housekeeping things: Please don't write and tell me there was no Temple of Isis in Ancient Egypt, because:

A. I know that's what the books say.

B. I don't believe it for a minute.

There had to be. Just because we haven't unearthed it, doesn't mean it wasn't there. But since there's no proof it was, I'm using what's known as poetic license here.

The second thing I expect to get mail about is that in this story, they don't eat meat or wear animal-derived clothing in the temple. I expect folks will think I put that in because I'm vegan. But no, it's a real fact. I actually stumbled upon it while researching other things about temple life in ancient Egypt.

There are now officially 24 stories in the Official Wings in the Night Universe. And I absolutely adore every single one of them.

But like its characters, this series will live on...

*and on...*

*and on...*

*and on...*

# PRAISE FOR MAGGIE SHAYNE

"My inspiration has always been Maggie Shayne and her Wings in the Night Series. Sexy, thrilling, a must-read!" ~***1 *New York Times* Bestselling Author CHRISTINE FEEHAN

"Maggie Shayne's books have a permanent spot on my keeper shelf. She writes wonderful stories combining romance with page-turning thrills, and I highly recommend her to any fan of romantic suspense." ~KAREN ROBARDS

"Readers will feel as if they can touch the connection sizzling between the duo. This story will have readers on the edge of their seats and begging for more." ~ RT BOOK-CLUB MAGAZINE (Review of Twilight Fulfilled)

"One of the strongest, most original voices in romance fiction today." ~ Bestselling Author ANNE STUART

"Creepy, chilling and compelling. Simply spellbinding!" ~ New York Times Bestselling Author SHANNON DRAKE

# CHAPTER I
# JEWELS OF THE GODDESS

I, Rhianikki, firstborn of Pharaoh, stood in a straight line with the other five-year-old girls, and not even at the *front* of the line. We all wore the same white linen dresses with straps over both shoulders. We wore no silk aprons, no golden girdles, no precious stones. Our sandals were woven papyrus with long, pointed toes that curled up and back around—every pair, just the same.

I hated it!

We'd been told to line up here, in the temple garden, which was rife with fruit trees, fragrant herbs, and flowers of all sorts. There were twisting stone paths all through it, with wider stone floors for gathering. It was open to the summer sky above but surrounded on all three sides by the gleaming Temple of Isis. Its fourth side was made of bushes and shrubs with an opening in the center for passing in and out, and beyond lay the desert. The temple's walls were made of white stone blocks bigger than I, and they blazed like the sun when the rays of Ra hit it just before sunset.

In one end of the garden, there was a fountain with a pool at its base. A golden statue of Isis stood on a raised stone dais as tall as a person. Her wings were spread wide, and arced forward, as if she were offering a hug. Her face, arms, and flowing skirt were carved of smooth black onyx. Her glorious wings, skirt, arm bands and headpiece were made of pure gold. Water flowed upward, as if by magic, bubbling out around her feet before tumbling down the head-high dais into the circular pool below.

A beautiful, dark-skinned woman with long black hair that hung in a thousand braids, stood before us. She wore white linen, too, but the front of her dress was pleated. Over one shoulder, she wore the red sash of the temple, and around her waist, the girdle of her station, a black cord shot through with threads of silver and gold.

"I am Priestess Elana," she said, and she walked slowly in front of us, pausing to examine each of our faces for long moments. When she came to me, I gazed right back into her eyes and did not blink. She did, though, and then she moved on.

"You have been given by your families in service to Isis, and to this, her temple. How you serve here reflects upon your family's honor."

*My family.* I seethed at the word. I was firstborn to Pharaoh, but my mother had died giving birth to me. My father had taken a new queen who had born him twin sons.

At first, I had adored the infants, despite their incessant squalling. But soon, my father had sent me away from the palace to serve in the temple. He said I could no longer be heir to the throne. His heirs would be the new queen's sons, in order of their birth.

A breeze stirred the air and I heard the ringing of chimes. The beautiful priestess went on as if she'd sensed the fury inside me. Or more likely, she'd seen it in my eyes.

"You must not be angry with your families for sending

you here," she said, and her words caught my attention despite my rage. "Gifts to the goddess must be the finest and the best we have to offer. The first fruits. Anything less would offend the goddess and invite her wrath."

I tilted my head and listened more closely.

"Only the best, the most gifted girls and boys are sent to serve the gods. You are special, every one of you."

Some more than others, I thought, looking at the girls around me. None of *them* had divine blood. I was born of Pharaoh, a god himself, although a cruel and shortsighted one. I would be ten times the leader those mewling runts could ever be.

"Here you will learn of the gods, their stories and their history. You'll learn how to properly serve them, and you will learn the secrets of magic."

My head swiveled toward her and I blurted, "Magic?" Then I clapped a hand over my mouth. My father would have slapped me for interrupting, had he been the one speaking.

But Priestess Elana smiled at me. "Yes. Magic."

Something in her eyes spoke to something in mine, but only for a moment. It was as if she recognized my greatness already. "That is all for now. You may enjoy your breakfast here in the garden and then we will begin your lessons.

I saw servants carrying trays laden with fruits and breads into the garden. These, they placed on flat-topped stands and pedestals.

The girls around me scattered, rushing to gather all they could carry. Some even used their skirts to carry more. Each went to the fountain to offer the very best piece to the goddess before finding a spot to sit and eat their own. I alone stayed behind, watching them.

"You are pensive, Rhianikki?"

I was stunned at Priestess Elana's familiarity. "I am called 'my lady, my sun, my princess,' or 'my goddess.'"

"Yes, by those who served you in the palace. But here, *you* serve. In that way, you are equal to the rest of us here."

I blinked very slowly because her words made no sense to me. None of the people here was my equal. Not Priestess Elana—not even Naiya, the high priestess herself. I was no longer convinced that even my father was my superior, having made the sand-headed decision to send me here.

To *serve*. Ha!

"You are only five years old. You will come to understand, in time."

Oh no I would not. But maybe *she* would. "I will eat now."

"Yes, you may get some breakfast.

"I was not asking." I lifted my chin as I went toward the nearest tray of food, the ridiculous sandals slapping the stone as I walked. A mountain of fruits and breads made from the grains grown along the banks of the Nile awaited me. I took the very biggest, most moist looking slice of bread and brought it to my mouth.

"Rhianikki, wait!"

I froze, thinking there must be a wasp about to sting or a cobra about to strike.

It was the High Priestess Naiya, who'd shouted, I realized as I found her with my eyes. She was far older and less friendly than Priestess Elana. She had come out into the garden and stood near the fountain that splashed endlessly by whatever magic lived in this place. Her hair was long, jet black and shot through with white as if she'd walked through a forest of spiderwebs. She wore it in a single braid that fell across her right shoulder. Her skin was sun-bronzed and wrinkled. She was making her way toward me.

Both red and gold sashes crossed over her linen dress, one over each shoulder, draping well past her knees, and her corded girdle looked to be mostly made of gold threads.

In spite of it all, she still wore the stupid papyrus sandals. Apparently, there was no hope of graduating past them here.

"What?" I asked.

She raised her eyebrows where light and dark seemed to be at war, maybe due to the note of impatience in my tone. "We give offerings and thanks *before* we eat. The gods must always be fed first. No doubt you chose the very best slice of bread. Bring it along, over here."

She turned, pointing. The statue of the great goddess stood there, wing and arms open wide. She looked like me, I thought. There was a basket on the dais above the water, for offerings.

As soon as High Priestess Naiya turned and started toward the goddess, I swapped my bread for a different slice.

She looked behind her. I held the bread in my palms in front of me and looked up at her with as much innocence as I could fake. Her eyebrows bent low, but she turned around again and kept walking, and I followed.

We stopped before Isis. High Priestess Naiya bowed deeply. "Accept this offering, oh great goddess Isis, lady of the dog star, eye of Ra, adored by men, envied by women, I offer you the finest part of my meal. Thank you for providing for your people, oh great Isis." Turning her head slightly, she said, "Repeat."

"Oh mighty Isis—"

"Oh *great* Isis," the high priestess corrected.

"Mighty is a far superior word to great."

She blinked down at me, then lifting her eyes slightly,

looked past me. I glanced over my shoulder in time to see Priestess Elana, her hands over her lips to hide her smile, but I could see it clearly in her eyes.

"Nonetheless, child—"

"Princess," I corrected. And then I repeated her stupid words verbatim, mostly, just to show her I was not stupid. "Accept this offering, oh great Isis, lady of the dog star, eye of Ra, adored by men, envied by women. I, Rhianniki, Daughter of Pharaoh, adored by all and rightful heir to the throne of Egypt, offer you the finest part of my meal. Thank you for providing for my people, o great... and *mighty* Isis."

I looked at the high priestess, who was watching me with one eyebrow crooked up higher than the other. I was thinking only about getting back to that tray before someone stole my perfect, wonderful slice of bread.

"Bless all who serve in this temple and teach them of your ways. So be it."

"So be it," I repeated. "I will eat now."

As I turned away, I heard the high priestess mutter, "Forgive her, oh Isis. She is... well she is Rhianikki."

I looked back at her, in case I wasn't supposed to go, but she nodded and waved me away. I sped to the food table and snatched my bread just as another hand reached for it.

The little girl I'd beaten sent me a surprised look, but when I glared, she backed away. I helped myself to a handful of dates and looked around the garden for a place to sit.

There were other girls gathered and talking as if they knew each other or were beginning to. I had no need for friendship, however. I had noticed something of interest back at the fountain, so I carried my food that way, and found a wide spot to sit atop its short stone wall. I gazed into the pool at the fountain's base as I ate.

There were jewels in there, gemstone beads and pieces that gleamed like gold. I took a bite of my bread as I studied them. Oh, it tasted even better than it looked!

"When people come here, they leave offerings in the goddess's pool to win her favor." Priestess Elana had come to join me. She sat on the stone wall, nibbling her own slice of bread.

"What does the goddess do with them?" I looked at the statue. Isis wore no jewelry at all, except that which was carved into her stone and engraved in her gold. "If I were her, I would not like that one bit—all those gifts at her feet and she can't even pick them up and put them on."

"It is the value of the gift, the sacrifice of giving it that the goddess imbibes, not its physical form. Like when we eat the nut but leave the shell."

"I see."

"Do you?"

"Yes, I do." I continued eating my bread, having finished the conversation.

The next morning, when we lined up as we did every morning in the temple garden, before the statue of Isis and her sacred fountain, I wore my white linen dress just like all the others. Around my waist, I'd tied a strand of precious gemstone lapis lazuli and golden topaz beads all strung on twine. Around my neck hung a strand of onyx beads, around my wrist, four silver bracelets, and holding my dress across my left shoulder, a golden buckle.

I still had no headpiece worthy of my station, so I'd

braided the blossoms from the hibiscus plants to create my own.

Priestess Elana stood before us, and when she saw me, her eyes widened. She kept opening her mouth and then closing it again.

High Priestess Naiya, noticing the silence as she passed the open archway between the temple and the garden, came out to join us, looked at me, and then clapped a hand over her mouth and turned away. Her shoulders were shaking. I thought she might be crying, and broke ranks to run to her and put my hand on her back.

"Do not weep, High Priestess Naiya. I gave the finest to Isis first! Look!" I pointed to the statue.

Priestess Elana came to stand on my right. High Priestess Naiya was on my left, both facing the statue of Isis, which was now draped in jewels I had rescued from the pool. I had strung amber with jet, and moonstone with blue topaz, and I'd draped strands all up and down her wings. I'd dangled golden cuffs from her headpiece and piled more at her feet.

"Isis is pleased," I said.

Both women looked at me sharply. "What makes you say so, Rhianikki?"

I shrugged. My jewels jingled like music. "Look at her. She's smiling, can't you see it?"

They looked at the statue, then at each other, and then they looked at me.

"Well, maybe *you* can't see it, but I can. Probably because I am part goddess myself, as you know." I turned to the other girls, who'd stayed in line waiting, because I wanted to make sure they had heard me clearly. "I am the daughter of Pharaoh, who is divine, which makes me divine, too," I said. Then I added, "Divine means *of the gods*," for the little girl who was frowning hardest.

I turned back to my teachers and my necklaces jangled again. "I am ready for the day's lessons now."

The two women were still staring at the statue. The high priestess frowned, tilting her head to one side and squinting. "Elana, do *you* think she is smiling?" she whispered as I walked away.

"I think... she might be," Priestess Elana replied. "Yes. I think she is."

CHAPTER 2

# LESSONS IN MAGIC

"I am bored."

The priest's shiny bald head was more interesting than the lessons. I had been staring at it for a while, but not a single hair had sprouted.

I was sitting upon a large silk pillow sent to me from my father the pharaoh. Other girls sat upon the gleaming white stone floor. Unlike our other teachers, Priest Zebet never bothered putting mats on the floor for his students. I was glad he was only a "visiting" teacher and would move on at the conclusion of the astrology class. The Temple of Isis was all women. No men resided here.

His droning about the positions of the stars was putting me to sleep. He wore white linen wrapped around his waist and a red sash crossways from his right shoulder to left hip as a sign of his station. The sash was also linen. We were forbidden to wear clothing derived from animals in the Temple, as was the case at all of Egypt's temples. Animal hides were unclean and carried with them the taint of death. It was the first lesson we had been taught.

"Can one die of boredom?" I asked, when my initial comment failed to get the priest's attention.

"There is nothing boring about astrology," Priest Zebet said. "It has been used to predict wars, famine, plague—"

"Predict. Who cares what you can predict? It is the person who can *cause* wars, famine, and plague who has the power."

He raised his eyebrows. "Or the one who can prevent them," he said, correcting me.

I shrugged. "That, too, I suppose."

"And yet the will of the gods is beyond our control, Princess Rhianikki. So there is no such person. This is why we give offerings and sacrifices, to placate the gods that they might show us their favor. Ultimately, however, we have no control."

Finger to my cheek in thought, I said, "I wonder..."

"You needn't *wonder*. I have just *told* you."

I lowered my head, having learned better than to argue with the priest, or any priest who might have cause to visit the Temple of Isis. They were impatient, filled with ego, and prone to punishing young priestesses-in-training for the smallest of reasons. But I disagreed with much of what they taught me, and I cared about *almost* none of it.

"You would do well to pay attention, Princess. You cannot move on to the lessons you long for until you have mastered the basics."

"I have been in this temple studying your basics for six months," I said. "I know all the gods, their names, their powers, and their unlikely stories. I know all the stars and constellations and how they are said to influence our lives. I know how to make offerings and keep the temple and its gardens, and I've shown you as much every time you have demanded it."

I had risen to my feet. The other girls scooted a little farther away from me, watching the two of us with wide eyes.

He opened his mouth but closed it again, deciding against his argument. "It is true," he said. "You have excelled in all your studies, and in all the tasks you've been assigned. But the rest of the class must still–"

"Obviously you cannot hold me to *their* pace. I am part goddess, after all. My father is—"

"I am well aware who your father is, Princess."

"Continuing to teach me what I already know is a waste of my time, is it not? The pharaoh sent me here to learn, not to die of boredom, not be a servant who sweeps the floors and cleans up the offerings when the gods have sucked all the life out of them. I do not think he would be pleased to know that I—"

He held up both hands, palms toward me. He might have intended it as a command for my silence, but it looked more like a plea from where I stood.

I went quiet, just to see if I had yet won.

He heaved a heavy sigh. "Tomorrow, you may observe the older girls' lesson in magic."

My smile went so wide it might have split my face.

"But you may not participate, Rhianikki—only observe."

"Yes, Priest Zebet. I understand. Thank you." I managed to sound humble and grateful, despite that as a princess of Egypt I ought to be able to do whatever I wanted in this temple. Still, I was small and could not physically force adults to comply.

Once I learned to wield magic, however, I expected that to change.

I was up before dawn, bathed, dressed in my best Kalasiris dress. It had been dyed light blue, the color that denoted the first year of study at the temple. We'd received them on our second day. But of course, mine was not plain like everyone else's. I had created a necklace and belt from deep blue lapis lazuli beads interspersed with white shells I had gathered along the banks of the Nile.

I was in the garden long before theh servants brought our breakfast. I paced for a while, then paused in front of Isis and her bubbling water and wondered what made it flow. I gazed up at her face, smiled at her, and spoke to her, goddess to goddess.

"Isis," I said. "I wish to wield magic. If you can help me, you should, for we are sisters, after all." I took off my necklace, held it in my hands and inspected it. It would make a very good offering—maybe the best offering ever. Extending my arm, I held it out over the water. Then I thought for a moment, brought it back in, and draped it around my neck once more. "I will give you the necklace *after* you give me my magic." That seemed a much more reliable system than the one most people used.

I heard voices and soft papyrus sandals shushing over stone. The other girls were coming outside in small groups. As they formed a line, I went to join them. I kept my eyes level, gazing at each of them as I approached, but they avoided my gaze, and if they caught it by chance, looked away quickly. They feared me, but only because of who my father was. They could not know how little he cared for his firstborn.

I took a spot in the line.

Priestess Elana came out and nodded, pleased to see

every single one of us where we were supposed to be, and even a little bit early. I loved the garden in the early morning. It was cool and there was always a breeze, and birds sang so loudly and beautifully that sometimes I would just sit and listen to their songs. I was beginning to learn which birds made which music.

"You all look so eager this morning!" Priestess Elana said.

They *did* seem unusually smiley now that she mentioned it. I realized why and my heart sank a little, even though I didn't care. "I get to move up to the next level of study today," I said. "They are relieved to be rid of me."

"Is that true, girls?" She looked at each face a bit sternly. "Makka, is it true?"

Makka was the unofficial leader of the students here. Most of us were six years old. Makka had turned seven, and the two youngest were still only five.

Makka said, "We are happy to know that Princess Rhianikki will get her wish. That is all, Priestess Elana."

"As you should be. Well, go on then, eat. Go on!" She clapped her hands twice, and the girls broke ranks and raced to the platters of food, eager to choose the very best pieces for the goddess.

I remained, and when they were out of earshot, I said, "Makka lies. They do not care that I got my wish."

"They might care a little," Elana said. She walked slowly toward the food, and I fell into step beside her. "But I think they also feel relief this morning."

"To be rid of me?" Like my father, I thought.

"To be rid of the fear of offending you. Imagine you are an ordinary girl in a classroom with a girl whose intellect is far beyond her years, a girl whose powers were whispered about even before she came here, a girl whose father has the power to order your own death. You would be always on guard; always afraid you might say or do the wrong thing."

She was wrong. I had no powers to make anyone whisper. I was smart, but only because I had decided to learn all there was to know. "My father does not behead children," I said. "Certainly not for offending me. My brothers, perhaps, but they are not here."

"The other girls have no way to know any of that. Do not let it hurt your feelings."

"Them? Hurt my feelings? Psssh."

The priestess laughed softly and plucked two pomegranates from the pile. She eyed them both while I helped myself to several and a hunk of crusty bread. We went together to the goddess, placed our offerings in the basket, and repeated the silly words of our offering prayer in unison.

Elana looked sideways at me. "Very good."

"Thank you. You did well also."

She smiled and we ate, and I watched the slow progression of the sun-dial's shadow. The instant it crept to the day's second hour, I ran through the archway into the temple, and straight to the room where magic was taught. I'd never been inside before. There was an arched opening in the stone with a deep purple curtain covering it from within. I was early, but there was someone inside, I could hear them moving around.

I pulled the curtain back to peer in.

A woman stood before a long and cluttered table. Her back was toward me. She wore a black linen wrap around her waist, and nothing on top. The stone table before her was littered with items that fascinated me—pottery vessels of every shape and size, piles and bundles of herbs in no order, mortars and pestles—a whole row of them, and bow-drills for making fire. From the belt round her waist hung ropes of gemstones in many lengths and in all the colors of the rainbow. Her hair was wild, a fluffy mass in of silver and gray that seemed almost purple in the light of the oil lamps around the room.

She'd stopped moving when I'd pulled back the curtain. She still hadn't moved as I stared at her back. And then she said, "Come in, Princess," in a voice like that of a bullfrog. "I've been expecting you."

I went inside, letting the curtain fall closed behind me. She turned around and looked me up and down. She wore layer upon layer of silver, gold, and lapis necklaces draped over and between her breasts. Her face was beautiful to me, despite its wrinkles. Her skin was desert bronze and her eyes, midnight brown. She had long, thick lashes, and dimples when she smiled, and her lips were thick and full.

"Who are you?" I asked. "I thought a visiting priest was the teacher of magic."

"The teacher of magic met with a tragic accident while out gathering herbs last night," she said. "I have come to take his place."

"Oh." I found it odd that I'd not heard of this from anyone in the temple. Priestess Elana had said nothing about a priest having an accident. "Is he dead?"

"Yes. Does that make you sad?"

"I did not know him," I said. "Are you as skilled at magic as he was?"

"More skilled by far. Magic... is strongest in females, you know."

"I did not know. But had I given it any thought, I'd have guessed. Magic is stronger yet in those of royal blood, yes?"

She laughed and it reminded me of the way chickens

cluck all at once when you disturbed their bug-pecking. "Magic is stronger in those chosen by the goddess," she said. "I believe you to be one of those."

"Obviously. I'm the daughter of Pharaoh."

"Would you be surprised to hear that has nothing to do with it?"

My eyes widened. Already I was learning things I'd never imagined. "Then, not *all* royals are so chosen?"

"I could be executed for saying such a thing. So I will not say it. Besides, all that should concern you are your own powers. No one else's matter."

"You're the second person today to suggest I have powers. Why have I never seen them?"

She shrugged one shoulder. "Your mother was the first to say so. She sensed it when you were still in her womb. Your nurse was the second. She said the room would shake when you were angry. The new queen recognized it, too. I do not know what she saw, but I know it frightened her. And that is why you are here."

The notion of the new queen being afraid of me filled me with dark satisfaction. I hated her. It was her fault I'd been exiled from my home.

"As we grow older, we lose the powers born to us because we doubt they were ever real, or forget them entirely. Already you have forgotten."

I could not argue with that. But if my mother believed me special, and my nurse, and that awful stepmother sitting on my throne, then perhaps it was true. "What do I call you?" I asked.

"Betta."

I bent my head, hand to my heart. "I am Rhianikki, first-born of Pharaoh, Princess of Egypt."

"I know." Her eyes sparkled as they gazed into mine. I

felt she was happier to see me than anyone had been since I'd left my home.

Other girls came in then, all of them far taller than I. They were thirteen, more or less. They wore pale lavender kalasiris, which represented that they had completed all the boring lessons I'd been taking and had advanced to magical studies. They paid me little notice as they took their places on the floor, sitting on the woven mats Betta had spread out for them. One or two sent curious looks my way, then whispered to a friend, but I didn't care.

I had forgotten to bring my cushion, but I did not wish to sit among them anyway. They were all so much taller, I would never be able to see. I remained standing in the back of the room so that I could see them all, but only the teacher could see me.

"I am called Betta. I will be your teacher of magic from now on." The girls muttered until Betta said, "Princess Rhianikki, firstborn of Pharaoh, please join me here."

I walked forward as the girls all started whispering.

"It's her."

"She's the one."

"The princess."

I walked through their midst up to the front of the room.

"Would you honor me by acting as my assistant, my lady?"

I adored Betta, I decided. "Yes, I would." I went behind the table but could not see anything over it.

A bench came sliding toward me, pushed by Betta's foot. I stepped up onto it and gazed out at the ordinary girls. Some of them smiled at me as if they found me cute. I hated people finding me cute, so I returned those smiles with a royal glare.

"I am going to teach you how to make fire," Betta said. "Come. Line up in front of the table."

They obeyed immediately, all rising and coming forward. There were seven of them, all of different heights and shapes and shades of brown. They all had dark hair—some with curls, some with fluff, and some with long, straight hair like mine. Their kalasiris were pretty, and I preferred the pale lilac hue to my own light blue, but none were adorned like my own.

Betta handed me a basket full of candles, after removing one for herself. "One for each girl, if you please."

I took the basket and walked along my bench, placing a candle in front of each girl. Betta came behind me, pushing a small dish of sand in front of each.

When I finished, one candle remained. Betta took it and placed it beside a bowl of sand on my side of the table. Then she handed me another basket, and without being told, I knew what to do. This basket held wooden drilling boards, two hands in length, narrow and flat. Each board had twelve holes drilled into it. As I handed them out, Betta moved behind me again, passing out the small drill-bows, already bent and strung, each with a wooden dowel wrapped in the very middle of its bowstring. Again, one of each remained, and Betta set them on my side of the table.

Finally, I handed out a basket of flat stones with depressions in them, capstones. When there was one stone left, I placed it with the other items near me, just in case Betta didn't know or didn't care that I was only supposed to observe.

"Place your candles into the sand, so they stand upright," she instructed.

The other girls stood their candles upright in their bowls of sand, the simplest of candle holders. I looked at

Betta, my hands hovering over my candle, eager, but waiting. She nodded at me, and I thrust my candle into the sand so fast I spilled a little.

"Now," Betta said, "Light your candle in the easiest way you can. You may use anything I have given to you, or anything else you see in this room."

One or two of the older girls reached for the drill bow. Others imitated them. But I looked around the room. There was an oil lamp on the far end of the table, its wick poking from its spout, its flame dancing brightly. I plucked my candle from the sand, walked along my bench to the lamp, and touched the candle's wick to the oil lamp's flame. Then I carried it back and stood it in the sand.

"Very good, Rhianikki," Betta said. "Not the easiest way, but certainly easier than the manner chosen by the others."

Several of them dropped their bows and grabbing their candles, started toward the lamp, but Betta held up her hands and they stopped.

Then she came to me and with her fingers, snuffed my candle. She went to the oil lamp and moved it up to a high shelf, out of reach. "Again," she said. "The easiest way, without using the lamps."

So, I picked up the bow drill. I had seen them used, of course, but I had never used one myself. The holes in the drilling board already held resin packed in tight. I could smell its rich, sharp scent. I inserted the dowel into one of the holes in the board. Placing the capstone atop it and pushing down to hold it in place, I moved the bow back and forth, and its string, wrapped 'round the dowel, caused the dowel to spin. After a few seconds the dowel began to squeak loudly against the wood. It hurt my ears, and my arm was getting tired.

I kept going. So did the others. The room was filled with

so many high-pitched squeals of wood against wood, it sounded like cats being tortured. Some of the girls began to whine or moan or pant with the effort.

"That is not the easiest way, either," Betta said at last, just as I managed to generate a puff of smoke.

But I was so close! I moved the bow faster.

"Bows down," Betta said.

I obeyed, though I regretted it. What other way could there be?

Betta took the candle she had saved for herself and placed it into an elaborate stone jackal with a hole in his back for this purpose. Then she gazed at the candle.

"What are you..." one of the girls began.

"Shhhh. Observe." She stared longer. Her eyes seemed to lose their focus, and to go blank. And then she spoke.

"Isis, great Isis, I, your loyal servant, beseech you to light the candle flame."

She stayed very still, her eyes unblinking, aimed at the wick, but I sensed she was not really seeing it. No one else in the room made a sound. Soon Betta began to rock very slightly back and forth on her feet. This continued for a time, and then she began to hum, just a single monotone note.

I held my breath, and I thought the others were as well, and then as we watched, the wick released a thin spiral of smoke. I almost gasped aloud, but managed not to, knowing the sound might break Betta's concentration. Within a few more seconds, the wick began to glow, its tip becoming a red-hot brand. Then, with a sudden *pop*, the flame came to life.

Everyone gasped, even I.

Every girl in the room resumed her position in front of

her candle, gazing at it, rocking, reciting the same words. Some of them even hummed.

Betta watched them, smiling indulgently, but then noticed me standing there doing nothing. "Well? Aren't you going to try?"

"Not until you tell me how you did it. It would be foolish to try until then."

"How very wise you are, child."

The other girls, hearing this, stopped what they were doing and listened.

"I asked the goddess, as you heard. I asked not just with my words, but with my whole heart. And then I emptied my mind, so that Isis could work through me to light the candle if it pleased her to do so."

"Oh." I thought for a long moment. "Would it be all right if I tried it my own way?"

She gave a single slow nod. Two of the other girls giggled, leaning close to each other and whispering, but when I looked their way, they pressed their lips tight.

Standing on my bench, I turned and faced my candle. I put my eyes upon it.

The other girls were doing likewise, muttering Betta's words again, no longer interested in my efforts. I held my hands over the candle and spoke my own words to Isis and to any of the other gods who might be listening.

"I am Rhianikki!" I said, and I said it so loudly and so strongly that the others fell silent. "Firstborn of Pharaoh, I am part goddess myself. I am divine. I do not need to ask Isis to light the candle. I have magic of my own."

Every eye was upon me as I gazed at the candle. I emptied my mind of every thought except one—the glowing light of a red and yellow flame popping to life on the wick of my candle. I could see it so clearly, that firelight dancing. I could feel it, all warm and hot and rising up my body, up into my chest, up into my neck, up into my face. My vision went hazy and my eyes felt as if they were pulsing with heat that wanted to push its way out.

"Ignite!" The word burst from my mouth without warning, and my voice sounded deeper than it ever had. I felt the energy pulse from my eyes, and my candle burst to life. One of the girls gasped, and when I looked her way, *her* candle popped to life, and so did the hem of her dress. She screamed and hopped backwards, slapping at her hem. But I could not stop. I swept my gaze over the whole row of candles, and one by one they popped to life, and so did the hair of a girl who still stood too close.

She shrieked and another girl dumped a vessel of water over her head, which made her shriek again. Betta put her hands on my shoulders and said, "Close your eyes."

I didn't close them, I *slammed* them, and held them tight lest I burn the temple down.

"Now let the fire energy drain down, down, down to the floor. Down, down, through the floor, and into the earth. Down, down, down. There, take those silly sandals off. Put your bare feet on the floor."

I did everything she said, my eyes still closed as I heeled off my sandals. I imagined the fire being quenched by the cool stone under my feet and the strong earth farther below.

"Good. Now open your eyes."

I reached out my hand and felt her standing in front of me. "You should step to the side, first."

She moved. I opened my eyes. Nothing caught fire. The older girls stood in a huddle at the opposite end of the table from me. They were all staring, their eyes revealing their fear.

"I am sorry I set you on fire," I said to the one with the burn marks on her kalasiris. "I didn't know I could do that. I will ask my father to send a new dress for you." Then I looked at the girl whose hair had caught fire. "And for you, I shall make a beautiful headpiece."

"Th-thank you, P-princess." The girls bowed, not from respect, from fear. I didn't hate it, but it wasn't ideal.

"Today's lesson is done," Betta said. "Tomorrow we will continue. You may go."

All the girls trooped out of the room, but I stayed behind. "How was I able to do that?" I asked.

"Think hard, Rhianikki. Has anything like this happened to you before?"

I lifted my head and looked her in the eyes. I could almost feel her willing me to remember.

"I was very angry when I heard my father tell his new queen that her wailing infants would be his successors instead of me. That I would be third in line, after them."

"Yes?"

"I felt anger well up in me and I stormed into the nursery to tell them so, even though they would not understand. The walls trembled and shook, and a pillar fell right across their beds. And their nurse ran in and saw me standing there, over them.

"An earthquake, do you think?" she asked.

"If an earthquake can strike a single room, perhaps. But it felt as if it came from my anger," I said. "It felt as if I did it to them."

"But they were not injured," she said, and I wondered how she knew. "Why do you think that is?"

"I would never hurt them. They are my brothers, partly."

"You did not wish to hurt them, so they were not hurt."

25

"But Betta," I said, searching her face. "I did not *wish* to hurt those girls I set on fire just now, either."

"No? Not even those two who giggled at you?"

"No, of course not, I... " I realized then, that the two girls who had laughed at me were the same two who'd been set alight.

"Ohhhhhhh." I shook my head in wonder. "Maybe I *was* angry with them. A little bit." Then I lifted my eyes. "How did you know?"

"I know many things," she said very softly. "The truth is that I am not here for those other girls. I'll teach them, of course, but it is not my purpose."

"What *is* your purpose?" I asked.

"Haven't you guessed by now, Princess Rhianikki?" She reached out a hand and ran it over my hair. "You are."

## CHAPTER 3
# FESTIVAL OF OSIRIS

ontrolling my temper was controlling my power. That was what Betta had taught me above all else during my first two years at the temple. To control my power, I would have to control my temper.

I *hated* controlling my temper!

It boiled inside me, sometimes. I would go for walks, far into the desert where I could hurt no one and just rail. And not once in all the times I'd done so had anything caught fire.

I turned that over in my seven-year-old mind, and I wondered if it was true that my temper and my power were so inseparable after all. But advanced as my brain was, I was still a child, and the distraction of the day was irresistible.

. . .

It was the first day of the Festival of Osiris. There would be a parade in the streets, and I would be in it. Always, the king and his family, carried upon elaborate litters of gold, were a part of the parade. At least, that had been the tradition until I'd come here. This was the pharaoh's first visit to Terne since I'd been banished.

I'd ridden in the parade with my father many times before *she* came.

As I ran ahead of the other girls, Priestess Elana caught me up, touched my shoulder. "Why the hurry, Princess? We can barely keep up."

"I must find my father!" I pulled from her grasp, stretching my head to try and see above the crowds. But there were so many people! In the distance, the pyramids stood, gleaming white in the sun, and when my panicked eyes fell on them, I calmed. "I will find him," I said. "Betta taught me how." Closing my eyes, I tried to feel for him.

The priestess spoke from nearer to me, as if bending down. "He won't let you ride with him in the parade, sweet Rhianikki. The high priestess has pled with him, but he will not bend."

I opened my mouth to deny it, but before I could speak, I knew. It settled in my mind. It was true. I knew truth when I heard it. Betta had taught me that, too. One must only listen with the inner ears, see with the inner eyes.

Lowering my head, I said, "He has shamed me, his first-born. He will be sorry one day."

"I will not permit you to be shamed, my princess. Nor will the high priestess. Stay with me, trust me." She reached down her hand and I hesitated for a moment. But I did trust her. So, I put my hand in hers, and we walked together.

She directed the other girls where to stand and put

some younger priestesses in charge of watching them, then, still holding my hand, kept walking.

"Where are we going?" I asked.

We'd wandered off the parade route and were winding through an area where floats and litters were being prepared for the march through the city. People were everywhere, and I began to feel suffocated, being so small. We passed litter after litter, many of them bearing statues of the gods from temples nearby. Our contribution was Isis, the very one from our own temple, which I so admired.

I spotted her up ahead, already elevated upon a grand litter that rested on stands made of sturdy reeds. It would be born upon the shoulders of young men from the village, later.

She stood tall upon her dais. No water spurted from around her feet, now, though. A mountain of flowers lay there instead, and a chair stood in front of her. Not a chair, a throne—my throne.

"You must change. Hurry, my lady, in here." We ducked into a tent, and Priestess Elana took the cloth bag from her shoulder and opened its flap. She pulled out a garment that shimmered like the gold in Isis' wings. "Quickly now!"

I pulled off my dress and put on the golden garment. When my arms and head poked through, she was placing sandals at my feet, each bearing a gold medallion with a sunstone in its center. It represented the eye of Ra, one of the many names for Isis.

I stepped into the sandals, which fit perfectly, and had plush, soft lining that felt luxurious on my feet. When I straightened, Elana affixed a belt around my waist. It was wide, beaded in lapis and moonstone and jet. It was the most beautiful girdle I'd ever seen.

Then she handed me a headdress—the headdress of a royal princess of Egypt—and not just any, but the next in line.

I pressed my hands together, tears springing into my eyes, and I bent my head toward her. "Thank you, Priestess Elana."

She placed it upon my head. I loved the weight of it. I felt much more like myself again as I opened my arms for her to adorn them in bracelets. I wore my own beads round my neck.

"Just for today, Rhianikki," the kind priestess reminded me. "You understand? This is not a coup. This is a statement that you exist and will not simply disappear. You are first-born. That is the truth. You are only reminding them of it." Then she bowed to me. My teacher bowed to me.

She pushed open the tent flap and called loudly, "Hail, Rhianikki, Firstborn of Pharaoh, Princess of Egypt, and Daughter of Isis."

Everyone within the sound of her voice stopped what they were doing. Some saluted, clapping a fist to their chests. Some bent a knee as I passed.

Two young men stood before the litter of Isis. They were bald and wore the lavender robes of students to the priesthood. The boys studied at the Temple of Ra in Luxor, and must've traveled here with the temple caravan. They dropped to one knee as I passed, so their bent knees created a step for me. When I went to use it, they took hold of my hands and assisted me up, onto the litter.

It was even more beautiful from up there. Isis, I saw, was held in place by thick, woven ropes. The flowers that surrounded her were piled deep enough for me to roll in, and it crossed my mind that I might do so before this was done. But first...

I walked to the chair where I would sit, with the goddess at my back, her wings spread wide and curved forward. The chair was of black wood, imported from the south. It was carved with glyphs that told of my birth, and how the earth had rumbled upon my first cry. Each engraving painted was in gold. It was my throne. It used to sit in the palace beside my father's.

T turned to Elana. "How is this here?"

"We borrowed it from the palace," she said.

I did not think that was all of it. I thought my father must've had my throne removed and stored away someplace, and so would not notice if it went missing. That was what I thought.

High Priestess Naiya leaned nearer Elana. "You're going to get us all killed." She took the younger priestess's arm and the two of them went over to the tent where I had changed. They went inside and closed the flap.

Something told me to go listen to whatever they were saying. Betta had taught me never to ignore my inner voice. So, I got down off the litter, a hand on each boy's shoulder before they had the chance to kneel. I hurried to the tent, moved around to one side, and pretended to adjust my gown.

"We are honoring our princess and student," Elana said. "The pharaoh cannot hold that against us. Why would we presume such a thing would incur his anger? And even without that, he would not risk the wrath of Isis by harming her priestesses."

"You cannot be sure of that. I never should have allowed this—"

"She's special," Elana said rather forcefully. "The High Priest of Hathor called her 'chosen' when he visited our temple. I never had the chance to ask him what he meant by it. However, from what I've seen... " She trailed off.

"Her intellect matches any adult in the temple," High Priestess Naiya agreed. "It was one of the things that so frightened the queen."

"Yes, and her powers. Her advancement in the area of magic is rapid."

"Betta has not reported this to me," the high priestess said.

"Betta must have her reasons," Elana said. "My sources are the other girls in her class. They're afraid of her, you know."

"Everyone is afraid of her, a seven-year-old girl. It's all nonsense. Magic is from the gods, and the gods will keep it controlled."

"Rhianikki believes herself equal to the gods," Elana said.

"Are you complaining? Are you not reinforcing that belief with this... display?" I heard the tent flap, and the women stepped out of it and looked toward the litter. "Where is she?" the high priestess asked. "Rhianikki?"

I angled outward, so I came back into their line of sight from further away. I explained nothing, just returned to my litter, stepped up on the knees of my attendants, and walked once again to my throne. This time, I turned and sat upon it. The cushions in its seat were as soft as I remembered. I placed my hands on its arms and straightened my spine.

I heard music and looked back toward the road where the musicians stood together. Some played flutes, others, lyres or small hand-harps. There were drummers, of course, and rattles that hissed like snakes. They played a song honoring Isis, sister and bride of Osiris, who had found all his parts and restored him to life.

They finished the song, then started a simpler one as they walked forward into the street.

Behind the musicians, fire dancers moved forward, some swinging ropes that blazed, others leaping through hoops set aflame. The young men from our village moved into position beneath my litter and lifted it. I saw other litters lining up ahead of us. In front of them all was the sparkling golden litter of the pharaoh. As it moved into position at the head of the line, it was, for a moment, angled toward me. I saw my father, his smile wide and white in his face, a fat, wriggling, two-year-old in his arms. And beside him, his queen, holding an identical child.

There was no place for me on that dais.

The litter turned, and the pharaoh was carried out into street to begin the parade. The crowds shouted and cheered. Other litters moved into place, bearing statues of the gods, their priests and priestesses walking ahead of them casting flower petals into their paths.

We took up position at the very end of the line. I held my head up high as my bearers carried Isis and me out into the street. Two baskets of flowers were poured upon my feet, and a smaller one, over my head, so that petals clung to my headdress, my hair, my shoulders, and littered my lap.

I was still laughing when we stepped into the street, and there was a moment of stunned silence, as if all of Egypt held its breath. And then, the cheers and shouts became deafening. People shouted my name and threw flowers. They spilled into the streets and ran along beside me. Women removed their jewelry and threw it into the flowers at my feet.

This continued all through the village. I kept glancing down at Priestess Elana and High Priestess Naiya who walked with the other priestesses of Isis beside me.

I could tell by their eyes they were worried.

As we neared the end of the parade route, the litters veered off into a field of tents set up among the tree-lined part of the riverbank. The Nile fed our orchards as a mother nursed a child, or so Betta had taught me.

One litter, though, had not veered off. It sat in the road, facing mine. My father the pharaoh watched my approach, and his face was angry. The queen was no longer upon the litter, nor were my brother usurpers.

But my father was furious. I knew that look on his face. Softly I said, "Oh great and mighty Isis, while I am myself divine, I am also young. Protect me."

I saw my father's eyes shift away from mine toward something off to the side, then they widened. I followed his gaze and saw a man with a crossbow pointed right at me, and even as I spotted it, the deadly bolt flew.

One of my bearers tripped and fell forward. My litter pitched. The cords holding the goddess snapped, and she toppled forward as I was thrown from my chair. All of this in a single instant in which I thought my life would end, and the mysteries of the afterlife would be mine to know.

I screamed and covered my head with my hands as the huge statue of stone and gold toppled right on top of me. I heard the wood of my throne splinter and I curled into a ball, sliding forward due to the pitch. And then I bumped into something hard and cold and stopped sliding.

*Everything* had stopped.

I lowered my arms as servants scrambled. The litter was straightened and lowered to the ground. I lifted my head.

The goddess had fallen right over my throne. The curve of her golden wings touched the earth on either side of me, holding her up so she did not crush me. I turned my head to look up, and right into her face. Her lapis eyes shone down upon me.

Men came and heaved her upward.

I rose to my feet. Shouts and cheer erupted from the crowd.

"The princess lives!"

"Isis protected her!"

"Wait, look! Look at the throne!"

I turned when I heard it. My throne's broken back lay face up on the litter, with a crossbow's bolt planted at the place where I estimated my heart would have been.

I turned to look for my father, but the royal family was no longer there.

# CHAPTER 4
# THE WISH-GRANTER

"Those bulging idiots are going to frighten the petitioners away," Priestess Elana said. "Why don't they stand somewhere else? The garden, perhaps? Surely the pharaoh's elite guard could do a better job if they were closer to the princess, and they would still be able to observe all who come and go."

"Then how would the people see *them*?" High Priestess Naiya asked. "I believe their entire purpose out there is to convince the public that the pharaoh is protecting his daughter, not trying to have her killed."

I paused just outside the sacred room where the two awaited me, to hear what else they would say. It had been two years since the bowman had fired a bolt at my chest during the parade. And I had often wondered if he took his orders from my father—or, more likely, from the queen. There was no way to be sure. The assassin had vanished. I had seen his face—only for an instant, but it was burned into my memory.

But now it was the anniversary of that event, and while

our own parade was still days away, my father had sent guards to watch over me.

"Do you really think he ordered it?" Elana whispered to the high priestess.

"The people certainly do," High Priestess Naiya said. "Or did, at first. Hence the show of force outside a peaceful temple both then and again now. Whether he ordered the attempt or not, those guards make him seem the protective father."

I was surprised to feel warm breath on my neck. Betta had come up behind me, crouched low, and whispered in my ear, "Anything interesting?"

I startle-jumped and sent her a scowl but she only grinned and nudged me through the arch into the room.

A wooden table with a bench on either side stood in the small, stone room's center. It held a vessel of water and wine, and cups. Its only window faced the front of the temple, letting the cool night breeze waft through. I went straight to it and jumped up, using my hands to balance so I could see below. Two large men stood at either side of the temple's elaborate front gate. They wore blue and gold kilts, leather sandals, and breastplates over their chests. Each held a large spear.

A small group of women approached the gate, looked at the men, then hurried away.

I dropped to the floor. "Priestess Elana is right," I said, "They are scaring petitioners. I will see to it." I dashed out of the room before any of them had time to reply, but I heard Betta say, "I'll go with her," and then as she came behind me, "because *this*, I must see."

I headed out through the entrance into the garden, emerging from the flowering vines that hid its small passage to the outside, then rounded the temple and approached the front and the guards. The straps that held their breastplates were chafing. I could see the marks on their backs.

I walked up behind them and took my stance, feet wide, hands on my hips, and said, "Guards!" in my most commanding tone.

They both turned immediately.

"I am Rhianikki, firstborn of Pharaoh, Princess of—"

"We know who you are, Princess," said the one on my left, smiling as if he found me cute, which made me want to take his spear and stab him with it.

The guard on the right, however, bowed deeply, and said, "How may we serve you, Princess Rhianikki?"

That was more like it. He straightened, and there was something about his eyes when they met mine that felt familiar. They were dark but shone as if lit from within. "Have we met before?"

"I have been in your father's service since your birth, my lady, and was frequently assigned to watch over you and your nurse, Kimaru."

At the mention of her name, my heart wept. I lowered my eyes, lest the guard see my weakness. "How is she? Caring for the twin usurpers now that they're too old for a wetnurse?"

"Yes, but missing her most beloved charge."

I thinned my lips. He was being kind, that was all.

"She sends her love for you," he went on.

It touched me deeply and I hoped it was true. But I swallowed my feelings and would not let him see them. "Your presence here is frightening away the petitioners. And besides, how would you protect me from way out here?"

"It's where your father bade us stand," said the first

one, and at my glare hastily added, "my princess."

"Yes, so one and all might witness his devotion. I am not so easily fooled. If he were truly devoted, I would be in my palace." I dismissed him by turning to his partner. "I am the one with assassins after her, am I not? And I am your princess, and my father, the only person in the kingdom with the power to countermand my orders, is not here. Is he?"

Behind me, Betta made a choking sound, then cleared her throat, drawing the men's gazes.

"Fine, I'm fine," she said, holding up a hand.

"Quite correct, my princess," said the guard with the shining eyes. "What would you have us do?"

"Follow me." I turned and started off, and I heard their footfalls behind me. I led them around the temple and into the garden through the passage in the outer wall. Our beautiful Isis stood in her place, a chip in one golden wing. I pointed to her. "They say the bolt hit her wing as she threw herself over me."

"I, too, would take a bolt for you, Princess," said the nice guard.

"Even if my father ordered you to let me die?"

He nodded. The other averted his eyes. "Have you been given any such order?" I asked, and both denied it.

I pointed to the smaller arched opening in one temple wall. "This entry leads straight to the petition room. Every petitioner will come by this route, so you can still see each of them. If you hear commotion inside, come. Until then, you may rest here. Even by night, it is the best place to linger. You'll be far more comfortable and much closer to me should I need help. And look. Fruit."

"Thank you, my lady." The nice one bowed, and the other one did, too, albeit an instant behind.

"Good. Just—try not to look so scary." I glanced at Betta, who had an approving twinkle in her beautiful eyes. Then I returned to the petition room.

"Ah, good, you're back," Priestess Elana said. "You did well, young princess. High Priestess Naiya is leading the first petitioners around, see?"

I leaned on the window and pushed myself up like before, arms braced, feet dangling a ponytail's length above the floor. Naiya was leading a group of village women through the front gate and around to the garden, where I hoped the guards were not standing rigid as stone statues.

"You are only beginning to learn the formalities of magic," Betta said, "although your natural abilities are as advanced as many four times your age. Still, as this is your first time hearing petitions, I advise you to listen, observe, and learn." She pointed to a stool in a corner, where I was expected to sit quietly.

"I am not to grant any wishes, today?"

"The gods grant the petitions," Elana said. "Priestesses hear them and bring them before the gods to be decided. You are not yet a priestess."

"You are correct," I replied. "I'm far more." But I went to my stool and sat down, even though I would probably not be quiet.

High Priestess Naiya brought a girl of about ten years old inside. Her petition was for a cure for her ailing little brother, and Betta peppered her with questions about his symptoms and recent history. She was skilled in the healing arts and understood which leaf, berry, bark, or root could soothe which illness.

As the girl explained, Betta nodded. "When you've finished here, wait in the garden, she said. Then she hurried from the room.

The priestesses accepted the girl's offering, a poppet she'd made, and promised to ask Isis to heal her brother.

The second woman who came in was old and leaned heavily on a walking stick. Elana helped her to sit and poured her a cup of water from a pottery vessel.

"Thank you, Priestess. High Priestess." She bent her head as she addressed them. "My request is a simple one. I wish for my life to be over. I wish rest. I am tired and in constant pain of the joints."

I noticed Betta just at the doorway, but she paused, shot me a look, then turned and headed back the way she'd come.

High Priestess Naiya covered the old woman's wrinkled hand with her own. "I will take your petition to the gods myself, dear woman, for in matters of life and death, only they may decide."

"Thank you," she said. She took a coin from her pocket. "This is my offering. It is all I have."

As she started to rise, Elana hurried to help her and pressed the coin back into her hand. "Isis accepts your love as your offering."

"It is a hot day," I said. "Rest in the cool of the garden for a while before you go. Have some fruit."

"I would like that, little priestess."

She left and Betta returned, three pouches affixed to her belt that hadn't been there before.

The third woman to come in was as foreign as any I'd seen, with skin so fair she might have been albino but for her tarnished copper hair, and eyes of sapphire blue.

She bowed deeply. "You honor me by hearing my request."

She spoke our language poorly, but with an accent that

enchanted me. I leaned forward on my stool, elbows on my knees, and hoped she would talk all day.

"I am Anya, from the northern lands. My husband, he wants children. If I cannot conceive, he will leave me and find another."

"We will give offerings to Isis for you," Priestess Elana said.

"Yes, and I can make a draught," Betta said. "There are certain roots I must gather that help with conception. A foul-tasting brew, but—"

"Why?" I asked, rising to my feet on my stool, so no one would perceive me as small and therefore unimportant. "Why do you wish to keep a husband who wants you only as a brood sow? Look at you! You are a rare and exotic woman. Men would line up to fight for you."

The priestesses spoke as one to scold me, but the northern woman interrupted. "This girl is wise beyond her years," she said, gazing up at me from her seat upon the bench. "I know what you say is true, though my appearance is common enough where I come from. But the thing is, I've loved him with all I am for such a long time now."

She looked so sad just then, with tears pooling ever deeper in her eyes until a fat one spilled over and rolled slowly downward, leaving a shiny trail of itself behind. "And I think he really loved me, too. It seemed to get better and better year by year between us. But then suddenly he was brooding all the time, and I kept asking why."

She stopped to wipe her tears with the edge of her headscarf, a simple white one she had made better by sewing in beads. Noticing that, I felt a kinship with her.

"Finally, he confessed that he's tormented by being childless and worried he's running out of time."

I gaped at her, then I turned to the three women I most admired, and asked in all sincerity, "Are all men idiots?"

They spoke all over one another, but I caught each reply.

High Priestess Naiya said, "We do not refer to others as 'idiots.'"

Priestess Elana said, "Not *idiots*, exactly."

And Betta said, "You're just noticing this now? How old are you?"

"Nine," I replied.

"So advanced in some ways, a *little* slow in others."

"I've barely known any men, to be fair," I said, crossing my arms over my chest. "But if my father's decisions are any indication, it must be true."

"Rhianikki!" the priestess and high priestess shouted as one.

Betta clapped a hand over her mouth and slapped her knee. "Come back tomorrow for the draught," Betta said.

Anya from the north put a few coins on the table and got to her feet, bowing and thanking us all.

"I'll walk her out!" I hurried to catch her and clasped her hand.

"Fetch back the next group, if you will, my princess!" Elana called after me.

The copper-haired woman with skin paler than sand smiled at me. "I must seem stupid to you. You'll understand one day, when you fall in love."

"If love makes you stupid, I will do without it."

We exited into the garden. As we passed them, my guards fell in behind us, and I turned to speak to them. Anya kept walking.

"Stay back ten paces," I told them, my voice low. I had words for Anya that I did not want them to hear.

"We can't stop an arrow from ten paces, my princess," said one.

"You can't stop an arrow from two," I replied. If you see someone trying to shoot me, yell 'down' and I will obey."

I saw that Betta had come outside, too, and she approached the old woman and the girl, who awaited her near the fountain. I bade the guards wait there, and moved closer to listen in.

Betta handed a pouch to the young girl with the ailing brother, who sat there beside the old woman. "Make a tea," Betta told her. "A handful per cup, four cups a day for three days. Your brother will be well soon. Now give us some privacy."

Clutching the pouch, the girl hurried away.

Betta watched her go, then handed two pouches to the old woman, one red, one green. "This one will ease your pain," she said, nodding at the green sack. "And this one will *end* it. Do you understand?"

The old woman met her eyes and nodded.

"Tell no one."

Why, I wondered, would she use the green pouch for temporary relief if the red pouch was a cure? And then I realized it might not be a cure at all. It might be death. If it was, Betta was defying both the priestesses and the gods.

"Princess?" my guard called. When I glanced his way, he nodded toward Anya, who waited for me up ahead.. I hurried to join her.

"Do you think the magic will work?" Anya asked when we resumed walking.

"I think it already has," I said. "When you return tomorrow, you will see for yourself. You will have a child. Maybe two!" And then I repeated my teacher's words to the old woman, doing my best to mimic her deep and serious tone. "Tell no one."

I lay still and quiet on my mat beneath my thin blanket, and was too warm even then. Eventually, I sensed sleep stealing into the sleeping room like a thief. One by one my fellow students, on mats all around me, succumbed. I rose and crept between them and out onto the balcony, where a warm breeze gave a little relief.

I climbed onto the tree limb and shimmied toward its trunk, then dropped to the ground as I had done many times before. It was different outside at night. Night birds called as soft as a mystery, and frogs sang a chorus. I walked in silence, out through the side gate where my guards would be unlikely to see.

My father would remain in the city throughout the week-long festival and the royal caravan always set up in the same place, alongside a fruit tree orchard on the river-bank. That was where I went. There was a wide bend in the Nile there, where the water moved slow and ran deep. I stood beneath the old olive tree that seemed to lean over for a sip. I'd tried to climb it in my younger days when my father and I had traveled here for the Osiris festival. I bet I could do it now. But there wasn't time, so I turned my attention to the large, elaborate tents pitched nearby. My father's was the largest, white and trimmed in blue and gold, with guards set in front. The other tents surrounding it were for their attendants, seers, soldiers, and scribes. Those who cooked and cleaned had their own little site, a short walk upriver, where they were likely still dancing 'round a fire and drinking beer.

The queen was in my father's tent, but not her sons. They were in the nursery tent, set a stone's throw away so their incessant demands would not disturb the pharaoh's rest. Everyone had retired, except for the guards on watch. I'd seen several of them on my way here; one near the road, one near the river, and one in between. Two stood outside my father's tent, another outside my brothers'.

I was a small shadow, moving from tree, to cart, to water cask, to tent. I passed one guard so close I heard him breathing—and yet he was unaware of me. Soon I stood outside the tent where the twin toddlers slept. I hid behind a wine cask as tall as my head, closer to my brothers than I had been in a long while. They had probably grown. Would they remember me? My throat tightened. I rubbed my eye with the heel of my hand.

"I only hope they haven't grown too fat for me to carry," I whispered, wishing I could feel as uncaring as I sounded.

"So it's to be an abduction, then?"

I jumped out of my own skin, then turned slowly. My guard, the one with the shining dark eyes, crouched there looking at me.

"They'll come to no harm," I said. He said nothing, just gazed at me. "They'll have a good home," I went on, "and parents who adore them and don't employ nurses to raise them."

He rubbed his chin. "Your father will search the entire kingdom for them."

"Obviously, I must leave one of their blankets near the water's edge."

"Ah, clever," he said. "And how will you get past the nurse?"

"Kimaru? She was my nurse, too, you know. I never had a problem getting past her before."

47

His smile was like a light in the darkness. "You are an amazing little girl. How old are you, Rhianikki?"

"Nine," I said.

"Your mind is far older, I think. Or perhaps, your soul."

He was very wise, for a soldier. "What is your name?"

"Today, my name is Luca. I change it every few decades. You'll do the same, one day."

I was dying to ask what he meant by that, but movement near the nursery tent caught my eye. A form, swathed in black attacked the guard from behind, knocked him senseless, then crept inside.

I sprang into a run, crossed the grasses. Luca came behind me but was attacked from our flank.

As he fought, I entered the dark tent, and my feet hit something soft. Clouds moved, and a beam of moonlight shone down on my dear nurse, Kimaru. She lay on her back, wide eyes unseeing, a blade in her chest. Her killer was leaning over my brothers, who were sound asleep and not even aware of my presence.

I stepped over Kimaru's body, swinging one hand low to pull the knife from her chest. And then, with a growl of fury, I sprang, and plunged it into the child-thief's back.

Howling, he whirled on me fist-first, pounding me in the jaw. I hit the floor some distance away as mayhem erupted. The child-thief fell to his knees. Guards alerted by the noise poured in.

Luca came to me. He leaned over me. "Princess?"

I tried to answer, but his face swam and my vision went dark.

I lay in a bed so soft it reminded me how hard was my mat at the temple. A cool compress that smelled of herbs lay across my face. I opened my eyes to see my father, the pharaoh himself, standing beside me. He wore no headpiece; only his thick, single braid adorned his shaved head.

He wasn't looking at me, though, but at my guard, who stood at my feet.

"I can only surmise her reasons, my king," Luca said. "She must have sensed the threat to her siblings, or perhaps she saw it in a dream. In the temple they say her skills in magic are quite advanced."

"I am aware."

"I followed to keep her safe. She saw the intruder enter the tent of your sons, and without hesitation, raced inside to defend them. Alas, it was already too late for her nurse, but—"

"But Rhianikki took the blade from Kimaru's chest and stabbed the attacker," my father said. "As many times as you've told me, I still have trouble comprehending—I thought she hated her brothers."

"Clearly, she does not," Luca said. "What of the attacker?"

"We kept him alive until he talked. Then we let him die from the wound the princess delivered. They planned to take the two princes back to Kussara to be sacrificed to the Hittite gods."

I gasped aloud and both men turned my way.

"You were brave and heroic, my daughter," my father said. He placed his hand on my head. "The queen is as grateful as I." I averted my eyes. That one's gratitude, I could do without. And then he said words I'd been longing

49

to hear. "Rhianikki, you may return with us to the palace, if you wish."

My eager eyes shot to his. "And to my rightful place as firstborn and heir?"

He looked away this time.

I took a deep breath. The pain of his ongoing rejection had hardened my heart. "Luca, take me back to the temple." I got up, still holding the poultice to my face.

"But Rhianikki—"

"No, Father. You and your family are unworthy of me. I will continue training as a priestess of Isis, for *she* is most worthy. She saved me from your wife's hired assassin, after all." I threw the poultice right at his chest and strode from the tent.

Luca came too, walking just behind me. No one followed.

"Are you all right, Princess?" he asked, when we'd reached the road.

"Know this, Luca. If I should decide I want the throne of Egypt, I will have it."

"I do not doubt it."

We'd rounded a bend in the road. "Can they still see us?" I asked.

Luca said, "No. Why?"

I fainted at his feet.

The northerner Anya returned the next morning for the miracle she'd been promised. I was permitted to greet her at the gate. Her alarm when she saw me revealed my bruises more clearly than Hathor's mirror could have.

"What happened to you, child?"

"I did something brave last night. Maybe two things," I said. For I had saved my brother's lives *and* chosen to return to the service of the goddess. Well, to my studies of magic, more accurately. "Isis owes me a boon. I've been telling her so since I woke before dawn and have asked her to give my reward to you in the form of a child."

"What a sweet girl you are," she said, and she cupped my unbruised cheek in her pale hand.

"I am not sweet," I said, removing her hand. "Let us go inside. Perhaps the priestesses have other solutions by now." I hadn't checked in, as I'd been conversing with Isis since I woke in my bed before sunrise. "This way."

I walked into the temple garden and through it. My guard was off duty today, taking a well-deserved rest. He preferred the night shift, he'd told me on the way home, and it made perfect sense to me. Assassins and thieves always struck by night.

I led Anya into the room of supplication. High Priestess Naiya stood near the window with her back to us. Elana and Betta flanked her. They all turned, and I yelped in surprise to see that Naiya held a wriggling baby.

Anya gasped and ran forward, reached for the babe, then hesitated. But then Naiya passed the infant into her arms. I had never seen such bliss as I saw in those strange blue eyes just then.

"But... how?" she asked.

"That's what I'd like to know," Betta said, her gaze on me.

"The infant was left at the gates by a distraught young girl, not an hour ago," Naiya said quickly. "Several saw her. One of the priestesses gave chase, caught her. Weeping, she begged us to care for the child. And so we shall... by giving her to you."

Anya looked up from the newborn for the first time, her tears flowing freely. Then she looked at me. I do not know how you did this. I... thank you."

"You are welcome," I said. "If I were you, Anya of the North, I would keep the child and leave the husband."

She was too enraptured by the baby in her arms to hear me. She said she knew the way out, and left.

All three women looked at me. High Priestess Naiya said, "A royal emissary came at dawn to tell us of your nocturnal adventure."

"I'll make a fresh poultice for your face," Betta said, hurrying from the room. She tugged Priestess Elana's arm, and the two left us alone.

High Priestess Naiya sat down and she patted the bench beside her. I sat. "Tell me, Princess Rhianikki, what did you do after returning to the temple last night?"

"I must have slept for a while, after Luca—my guard—brought me back. Then I woke before dawn and went to the garden to speak to Isis."

"You prayed," she said.

"I spoke to her. I told her I had saved the lives of two royal infants, and she could repay me by giving just one ordinary child to Anya."

The high priestess nodded slowly. "Did she answer you?"

"Of course."

Her eyes opened a little wider. "She spoke to you?"

I was confused by her question. "You witnessed her answer yourself. You saw her answer leave here with its new mother just now. How can you doubt?" I sighed, wondering how adults could be so blind. "May I go?"

"Yes, of course. You should rest after such a long night. You are excused from classes today, Rhianikki."

"Thank you. But today my name shall be Hella." I turned and walked away, belatedly adding, "Or perhaps Mari." When I glanced back at her, the High Priestess wore a most puzzled expression.

## CHAPTER 5
# THE ABDUCTION

"I can't figure it out," I said. I was walking along the riverbank in search of heart-shaped leaves with spots, for treating ailments of the heart.

"I doubt there's anything you can't figure out. You have a mind far beyond your meager nine years of life," Betta said.

She was barefoot and wore a simple dress of undyed cotton. Her wild hair was held off her face by the strip of pretty blue cloth she'd tied round her head. The band made her springy gray and silver curls stand up even higher than usual.

Betta paused in yanking on a thick stem to harvest what she called lung root. "Tell me, young princess, what is it you wish to know?"

I gazed at her familiar face, as dark and rippled as the Nile on a moonless night. "You and the priestesses... differ in some ways."

"Good. Very good observation."

"They counsel the old, the suffering, and the pregnant that only the gods may decide on things like life, birth, and death. But I think... you give them potions that put those decisions in their own hands."

She nodded. "This is true. You've observed well. Oh, sometimes the priestesses will look the other way whilst I offer concoctions to help a woman conceive. But as for any other decision... " She shrugged her frail shoulders. "Who do *you* think should decide when a life is too painful to live anymore, or a pregnancy too difficult to bear, Rhianikki?"

Raising my head, I pondered the question. I had learned that Betta's questions were lessons in themselves and must be treated as such. I found another patch of heart-balm leaves and picked a handful, but left most of the leaves alone, so that the plants would continue to grow.

"Who can know what is too much to bear, besides the person who bears it?" I asked. "The temple does not forbid us to end the suffering of an animal, a goat or pig, even an ailing cat would be granted respite, would it not?"

"Oh, indeed, with great ceremony, I expect."

I nodded. "Humans are wise enough to decide for themselves. On that matter, we agree. But on the other—"

"What other?" She was shaking and brushing the dirt off a handful of lung root.

"If the temple forbids something and you assist in it, do you not risk incurring the wrath of the gods?"

"I've been following my own sense of what is right and what is wrong for a great many years now. The gods have shown me only blessings."

"So, it is the priestesses who are wrong?"

"Oh, no, child, the priestesses are also right."

I tucked a bundle of leaves into my bag, which was slung over one shoulder and across my chest. "How can you both be right?"

Betta looked around for a stump, limped over to it and

took a seat. I hurried to sit at her feet on the grassy ground near the bank of the river. The water's rushing and splashing was asplayful and exciting to me, and its scent saturated the air with fish, with seaweed, with river water and mud—it smelled different from anywhere in the world.

"If the priestesses helped a suffering person to die, it would be wrong," Betta said. "And the reason it would be wrong, is because they believe it is wrong. When you believe in your heart that something is wrong and yet you do it anyway, you sin. Likewise, when you believe in your heart that something is right, and though capable, you do not do it, you also sin. Do you understand?"

I blinked and nodded. And then something else occurred to me and I could not keep my eyes from widening.

"Go on, say it," Betta said. "I know those eyes too well. They're the most expressive eyes I've ever seen."

"You are not a priestess," I said.

"I have never claimed to be."

"And yet you teach magic."

"That I do."

"I have heard it said that one who practices magic but is not a priestess can only be a witch."

"I have heard that, too," she said. "But it is only said of women. A *woman* who practices magic but is not a priestess is a witch. A man who does the same, is a mage. Greatly respected and paid for his services. A woman is a witch, feared and avoided in some parts of your father's kingdom, tolerated in others, driven out of the most backward cities."

"Sometimes killed," I said. I'd heard stories. The thought made me shiver. Are you a witch, Betta?"

"I am a practitioner of magic who is not a priestess,"

she said. "What others call me, well, I have no control over that."

"But if the high priestess finds out—"

"The high priestess is a wise woman who misses very little. She cannot condone all that I do. But she knows I was sent for you, Rhianikki. And she knows you need me, so she pretends not to notice, and I do my best to be discreet."

She started to get up. I hurried to grab her walking stick from where she'd leaned it and handed it to her. Our bags were full, so we started back. As we walked along the road, she said, "You are deep in thought."

"I am contemplating whether the gods are real."

"Oh, the gods are real, child. Make no mistake about that. But it is humans who make up the tales about the gods, who interpret the will of the gods, who create religion and rules they later say were given to them by the gods."

I was stunned. "But I thought the tales *were* inspired by the gods!"

"Some are, some by other motivations. Greed, mainly, or the lust for power."

"Then how do I know what to believe?"

She stopped walking and gazed down at me. "Have I not just told you?"

I frowned, perplexed and playing her words over and over in my mind. "I am to believe what my heart tells me is true and act accordingly."

There was a gentle breeze that picked up as day began to fade. The sky was red near the horizon, and deepening to purple.

"You have told everyone in the temple that you are part goddess yourself, have you not?" Answering my question with a question of her own was a practice Betta employed often.

"Am I, truly, though?" I asked, lowering my head. I could not look into her eyes as I awaited her reply, lest she strip me of my divinity with a single word.

She took my chin in one hand, tipped it up so she could gaze into my eyes and said, "It is the truest thing I have ever heard, child. When you speak what is in your heart, it cannot be otherwise."

Then she started off again, walking ahead while I pondered her words.

I felt danger in the instant before I saw it. I even yelped, "Betta!" before the hooded man sprang upon her, swinging a club at her head. It hit with a thud, knocking Betta onto her side so hard her old bones might've broken.

I launched myself at the lumbering, masked villain, screeching like a sandstorm. He turned toward me, opened his huge arms as if I were stupid enough to run straight into them, but I was *not* stupid. I dove, sliding under his legs and punching straight up at his groin. He dropped to his knees, as I scrambled to my feet behind him. I spotted the club he'd dropped and used it to wallop him in the head.

He toppled over sideways and lay there, eyes closed. I watched him only for a moment before leaping over him and falling to my knees beside Betta. There was blood in her wild gray and silver hair, and her pretty blue band had been knocked askew. "Betta." I touched her shoulders. Her breath on my face told me she yet lived. "Betta, wake up. Do not die." I tipped my head backward and shouted at the sky. "She must not die. Do you hear me, Isis? She must not die!"

A sack came over my head from behind, and my hands were clasped in one large one, then bound with a rope as I struggled.

"This one, however, I will kill myself," I promised the goddess.

The man laughed and the sound echoed, amplified, from deep within his cavernous chest. I twisted and kicked him in the shin. He yelped, then cuffed me upside the head and knocked me flat to the ground. The air was forced from my lungs, and for a moment I couldn't suck it back. And then he grabbed me by the front of my dress and lifted me to my feet. I bent slightly, gasping for breath. I could see a thin bit of light through the bottom of the sack, and I turned in search of Betta.

"Your priestess is not dead," the man said. "I can make her that way if you keep fighting me. Or you can come along like you should."

"Come along where?"

He yanked the sack off my head, then with one hand on my skull, turned me toward him. He'd picked up the club, and he went toward Betta and raised it over his head.

I screamed so loudly it should've made his ears bleed. It did make him stop mid-swing. "I'll go with you," I cried. "Let her live!"

He studied me from inside the black hood. There were eye-holes torn in it. It was terrifying. "All right, then. No tricks." Then he lowered the club and adjusted his crotch, wincing a little as he did. He put the sack over my head again, took me by the arm, and marched me along. I could hear the river, calm and lapping at its banks. I could smell it as we drew near.

"If you plan to drown me—"

"If I'd wanted you dead, Princess, I'd have killed you back there."

Then he was not an assassin sent by my father or his murderous wife? That had been what I'd assumed. The queen had left me alone since I'd saved her twin whelps from the child-thief, but I'd expected her gratitude would wear off once she realized I was as much a threat to their claims of kingship as I had ever been.

More so, perhaps. My reputation had spread through the city ever since Anya of the North had received the miracle of a baby on the very day I had promised her one.

"What do you want with me?" I demanded. Perhaps he was in desperate need of some boon from the goddess and had heard of the young royal priestess with the uncanny magical skills. Many had. I was talked about in the city. The people held me in high esteem, and those with dire needs often requested my presence in the petition room when they came to beg favors of Isis.

"Is it a wish you need granted, then?" I asked the oaf. "This is hardly a good way to curry my favor."

"Curry your favor?" He slapped his thigh and laughed that booming laugh again. "Aren't you full of yourself? No, I've not taken you for your wish-granting skills, but for ransom."

I rolled my eyes. "Then you're an idiot."

"An idiot I might be, but you are a princess."

"I am. And who is it you think is going to pay you for my release?"

He scooped me up without warning and I expected to be thrown into the river and began pulling at the rope that bound my hands so I wouldn't drown. But then he lowered me again into a wooden boat. I felt the texture and its rocking motions and saw glimpses of the bottom beneath the sack over my head. He got in too, and it rocked up sideways. Then I felt us move away from shore and into the flow of the current.

"Your father the pharaoh will pay for your return."

"My father the pharaoh who tried to have me killed two years ago, you mean? Either him or his treacherous queen.

I've not decided which," I wriggled my hands in the ropes, then remembered a simple charm Betta had taught me. I stopped twisting my hands, closed my eyes, and imagined the goddess alive and well within me. I imagined the tight knots loosening. "Knot of one, come undone," I said. When I plucked at the knot again, it untied easily. I threw the rope overboard, then took off the hood.

"Hey! You little—"

"If the boat overturns, I will need my hands to stay alive. You cannot ransom a dead princess, oaf."

He had removed his hood, as well, confident that I wouldn't be able to see his face. Of course, I saw it then. He was an Egyptian, one of my own subjects. His dark skin, raven hair, thick eyebrows, and brown eyes were typical of my people. His head was shaved except for a single plait in the back. His jaw was wide, and his neck the size of a thigh. But his eyes were looking worried because of what I'd told him.

"The king will pay to get you back," he said. "He would not want his own daughter dead."

"The entire city saw the attempt on my life at the Festival of Osiris two summers ago. Did you not hear if it?"

He lowered his head. "I keep to myself."

"Isis pushed her statue on top of me to protect me. Only its wing kept it from crushing me." I shrugged. "No, the pharaoh won't pay you a nickel to get me back. He might offer to pay you to finish me off, though."

"Why would he—"

"He wants one or both of his twin sons on his throne, not me. Although... I suppose if you make a public enough case, he'd have to at least pretend to care." He was searching my face, frowning as if he didn't know whether to believe me. Then I nodded past him and said, "Rocks."

He turned quickly and used an oar to steer us around the boulders. Then he turned us into one of a dozen small tributaries that split off from the Nile, and we followed that for a while, and then another, and yet a third, before he finally beached the craft on the shore and helped me out. He pulled a net with a half dozen fish in it from the side of the boat. He'd had it tied on, dangling in the water to keep them cool.

"This way," he said.

I crossed my arms. "It's been hours. Betta could have died by now. Send a message to the temple or to anyone in the city so they will go find her."

He waved a hand at me, blowing air through his teeth. "You needn't worry about your friend. Do you think nobody heard your wailing and roaring at me like a panther out there? I was lucky to get you away before your guards came running."

"*My* guard Luca, would've killed you by now and had me back at the temple eating dates in the garden. But he was called away, and I'm stuck with an imbecile in his place."

"You're a little bit mean, aren't you, Princess?"

"*I'm* mean? *You* hit an old woman in the head with a club, and *I'm* mean?"

"I didn't hit her that hard."

I said a curse word, and he widened his eyes more than when I'd punched him in the testes. Then, shaking his head, he grabbed up the boat, which was as big as three of him, and carried it off. He placed it behind a stand of scrubby brush, glanced back at me, and said through clenched teeth, "This way."

I followed him because we were in a place I did not know. There were a few scraggly trees, no grass, but plenty of shrubs and scrub brush, and a few weeds here and there. I was already contemplating my escape. I would find a way to disable, trick, or distract him. That part would be easy, as I was clearly far smarter than he. Then, somehow, I'd have to drag that boat back to the water's edge. It was heavy, but I thought with enough time, I could do it. After that, I would paddle upstream, against the current, back the way we had come.

"Come along or I'll tie you up again."

"Then I would get free again." I had stopped walking to ponder my options. Maybe I should float *down*stream, for he'd surely expect me to go up. I could find a village, identify myself and command someone return me to the temple.

He barked at me again, and I got moving. Soon we were approaching a small mud-brick house so cleverly tucked into the landscape that I couldn't even see it until we were nearly upon it. It had a thatched roof and a blanket hanging in its doorway. He held the blanket back and ushered me inside.

There, lying on a mat on the floor, was a little girl of five or six, with a dirty face and hair that had seldom seen a comb. She was skin and bone, and did not get up from her place curled in the corner, wrapped in a blanket. The dwindling coals of a fire burned in a pit nearby. A thin stream of smoke was drawn out through a hole in the low ceiling right above the fire pit, but not all the smoke went out. I could taste and smell it in the air.

I looked up at the man as he dropped his netful of fish onto a small wooden table.

"If this poor child is how your prisoners fare," I said, "I will not be staying long."

"Prisoners?" the little girl asked. "Father?"

I looked at her quickly, stunned. *Father*? The oaf was her father?

Her eyes were brimming with tears. "What does she mean, prisoners?"

"This is your own child?" I asked. "By the gods, oaf, what have you done to her?"

"Do not call me oaf. My name is Beck."

"You are an oaf and that is what I shall call you. By the wings of Isis, at least *my* father tried to kill me quickly—a bolt to the heart. But to starve your own child—"

He clapped his flat hand to the side of my head hard enough to make my ears ring as I stumbled sideways and caught myself on the wooden table. Water sprang into my eyes—not tears.

"Father!" The girl cried, louder than I'd have expected, given her obvious weakened state. Then she came to me, and I realized she was older than I'd thought. She stood nearly as tall as I but was so thin I could count her bones. She took me by my arm and led me back to her spot near the fire, pulled me to sit down beside her on her cushion. "I am not starving, nor a prisoner," she said. "I am only sick. My name is Meela."

"I am Rhianikki," I said.

"Do not talk to her!" the oaf shouted, and then he leaned over me, gripped my arm and tugged me across the small abode to the corner farthest from the girl. "Stay there. You move, I'll tie you up gain."

"Tie me up again and I will kill you in your sleep."

"Father, stop!" The girl started to cough. She bent over herself, hugging her waist, coughing so hard I thought she would die from lack of a breath. The big man went to her, knelt and held her, rubbing her back until the spasm passed. Then he reached for a rag to dab the blood from her lips.

She huddled there, bent over, breathing as if she were air-starved. When she could lift her head again, she looked up at him. "W-why have you brought her here?" Her eyes were stricken with heartbreak and pain... and with love for the oaf. "What have you done, Father?"

He shifted his eyes away from hers, and I saw shame in his face. Before he could answer there was a plaintive mewling sound from where we'd entered, and an animal, a cat, came partway in. It had a sleek black coat, and stood half in, half out, with the blanket that blocked the doorway draped over its back. Oh, such a beautiful creature I had never seen! It lifted its chin, sniffing the air, clearly smelling the fish.

The little girl's father looked down at it. I expected him to kick the poor animal and was ready to bury him if he did. But instead, he said, "Yes, yes." Then he went to the table, took the smallest fish from the pile and carried it to the cat. He pulled the blanket aside and tossed the fish out. The cat spun around and bolted after it, and I was able to see it more fully. She was female, with an expanded belly and swollen teats hanging low. She was carrying kittens.

"I call her Bast, like the goddess," Meela said. "She just showed up here one day."

"It's a good name."

She smiled at me, but then lay down again, exhausted, I thought, from all the excitement and the coughing fit. I doubted she saw many people besides her father, nor was it likely she'd traveled far from this hovel.

"Will you tell me, Rhianikki, since my father won't? What has he done to you? Why has he brought you here?

Did he take you against your will?" She sent the man a disappointed look. He could not hold her gaze.

I knew I could hurt the oaf more by telling his child the truth than by driving a knife into his heart. But while Betta had been teaching me about magic, and plants, and powers, Priestess Elana had been teaching me about compassion. One of her lessons, one that I had been attempting to put into practice since she called it my weak spot, was to measure my words against the good or harm that uttering them would bring. In this case, I thought that blurting the truth might hurt the little girl even more than it would hurt her beastly father. And the child was already ill, suffering, and born to an oaf. She had enough problems. She was not my enemy.

He said nothing but hung his head, knowing his little girl would soon hear the truth. That he'd pummeled an old woman and kidnapped a young priestess. He was donkey dung, a useless idiot with a cruel streak and more brawn than brain.

But he had fed that cat.

I sighed, closing my eyes, and hating what I was about to do. And yet, my heart told me it was the right thing. And had that not been the lesson of this very day? To listen to what my heart told me was right?

I looked the little girl in the eyes. "I have been studying the healing arts at the Temple of Isis," I said. "I am here to help you get strong and well again."

I met the oaf's stunned gaze, daring him to disagree. Then he looked at his daughter.

She studied him, skepticism clear in her face. She was intelligent. It must have come from her mother's side. "If we want Rhianikki's help, Father, should we not treat her as an honored guest rather than as a prisoner?"

He lowered his head. "The journey was long and I am overly tired, and worried for you, Meela." Then he turned to me. "I am sorry."

"As well you should be," I said. Then I returned to the spot near the girl and the fire.

The man went to the table, sat on one of the two wooden benches that flanked it, and pulled a knife from his belt to begin cleaning the fish.

He was still my captor, and I was still his prisoner. He would likely kill me when he realized he would receive no ransom. But there was no reason I couldn't try to help the girl while I awaited my chance to escape.

And if I returned to the temple to find that my beloved Betta had died, I would come back to this place and kill him.

# CHAPTER 6
## THE CAT

Beck, the oaf, cooked fish over the fire. Every time he added fuel—dried dung, moss, and other litter, my eyes and nose burned a little more. When he deemed the fish done, he divided it onto three plates, two fish for each of us, and three for him. He set the plates on the small table, which, to his credit, he had washed off after the fish-gutting.

Meela started to get up from her nest on the floor. I moved closer, ready to offer help should she stumble. Her legs were thin and weak, and she limped when she walked.

I had touched her face to check for a fever, the way Betta had taught me to do, but her skin was cool. I'd noticed a whistling sound to her breaths. Her eyes were dull and red, another sign of illness.

She noticed my close observation and offered a small smile, then limped to the table and slid onto the bench across from her father.

I stood looking at the plate in front of me. It was pottery, and fish-shaped itself. Then I looked around the hovel. "Is there anything else?"

"It's all we have," Beck said, and I could hear the edge of irritation in his tone. He thought I should be grateful and eat what I was given. "I'm sure you're used to far better food in the temple, but here we only eat what I can catch or kill myself. And this is all I caught today. Eat the fish, Princess."

"The eating of flesh is forbidden in the temple. We do not even wear leather sandals." I lifted one of my feet so he could see the bamboo sandals I wore. This was the custom in all the temples, according to the priestesses. "If I am to be a priestess, I must keep my body pure."

"But—what do you eat, then?" Meela asked, her eyes wide.

I frowned at her. "Vegetables, fruits, nuts, breads—many things." I looked at the oaf. "There are roots and herbs that grow wild. I can go out and gather some if you—"

"No."

"You may come along, watch that I don't run away."

"Eat the fish or go hungry." He tucked into his own meal and I silently wished he would choke on a bone. I went to my plate and pushed it across to him. "Have my share, too."

He took my two fish and dropped one onto Meela's plate, the other onto his own. I sighed and returned to the fireplace.

The oaf snored like a roaring bull. He had cleverly positioned himself on the floor right across the hovel's only opening, the idiot. I hopped over him without making a sound and slipped through the blanket outside into the night.

Fresh air filled my lungs for the first time in hours. The smoky air inside and the girl's wheezing must be related. I would mull on a solution while I sought sustenance.

The moon was full, still low on the horizon and spilling plenty of light to assist in my efforts. I walked to the river's edge, then along its banks, where the soil was rich and fertile. The splashing current was like a song, the fishy aroma like the scent of flowers to me. There were leeks and wild garlic in abundance. Further from the edge, I found wild turnips, as well. I gathered them into my skirt, carried them back and dumped them on the ground near the well.

Then I brushed the dirt away from my skirt, and returned to my hunt, this time gathering numerous greens. I picked ripe berries to add sweetness, carried all of it back and dumped it beside the rest. There was a large rock that was near the well. It would make a good seat and was near a circle of stones where there had clearly been fires.

Taking the river walk in a different direction, I located herbs for seasoning, and then a beam of moon glow illuminated the spotted leaves of the lung root plant! I nearly shouted for joy. "Thank you, Lady Isis! This is exactly what Meela needs." As soon as I breathed the words, I knew that she needed much more than just the root, and I felt, too, that the goddess had sent me that knowledge.

I had to sneak back into that hovel, over the sleeping oaf, and I could have kicked myself for it. I should've brought a cook-pot out with me. If I woke him, he would ruin everything.

I pulled back the blanket and noticed the smoky air immediately. After breathing outside for hours, it nearly made me cough, and I held my forearm over my mouth to muffle it in case I couldn't hold it back. My eyes watered.

Meela was awake, watching me with wide, curious eyes. I put my finger to my lips to signal silence, then deftly stepped over her father and went to crouch low beside her.

"I thought you must've run away," she whispered, leaning close to my ear so I could hear her.

"I've been gathering vegetables and herbs. And now I'm going to cook for us. But I need a pot. Two pots." I looked at the stacks of pottery vessels under the table. There were cups and pitchers, plates and bowls, pots of all sizes. Many had swirls or flowers etched into them. There were no glyphs or writing. It was odd, considering how very poor this family seemed to be.

"I want to help," Meela whispered.

I should say no, I thought, but my heart wanted to say yes, so I must act accordingly.

I looked at her, then at the stack of pottery, then at her father's bulk blocking the doorway. Then I shrugged. "Okay. Wait here." I crept to the table, and moved the pots around as quietly as I could manage, finding two large ones to suit my needs, one of which fit inside the other. I put two cups inside the smaller pot, and found a large wooden spoon, as well. I carried this back to the fireplace inside the house, crouching low again. Taking one of the cups, I dipped it into the fire to scoop out a few coals, then placed it carefully inside the other pots. Holding the nested pots in my arms, I crouched down in front of Meela.

"Hug my neck and hold on tight. Oh, and bring your blanket."

She wrapped her blanket around her, then put her arms around my neck. "My big brother used to carry me like this," she whispered. As I rose, she locked her legs around my waist.

I carried her as easily as I might've carried that stray black cat. Then with great care, I stepped over the sleeping man. As soon as I put my first foot on the other side of him, he released a sudden snore, and I jumped so hard I nearly dropped the pots. I froze where I was, one leg on either side of his big belly, and he started to roll.

I lifted my back foot as he rolled toward it, and his bulk brushed my ankle. I clenched my teeth, looking down, startled, freezing in mid-motion. And there I saw his knife, its blade wrapped in leather. It was stuck through the rope belt he wore around his waist. I reached down, took hold of the knife hilt, and slid it free as I pulled my leg over him. Then I ducked through the blanketed doorway and outside, where I released my pent-up breath.

I expected him to come roaring out of the hut like a bull, and stood for a moment, very still, silent, turning only my head and my eyes to watch the doorway. But the blanket just settled back into position, and no sound or movement came from the oaf.

"Thank you, Isis," I whispered. My knees went so weak I nearly dropped the girl, but then I stiffened them up and walked toward my cooking station. I lowered Meela onto the boulder near the well and adjusted her blanket over her legs.

"If you watch what I do, you'll be able to do it yourself," I told her, and then I gathered the driest bits of moss, twigs and debris I could find, and piled them into the charred stone circle. I had intended to start the fire with my will, but Betta had warned me about doing anything like that in front of outsiders. She said it was dangerous, and I believed her.

Besides, this way, Meela would always know how to start a new fire from old coals.

When my fuel was ready, I made a hole within the pile, and shook the coals from the cup into it. Kneeling, I blew on it. The flames caught quickly, and soon a small fire was going. I fed it with twigs, then left it to burn while I dipped water from the well and used it to wash the bounty I'd gathered.

"My teachers at the temple insist we wash our food before eating it. Everything must be purified before it enters our bodies. They say it is not for spiritual reasons alone, but that it is also a practice for good health. So, you should do this, too."

I used the blade I'd taken from the oaf to scrape, peel, and chop the mushrooms, garlic, turnips, leeks, and greens I'd gathered, adding some other plants to lend flavor. All of this I put into a clean pot of water for cooking.

Next I rinsed the most flavorful herbs, tore them to bits and dropped them into the two pottery mugs. To one mug, I added minced bits of the lung root.

I placed three large rocks near the edges of my fire, and balanced the pot between them, so the fire could burn underneath, then I added more fuel. Dipping our cups full of water, I put them near the flames as well, to steep our tea. Then I sat beside the girl, adjusted her blanket again, and watched the fire. It was reflected in her brown eyes.

She watched me in a way no one ever had. She watched me as if she adored me.

A short while later, Meela and I were sipping our tea.

Hers was mostly lung root and mint. Mine had mint too, and the steeped leaves of a calming plant I hoped would keep me from losing my temper and killing the oaf.

As soon as I thought of him, he emerged from the hut, bellowing. "Just what do you think you're doing outside!"

"Good morning, oaf," I said. "The goddess has told me that Meela needs to breathe clean air. Can you not hear the cries of her breaths, how they squeal in and out of her body?"

"She needs to be inside, warm and safe. What do you know about it, anyway? You're only a few years older yourself."

"I am nine," I said. "This is what a healthy nine-year-old looks like. Meela looks like a sickly five-year-old."

"You will watch your tongue—" He raised his hand to slap me.

I pulled his knife from my sash and held it up so suddenly that he struck it instead of my face—the dull side, and with his forearm. Then he held onto his own wrist and hopped in a circle, cursing.

"Father!" The girl jumped to her feet.

"How did you get my knife! You little demon, I'll—"

"You'll stop fussing, sit down, and eat some of the breakfast Meela and I have made for you." I'd given her the spoon and told her to stir the pot. She'd done so as if it were the most important job in the world. I tucked the blade back into the sash wrapped around my filthy dress, and went inside to get bowls.

Meela was speaking to him as I emerged. "She made this tea to help my lungs, and father, I think it's working. I feel better this morning. My head doesn't hurt so much."

I poured the soup into bowls and handed them around.

The oaf sniffed at his, then looked at me suspiciously. "What's in it?"

"Plants," I said.

"Some plants can make you sick."

"Yes, that's true. Don't eat those kinds." I tipped my bowl to my lips and took a large, noisy slurp.

Meela did exactly as I did, and then her eyes widened. "It's *good*!"

"It needs salt," I said, then I looked at the oaf with my eyebrows raised.

He took a sip, his expression the same as if he were being forced to taste swamp water. But then his brows rose and he sipped again.

"At the temple, we are taught that plants have all that is required to keep us healthy and strong, and that for any ailment we might suffer, there is a plant that holds the cure. If you eat only meat, you miss all the medicine the gods put into plants for us."

"They teach this at the temple?"

I nodded. "And more, I found lung root here. It's for problems involving the breath. Breath is spirit, you know. It is life."

"I didn't know that," Meela said, looking up from her bowl, which was already half empty. "Did you know that, Father?"

"I did not."

"That's what's in Meela's tea, lung root and some mint. If she drinks it every day from now on, it will gradually ease her breathing, which will, in turn, increase her vitality as more spirit is able to infuse her body." I sat back and smiled, pleased with myself for having known how to help the girl, thanks to my dear Betta.

He sat there watching me as we ate our soup, as if he

was unsure what to make of me. Then suddenly there came the loudest shriek I'd ever heard in all my life. I set my bowl aside and jumped to my feet. It was coming from the little hovel. But there was no one inside.

"Bast!" The girl shouted. "It's the cat! Something's killing her. Do something, Father!"

The oaf surged into action. As he passed me, he yanked his knife from my belt, and I cursed myself for not stepping aside in time. But the sound was truly horrifying.

He was almost to the entrance, when he stopped, then crouched and looked at the ground near the bottom of the front wall, to the left of the doorway. I saw that a hole had been dug in the ground against and beneath the wall.

"It's her time," he said softly, and we heard him well, since we stood only a half-step behind him, leaning in either direction, trying to see around his bulk. "The kittens are coming."

❧

When the shrieking was done, I watched in stunned silence as the oaf gathered the cat and her three newborns into a wide, shallow, basket he'd had Meela fetch from the hovel. He'd lined it with dried rushes from a pile he kept inside for wrapping food and starting fires. As the cat stood in the basket, licking her kits, he called, "Meela, come soothe her while I clean the nest."

"But... can't we take them inside, father? It gets cold at night."

He looked at the girl, then at me, then he put his back to

77

us both. He used a broken piece of pottery to dig dirt from under the wall, removing the mess left by birthing.

Meela knelt near the basket, stroking the mother cat. Bast pushed against Meela's hand with her head, obviously loving the affection. After a few more strokes, the cat lay down and stretched out on her side. The kittens, each as black as night, rooted around until they found her and began to nurse.

After a few minutes, Meela's father stopped digging and turned to me. "You said the air in the house is bad."

I hadn't said, "house," but I nodded. "From the smoke. But I thought you didn't believe me."

He nodded at Meela. "How can I not believe my own eyes?"

Even I could see the improvement in her, just from being outside for most of the night and morning.

"But unlike the cat, we cannot live outside forever," he added.

"One of my teachers, dear Betta, says there is no such thing as a problem without a solution." I looked around. "You have a lot of pottery. How did you collect so much?" They were obviously too poor to afford to buy it.

"I make it," he said. It probably offended him that I gasped in surprise. "It's not difficult, and there's plenty of clay soil nearby. Even an oaf can shape a pot from clay." He took the basket up and tucked it back into the dirt cave beneath the wall of his home with great care, cat, kittens and all.

"Not all of them," I said softly. "In the temple, we have fires for cooking and kilns outside the building."

"But the nights get cold and Meela's so frail."

"Our nights get barely cool, much less cold. My friend from the north spoke of such cold that the water turns hard, and the rain falls as small white bits of fluff. Here, cold is refreshing and good. If it's too cool, use more blankets. If it's not enough, gather coals from the outside fire and bring them in to warm the place. But mind the smoke goes out," I said, "And only hang the blanket over the door when it's very cold. Mostly, leave it open. And when the nights are warm, sleep on the roof. The clean air will heal her. She needs it more than she needs heat."

He gazed at me. "How do you know all this?"

"I've been talking to Isis about it most of the night."

He'd risen from his crouch in front of the cat at long last. Meela and I crawled nearer, on all fours like cats ourselves, to peer in at her.

He said, "The goddess speaks to you?"

"Not precisely," I said. "I talk to her inside my mind. Like a prayer. But more like a discussion, not begging, the way most pray. Later, when I'm thinking about something else, I realize that I know what to do. The answer I sought is right there where I thought it wasn't."

He blinked at me, and it was gratifying to see that he was listening.

Encouraged, I went on. "While I was cooking, my mind kept picturing our ovens and cook fires at the temple. And I kept feeling the breeze coming in through our uncovered windows and doorways. Only just now as you spoke, did I understand that those images were the answer to the question I'd asked of Isis."

He looked at me, then looked down at his daughter, still kneeling by the kittens.

"It is also in my mind that Meela needs to eat plants, not meat alone. As do all people. And you have plenty of good rich dirt in which to grow beans and peas, herbs and greens. Leeks grow wild along the shore. And there's parsnip, turnip, garlic, aplenty if you know how to find them. I'll show you."

He nodded, but he looked troubled. Then he shifted his gaze to Meela, lying on her belly to pet the cat.

"If you pester her, she'll take her kits away and hide them," he called to his daughter.

Meela quickly withdrew her hand, looking alarmed.

"Here," I said. "Give her some broth to make up for it." I dipped a very small amount of broth into my empty bowl and gave it to the girl. She slid it carefully into Bast's den.

"Cats don't eat vegetables," the oaf said.

"Animals know what is good for them," I replied. "They have an inner knowing that is not drowned out by logic, as it is with us." As if to prove my wisdom, the cat sniffed at the broth, and then lapped up a bit of it.

I returned to my spot near the fire. "If we bury the fire in sand, the coals might still be warm come nightfall," I said. "I've seen the temple servants do it."

"That much, even I know." The oaf came over, and with a glance back at Meela to be sure she was out of earshot, said, "You are favored by Isis. I made a terrible mistake in wronging you. I will surely be cursed for this."

"Yes, you probably will," I said, and in my mind, I was composing the horrible list of ways in which that curse might manifest to tell him about. Meela giggled, and I glanced her way.

She was looking from the kittens to her father, smiling, beaming. My heart disagreed with my mind, yet again.

I took a deep breath and allowed it to speak instead. "You thought to ransom me to help Meela, yes?"

He nodded. "That was part of it. There is a healer I've heard of a day's journey by river. But I've been told his price is dear."

"That's not the point. You abducted me to help Meela. How can you be so sure it wasn't Isis who gave you the idea?"

"To abduct a young priestess?"

"To bring me here. Which you did. And now Meela has my help and I will teach you how to ensure that her healing continues, even after I'm gone. It is the answer to your prayer, is it not?"

He blinked in disbelief. "It is the answer to part of my prayer, yes."

"Well, there you have it. It is surprising how many people do not even recognize when their prayers are answered. They always seem so shocked when I point it out to them." I shrugged my shoulders. "It was not Isis' idea to pummel my teacher, however. I have no idea what your punishment for that might be. But if Betta is not seriously injured, then the punch to your manly parts I delivered was probably sufficient." I smiled at him when I said it.

He smiled back. It was my first glimpse of his smile. The teeth that were not brown, were missing.

Behind him, Meela giggled. She had come back over to us and heard the latter part of our conversation. Her face turned serious and she asked, "Do you really think the goddess answers prayers, Rhianikki?"

"Did you pray to be well again?" I asked.

"Every day!"

"And are you beginning to feel well again?"

She opened her mouth, then closed it again, then smiled and nodded.

I said, "See?" And then as I thought about it, I found a new understanding in my heart. "I was sent away from my home and my family to live in the temple in a far-away place. It seemed disastrous at the time. But now I believe it was always what I was supposed to do, and that it was all by Isis' hand."

Meela looked at her father, asking him something with her round, brown eyes, and he gave a slight nod as his answer.

"Then perhaps Isis will find a way to bring my brother back to us," she said very softly.

"Your brother?" I frowned and recalled she had mentioned an older brother last night. "Did he not grow up and move away?"

"Kiko is only twelve. And he did not move away. He was taken."

I swung my gaze to the oaf, who looked surprised, not at the news, but at his daughter's knowledge of it.

"Where is he?" I asked. "What became of him?"

"He was caught stealing bread," Meela said. "Father has told me he went on a journey and will return, but I know the truth. I am small and sickly, but I am not stupid." She swung her eyes from her father's to mine. "Six moons, he's been gone."

"For stealing bread?"

The oaf sighed, lowering his head and shaking it slowly. "It was the pharaoh's bread," he said. "The king was visiting a nearby village, staying at the home of the magistrate. There was to be a feast in his honor, and Kiko saw the parade of local cooks and bakers lined up outside with offerings of breads, and fruits, and casks of wine."

"That's how it always is, wherever he goes," I said.

"A baker had a sack over his shoulder, bulging with breads," the father went on. "He stood at the back of the line. Kiko snatched a loaf of bread from the sack and ran with it. A shout went up, and the pharaoh's guards chased him down. They shackled him. The bread, they fed to the magistrate's dogs." His voice broke. "A villager who saw it all came to tell us what had happened."

My temper rose. "And where is Kiko now?"

The oaf looked at Meela, clearly not wanting to say in front of her. She spoke instead. "It was said that when the pharaoh's caravan left the village, my brother was bound and walking behind."

Anger covered my mind like a dark cloud. I told myself to check my heart for its feelings on the matter. But my heart swirled with flames of rage. If I was to trust the feelings in my heart, and to act accordingly, as my teacher had told me I should, then there was going to be some very big trouble in my father's palace.

# CHAPTER 7
## THE STOWAWAY

Meela and I had discovered a huge patch of mushrooms and were gathering them for the evening meal. "Once more," I said. "Which one is for healing?"

The girl scanned the ground and quickly snatched up the correct fungus. Then I pointed, "And that one is for eating. And those over there, with the dark spots are poison and never to be touched at all. It's important to know which is which so you do not pick the wrong ones when I am no longer here."

She lowered her head and stuck out her lip. "I don't want you to go, Rhianikki. Life is so much better when you are here."

I'd been with Meela and the oaf for ten days, and she had improved beyond measure in that time. We'd made beds on the roof, where it was cool and breezy. I'd sewn together scraps of cloth to make long skirts and wraps for her, to keep the chill away, but I noticed the better she felt, the less she shivered and complained of cold. Her color was better, all hints of yellow completely erased. And most noticeable of all, her eyes were bright and clearl now.

"I know you feel sad that I must leave, so I'm going to tell you a secret."

"A secret?" She moved nearer me, taking a seat on the ground. It was a beautiful autumn day, the air was fresh, the breeze gentle and warm.

I knew there was nothing that bothered Meela more than being kept in the dark about things. It was true, I thought, of most children. Even when I had lived in my father's palace, there had been infuriating whispers among the adults that were "not meant for young ears." I suspected that many of them had been about me.

"Your father doesn't want you to know where I am going when I leave you. He is afraid that if I fail in my mission, your heart will be broken."

She lowered her chin to hide her smile and whispered, "I knew it."

"What did you know?" I asked.

"You're going to rescue my brother." Then she lifted her chin and met my eyes. "You are, aren't you, Rhianikki? I knew it. I knew you would."

I could not keep the grin from my lips. The girl was too sharp to be fooled for very long. "How did you guess?"

She shrugged. "I prayed to Isis. Then I dreamed that you saved him." I nodded. "Do you really think you can?"

"Of course I can." I knew where most prisoners went— wherever there was a building project in need of workers. If they were terribly dangerous, they might be kept in a stone quarry too deep in the desert to escape alive.

Much crashing came from the brush behind us, but we were not startled. The oaf was a noisy walker. However, he emerged from the scrubby bushes with a skinny bald man walking close beside him, and I jumped to my feet at the sight of the young stranger.

"It is Cobb," Meela said, getting up to stand beside me. "He's Kiko's friend from the village."

The oaf said, "I sent him to the temple to check on your teacher as you asked."

"And?"

I met the young man's eyes. He nodded and said, "I dared not ask after her, as the place was bustling, guards in and out, everyone buzzing about a missing priestess." He shifted his eyes between mine and the oaf's. "So I just hid myself and observed. They took breakfast in the courtyard, and I could see within from the top of the dune behind the temple. There was a woman with dark skin, her hair wild, all gray and silver, her eyes very large and set wide in her face. I heard another woman call her Betta."

I blinked rapidly against the hot rush that flooded my eyes. I looked at the oaf. "How do I know you did not tell him what to say?"

He lifted his eyebrows almost helplessly. "I didn't, I vow it."

"We'll see," I said. Then, to Cobb, "What was she wearing?"

He lowered his eyes as if thinking. "Her dress was light blue, as if most of the dye had been washed away. No sash. No headdress." Then his head rose, his eyes wider. "Oh, and around her neck, a long strand of beads, black and honey colored."

Her power beads. Betta only wore the amber and jet when serious magic was afoot. He couldn't have known that, nor could the oaf.

"And she was well?" I asked.

"She seemed well, for a woman of her age."

I nodded, looking from the boy to the oaf. "Thank you." Looking relieved, the boy ran off.

"I am as glad of this news as you are, Princess," Meela's father said.

"You should be," I replied. "Have you finished your pottery for the day?"

"Yes, but I've no need for so much. It will crowd us out of our home."

"Go and pile it all into the boat, and fresh water for drinking, and some of those wild figs we picked yesterday, and let us travel to the nearby village."

"With the pottery?"

"Yes," I replied. And when he continued to gaze at me blankly, I said, "Though it pains me to admit it, oaf, you are an unusually gifted potter."

"No, I'm not, I just—"

"Yes, Beck, you are." It got his attention, my using his name. "I've lived in a palace, have I not?"

He nodded.

"I have seen the work of the finest artisans at my father's table. Yours is equal to it, minus the fancy glazes and inlaid gemstones. Certainly, better than what most of the villagers are using."

"It's not," he said.

"Why do you argue so vigorously against your own value?" I asked. "You cannot get by in this world by cowering beneath your weaknesses, only by recognizing and using your strengths. Proudly. With confidence." I emphasized the last with a punch to the air, exactly the way Betta had done when she'd said the same lines to a student-priestess who had no confidence in her own skills. Then I brushed the dirt from my hands, picked up the basket of mushrooms, and said, "Come, Meela, let us wash up for our trip to the village."

At the edge of the marketplace, Meela and I stood her father's pots on the side of a well-worn and mostly flat road, while he carried them from the boat. There was a dress maker beside us, with racks to hold her wares. We had no rack, no table, no tent. But we lined up our pots all the same.

I was merely standing items in straight rows, but Meela kept taking them from where I had put them and arranging them into small groupings. Four bowls with spoons, a pitcher with several drinking vessels surrounding it, cook pots with large stirring paddles. Behind each grouping, she stacked like items.

People were stopping to look even as we set things up, so I said to one of them, "The potter is gifted, is he not? And he is willing to barter."

"Is he now?"

"Yes," I said, but she was still looking at me curiously.

Others came to trade for the pots. Someone offered bread in exchange for a pitcher. Another offered bits of silver. Our neighbor traded two dresses for two large bowls. And on and on it went.

As the oaf came huffing up from the shore, his arms laden with all he could carry, there were numerous empty spaces in front of us, and goods piling up behind us.

"Father!" Meela called. "We have three loaves of bread and five chickens. Chickens, father!"

"Chickens need feed," he moped.

"Large cook-pots over here," I called out toward the crowd, near giddy with the wild success of our journey. It was beyond even my expectations. "We'll trade for chicken feed!"

Meela laughed and laughed. Her father only scowled, until a man walked up with a sack over his shoulder. "Corn, ground fine," he said. "Test the weight." He handed it to Beck, who held the sack by its neck to judge its heft. "For that pot there, with the flower?" the man asked. "And throw in the spoon?"

Nodding as if not quite comprehending events, the silly oaf just stood there. Meela said, "Deal," and quickly handed the man the pot, spoon and all.

"My wife will be overjoyed!" He walked away humming.

"Are you beginning to see your worth yet, oaf?"

"I... I have chickens. And feed for them. And three loaves of bread."

"And fruits, father," Meela said. "A whole basketful."

"And silver," I added, shaking the cloth pouch I held. "And more customers, lining up."

I could not stop smiling as I watched the oaf trade his pottery until every last piece was gone, and the supplies piled behind us were like a treasure trove. There were meats and salted fish, vegetables and fruits, grains and breads, oils and honey, beer and wine, fabric for clothing, carpets and cushions and tools.

"I feel like a rich man," he said.

"Keep doing this every so often, and you soon will be," I said.

He looked at the pile, then at me. "We'll never get it all into the boat."

"Yes, you will," I said, "for I am not going back with you. It is time for me to leave on my journey to my father's palace in Luxor to free young Kiko and bring him back to you."

Meela lowered her eyes while her father shook his head. "It is too far for a young girl alone," the oaf said.

"I won't be alone. I'll be on that barge near where we left your boat. It's being loaded with goods bound for Luxor. And I'll be onboard when it leaves."

Meela came and hugged my neck. "I will miss you."

"I will return, I promise. And now you know how to be healthy. How to make the lung root tea. How to eat a wider variety of foods. How to sleep where the air is clear. You must keep doing all those things."

"I will, I promise."

She ran to the pile of goods, located a sack and began putting foods into it, fruits and a loaf of the bread. She glanced at her father before handing it to me, and he nodded his consent. Then he took the small sack of silver, poured a few pieces into his palm, and handed them to me. "To help you on your journey."

"Thank you." Meela's eyes were welling. This goodbye was becoming too sad. "Let us help your father load the boat," I said, because she needed distraction.

We began picking things up and piling them in. The oaf was skilled at balancing a load, and soon I stood on the shore, waving them goodbye as they set off on the river, back toward their home. I'd memorized the way. Bear right at the second fork, then left at the third.

From a short distance away, I heard a woman say, "There, that's her. She's been here all day. Do you think she's the one those soldiers were asking after?"

"There's a reward, you know," said another.

A chill danced along my spine. I was found.

"Hey, little girl." The two were coming toward me,

another following behind. "You, yes, you. Are you the missing priestess?"

"There is a missing priestess?" I looked around as if I might spot her hiding in the rushes and reeds. I noted they'd said "priestess" not "princess." Someone was keeping my disappearance quiet. Perhaps the priestesses had not yet told my father. Or perhaps they had, and my father did not wish to make my vanishing public knowledge.

"You fit her description," the second woman said.

"Dark hair, dark eyes, dark brows, dark skin... It's the description of every nine—" I caught myself, pretended to cough to cover the word, then completed the sentence. "Every twelve-year-old girl in the village."

"That's true," a man who'd followed a few steps behind them said.

"Striking eyes, they said, full of fire." The first woman gazed into my eyes. I tried to bank my inner flame.

"Sure, but nine years old, they said," the man reminded her. "This one's twelve."

I wondered why she let herself be corrected by her intellectual inferior. She looked at him as if he'd sprouted fish scales but said not a word.

"My father is calling me," I said. "His temper is short. I must go." I turned on my heel and ran straight back into the marketplace, heading for the booths with the most people. "Coming, Father!" I waved a hand as if at him, then dove into the crowd.

I was tall for my age, so my head was about chest level with the adults. I found myself fighting for a breath amid a throng of breasts and chests as I elbowed my way through.

*Stay upright, stay upright,* I told myself. *Do not fall down! Falling down is death.*

I aimed for what I hoped was the shortest path through, rather than the length of the shoppers, stomping on feet to get the last few bodies out of my way, and emerged at last into open space. Pressing my hands to my knees, I bent and drank in big, full breaths of air. Of spirit.

After I few seconds, I straightened and realized I must disguise myself. If soldiers had been searching this village for a missing little priestess, a strange girl all alone would rouse suspicion. I put on the new dress and used a piece of the silver to purchase a long blue sari I could wrap in myriad ways, including as a hooded cloak, which I did. It covered my face and hair, and I kept my eyes downcast, lest anyone else notice my "striking eyes full of fire."

I took a meandering path amid stands of sellers, holding my sack full of food within the cloak's voluminous folds. The sun was setting now, and the marketplace was coming to full boisterous life. I'd thought it busy before, but by night, its energy shifted entirely. Musicians came out with fire dancers and belly dancers, performing for their living. There were poets and bards standing far apart, reciting their beautiful words. The sellers of fruits and vegetables were packing up their carts and pushing them away, while those selling clothing and jewelry seemed to multiply. Other booths sold beer and wine, still others, opium and ashwagandha.

I was sorry Meela had gone. She would have loved to have seen this. But I would return and bring her another time. I smelled the smoke of Acacia, a sacred herb used by the most experienced of priestesses to induce visions and walk, for a time, among the gods. And there was a woman telling fortunes. She had a sphere of clear crystal in front of her on a metal stand, and she stroked it the way Meela stroked her cat. I deliberately avoided looking at her as I headed that way. I must pass her stand to get to the river, down the gentle slope behind her.

"I shall tell your future, girl. Would you like to know your fate? Or the name of your one true love?"

I looked past her. The barge was directly below us. She was the last thing standing between me and my goal, and I should hurry. People were looking for me here.

And yet...

"Come now. Sit yourself. It won't take long, and you can keep that cloak over your head. No one will recognize you, and I can keep a secret. Ohhh, the secrets I've kept."

She was not a fake. I knew this in that way I sometimes knew things. She was like Betta in some odd way I could not quite identify.

"Sit, child."

I sat, glancing behind me, seeing no threat. The villagers were speaking louder as they indulged in their intoxicants of choice. Maybe I wouldn't bring Meela back by night after all.

She took my hand, then drew hers away. "You are... you are unique. Unlike anyone else."

"In so many ways," I said.

"Your lifetime is made up of many lifetimes. It is so long, so very *very* long... " There she frowned, released my hand, and sat quiet, as if mulling on me.

"And my true love?" I prompted, because my back was starting to feel itchy and twitchy. I needed to put this village behind me.

"Ahh," she said, and she moved her hand over the crystal sphere. It seemed to be filled with swirling mists and then a face appeared in the depths of the thing. The most beautiful man I had ever seen, his dark hair was long and pulled back and tied there. He had rich brown eyes and thick lashes. His lips... they were the most beautiful lips I could imagine. Something in my heart fluttered like a trapped bird.

He was there and gone so quickly, that I caught my hand reaching out to the crystal as if to grab him and bring him back.

"He is not yet born, your love."

"He is that much younger than me?"

"*So much* younger," she said.

"What is his name?"

"He has not been born, so he has no name, not yet. You will love many before he comes to you, but when you see him, you will know him, and the love between you will be like no other, and for you there will be no one else from then on and on and on... "

She gazed into the distance, a tear welling in her eye. And then she blinked it away and held out her hand.

I dug out a bigger piece of silver than I'd intended, because her message had touched me deeply. The deepest part of my soul received it, and recognized it as truth. And I'd glimpsed his face, just for a moment, and hoped it had been burned into my memory as deeply as it had been burned into my heart.

She closed her palm around the silver. "You can cut through here to get to the barge," she said. "No one will see you in the darkness. You chose a good color."

I hesitated, startled that she knew my plan.

"Go on. I will tell no one. We women of magic must care for one another."

I started to walk away, and then turned back as something came irresistibly to my mind. "Your oil lamp will set fire to your tent tonight," I said. "But not if you never light it."

She gazed at me, knowing me for what I was, I think, in that same odd way that I knew her, and she said, "Thank you, little priestess. I will take your advice."

I bent my head slightly, and turning, hurried all the way down to the edge of the Nile. There I removed my new sari and rolled it up so I could carry it over my head and keep it dry while I waded through the shallows, through the rushes where I would not be seen, chanting Betta's anti-crocodile charm as I did.

"Sure as Horus bested Seth, biting me ensures your death."

I made it to the boat with all my limbs intact and used dangling ropes to pull myself up over the side. Then, staying low, I ducked in amongst the cargo. I found a perfect spot, hidden from all sides. Rolled carpets were my bed, crates filled with wine and oil casks, my walls. I removed my wet sandals and pretty new dress, hanging them from the crate beside me in hopes they would dry. I wore the new sari, wrapped around me, twisted secure, then draped over my shoulders for warmth.

My temporary quarters were as comfortable as my bed at the temple—and more comfortable than the oaf's hovel floor had been. Thank Isis Meela had a bed on the roof now. I ate a chunk of the bread, then curled up to sleep.

I didn't rouse myself much when I heard voices and felt the vibrations of footsteps. I started for just a moment, then reminded myself how deeply I'd crawled into the stacked cargo. I was entirely safe here.

Soon the boat was gliding into motion, the voices above quieted, aside from soft murmurs between the orders called out by the boat master, and I settled in for the journey home, to reunite with my family.

I wondered if the queen still wanted me dead.

CHAPTER 8

# THE RIVER

I realized that my bed was a little bit *too* comfortable, when I was startled awake by a sliding sound, as if something heavy were being moved...

Sunlight poured through every opening. Cargo was moving. They were unloading the barge! I had slept the night through!

I came to full alert all at once, grabbed my dress and sandals, my little bag of fruit and the smaller sack with a few bits of silver still left inside, then paused to get my bearings.

The boat was rocking gently in place. The sounds were coming from my left, so I would have to make my way to the very back of the cargo and slip quietly over the side and into the Nile. It would not be easy.

Bright sunlight reached me as I wove between stacks of goods. Some of the fruits were beginning to ferment in the heat, the smell unmistakable and not unlike the aroma of wine.

The boatmen were getting closer to me with every basket, cask, or crate they moved. There must be a dozen of them to make progress so quickly. They spoke in low voices. One hummed a tune. I was between a stack of clay lanterns and the basket of fruit with some of it rotting when the lanterns were unceremoniously pulled outward. I zipped ahead, then into a gap between I don't know what, but then I got confused as to which way was which.

I did what Betta had taught me to do when in a state of fear or panic. I closed my eyes and took a deep breath. "Breath is life," she would say, "and life is what the Gods are."

Life force filled me when I inhaled. I expelled the breath slowly, and once again, tried to get my bearings. This time I knew exactly which way to go.

I crept amongst the crates, and into a forest of wine casks tall as I, and twice as big around. As one was tilted forward, then rolled along on its bottom rim, I rolled too, behind another cask and onward. One by one, the casks rolled and I rolled, and then I found the back of the boat.

The cask in front of me tilted. There was nowhere to go but over, and no time to be quiet. I slithered over the side and splashed into the Nile.

"Hey!" a man shouted. "Hey, stowaway! Stowaway!"

I did not look back. However, other men gathered at the riverbank where I was heading. So, I had no choice but to turn and swim away from the shore instead. I was swept into the river's flow at once, and it wasn't so bad. Quick, but I could keep my head above—ow! My foot hit a rock. The current I'd thought fast, became faster. The rains had been recent and the river was high. I was carried swiftly around a bend, banging my arm, my knee, my head on rocks as the Nile had its way with me.

I had a notion of where I might be able to beach myself, if I survived the journey, and tried to keep my thoughts on it, rather than on the water I was swallowing and upon which I was choking. It was a place I'd visited as a child. The river had its own ideas about that. It hefted me up high, then slammed me down, and I went under. I flailed my arms in an effort to find air and failed. When I stopped flailing, I was elevated again. My head broke the surface, and I sucked in a breath of air, and then someone grabbed me by my reaching arm, hauled me right up out of the water, and dropped me into the bottom of a boat.

I coughed, gulped air, and pushed my wet hair off my face as I looked up to see my savior.

The oaf!

Meela crouched beside me as I choked out some more water. When I could finally control the spasm, I wiped my face with the back of my hand.

"Father, we must get her dry. We need a fire."

"Mm." He aimed the boat toward the shore, and soon he was dragging it up onto the riverbank. He went to gather fuel for a fire and while he worked, Meela helped me out of the boat. She took my bags off my shoulder, untied my sash, and peeled off my wrap dress, replacing it with her own dry blanket.

Then she stretched the dress over a low tree limb.

"What are you doing here?" I asked. "And where are all your riches?"

"We only went back as far as some friends partway back," Meela said. "They agreed to store our things at their house until we return. Father will give them a share for their trouble." She was unpacking my shoulder bag, taking out my clothes, and stretching my dress out on a rock to dry, placing my bamboo sandals near it. Poking through my bag, she salvaged two pomegranates and a handful of figs.

Her father knelt nearby, his kindling stacked just so, as he struck a piece of flint over and over.

"But why?" I asked.

Meela shrugged, but the oaf paused in his rhythmic work and said, "We couldn't see you going up against the pharaoh on your own for our sake. Kiko is my boy. It's my job."

"The pharaoh is my father. That makes it my job," I replied.

He grunted and returned to striking the flint. Sparks flew from the stone with each strike, and soon they caught some of the dried moss and reeds. He blew gently until flames took hold, then added larger fuel. "Come closer, girl. Your lips are blue," he said.

I did, hugging Meela's blanket around me. Then he handed me what looked like a meat pie. I frowned and sniffed at it.

"We each got one in the village before heading back," Meela said, "to celebrate our good fortune. Father asked for one with only vegetables to bring back for you."

I looked at him with raised eyebrows. First, he'd shown kindness to the mother cat, and now he was showing it to me. He was not the oaf he pretended to be at all, was he?

The fire began to throw off heat and I sat as near it as I dared, my hands outstretched to soak its warmth into my body. Ever so slowly, it seeped into my bones and pushed out the chill.

"Look," Meela said.

As the sun had climbed higher, it illuminated my father's palace far in the distance across the river. It reflected from the white stone and gold edging near its top. It winked and flashed, and looked nearer than it was.

"We should wait until night to rescue Kiko," I said, finally warm enough to enjoy the pie.

"And then what?" Meela asked.

"I've been thinking on it. Minor offenders work off their sentences with the stone workers and monument builders. I think that's where he'll be. And that," I said pointing, "Is that way."

"On this side of the river?"

"Yes. The workers' camp moves wherever the building project is. I glimpsed it in the distance while tumbling in the river. We can walk there in an hour. It's not far."

"Is the camp not guarded?"

"Not in any serious way," I said, and the oaf looked at me with suspicion.

I finished my meal and brushed the crumbs from my hands. "Thank you for the pie. It was good."

He grumbled something that might've been, "You're welcome."

"Now we should rest," I said, despite that I'd slept like the dead on the barge. "Tonight, under cover of darkness, we can go get Kiko."

I knew I could not take them with me. The oaf couldn't move stealthily if his life depended on it—which it would. And Meela would be unable to contain herself when she caught sight of her brother. I knew, though, that the two of them had not slept. There wouldn't have been time for them to travel, unload, and return if they had napped. I was amazed they'd managed to fit in the time to purchase the meal. They must have and eaten theirs while they'd journeyed. I, on the other hand, had slept well, almost too well.

They agreed that a nap would be a good idea, followed by a nighttime visit to the workers' camp. And I could tell by how quickly, and how deeply they slept that they needed it.

As soon as the oaf was snoring, I gathered what I would need, and set off toward the work site where I suspected Kiko would be.

I passed the current building project on my way inland from the river. The statue had feet, legs, thighs, and the beginnings of clothing.

I stopped to look at the great pyramid in the distance. It gleamed, yes, but in a few more hours, as the sun went down, it would glow as if with pure white fire. I had missed seeing the sun set on the pyramid. My father's favorite palace was here, within sight of it. But not too close. He wouldn't want to offend the gods by encroaching.

He was superstitious, my father was. He did not understand the gods as I did—as a force flowing to us and through us, not separate from us. Bella said knowing that, and knowing what to do about it, was the source of all power.

The statue I passed was built only as high as its seat. A king on a throne, probably my father. Why else would he spend his wealth on it? His vanity knew no bounds.

I walked past the statue, following well-worn tracks in the earth where the men walked back and forth each day, and followed it.

There was no cover, other than the shape of the desert itself. I was far from the verdant riverbanks. Why anyone would put a monument way out here was beyond my understanding. Sometimes the things adults did confounded me. I always thought it would be better to put the statues closer to the city, where everyone could enjoy them.

There was hard-packed earth and sand beneath my feet. Here and there the path disappeared beneath it, but I was patient and stayed on course and each time, it reappeared. There was a vast, blue sky above me, and the sun was pounding down. It wouldn't be easy to go unseen.

As I got closer to the camp, the trail widened and turned into many, meandering among the tents where the men would return. They'd chosen a spot with a natural spring, where vegetation grew. I saw the huwa plant with dark green leaves larger than my head, and its fernlike cousin, with lighter green leaves made of lace. There was even an olive tree.

I plucked some of the leaves and tucked them around my dress, using my belt to hold them. I held one large leaf in my hands to cover my face and head. Then I found a spot amid the plants close to the trail's edge, just where it widened, but before it split, and hid myself behind there.

It was cooler among the plants. I took a long drink of water from the flask I'd brought with me and settled in to wait.

That's when a hand grabbed me by the nape of my neck and lifted to my feet. "What have we here?"

"Release me or suffer my wrath!"

"Your what?"

"Wrath," I said and I kicked him squarely in the groin. He dropped me and bent double, howling in pain. I'd landed a good one!

I sprang up and ran with everything I had, out into the darkness, willing the shifting sands and the night itself to block me from his view.

I once again entered the cool, green valley that

extended out into the desert from the banks of the Nile. Here there were farms, orchards, and livestock, and further in, the boat makers and the docks where goods came in. The city unfurled from the opposite bank. And my father's palace, the place where I had once lived, stood at its center, like a jewel.

I sighed and hid and waited a long time to be sure I had not been followed, and then I returned to my companions.

They were awake and discussing me when I arrived. I caught only the tail of Meela's question. "...think she went without us?"

"I tried to, Meela," I said. "You're too smart for me. But I was nearly caught. So now we'll have to—"

I stopped mid-sentence when men came at us from the darkness, swords drawn. I weaved, dodging one grasping hand, only to feel my upper arm clutched by another. One had Meela by her arm, too, and I said, "Be gentle with her. She's been ill, and she's fragile. Please..."

The one holding Meela looked at me, then at Meela, who still pulled against him. "Meela, be still so he doesn't have to hold so tightly."

She stilled instantly, so did the oaf, who'd been resisting the two who had hold of him, one on each side.

"What do you want of us?" I asked, addressing the fifth man, who wasn't holding anyone. He was a big man, muscular, dark-skinned, dressed in nicer, whiter fabric than the others. His sash was multi-colored and strung with beads. He seemed like the leader to me.

"I want to know what you were doing sneaking around the workers' camp," he said.

"I brought these two to see their son and brother, if he's there. I was only going to watch the workers when they returned at day's end, to see whether he was truly among them."

He studied me, maybe surprised by my answer. His brown eyes looked me up and down. "So, you are the leader of this little gang of rebels?"

"Do not harm her," the oaf said. "She is–"

"The boy's name is Kiko and he knows nothing about any of this. It was my idea to come here. I thought perhaps I could persuade my father to set him free, but first I had to be sure he was here."

His eyebrows pressed together. "Your father?"

"My father, the pharaoh," I said. "I am Princess Rhianikki, firstborn of Pharaoh and priestess of Isis, and I will *not* be leaving this place without the boy, his sister Meela, and his father, the o—his father, Beck."

The men around me were stunned silent, and then the leader said, "I should have known, shouldn't I? You *look* like a princess. Doesn't she, boys?"

Then they all burst into gales of laughter. I looked down at myself, the leaves and ferns poking every which way, up and down and sideways from my belt. I ran a hand over my hair, and found bits of foliage clinging there.

"Come along, then. We'll see what the general has to say about all this."

"You'd better see what the pharaoh has to say about this," I warned.

"King's on a trip, little princess. The highest we can go is the queen."

"If I were you," the one holding my arm whispered for my ears alone, "I'd take my chances with the general."

# CHAPTER 9
# THE RESCUE

They took us by ferry across the Nile to the city itself, where oil lamps glowed from the mud-brick buildings where the citizens dwelled. Some were the workshops of craftsmen, a goldsmith, a brewery, a weaver who made fine linens. Others were residences. The streets were smooth slabs of sandstone, not like the packed earth roads in other places. Everything had to be better in the home of the pharaoh.

The city was quiet this night. It must be late; I'd lost track of the hour. A donkey cart carrying three wine casks rattled slowly along the road, and the beast's warm, earthy scent was comforting to me. The driver was a small man whose back was stooped and hair was gray.

Taller buildings stood in the darkness, the homes of the wealthy and those in my father's favor. And furthest back, the palace commanded the sky. Two rectangular brick towers rose high, each bearing images of the gods in bright blue lapis and onyx and gold. By night, the gods appeared dark and demonic, dancing as they did in the torchlight from below.

My hands were bound at the wrists in front of me, by ropes so rough they scraped my skin. There were four soldiers with us, one to escort each of us and the leader, who walked in front. Our soldiers, Meela's and mine, held us by our upper arms in exactly the same manner. But the oaf's soldier did not have hold of him. He probably didn't dare. The oaf... Beck, I corrected. He had come back for me. I should not call him oaf anymore. Beck was a big man, and intimidating when he chose to be. The soldiers had no way of knowing he was not what he appeared. He was not a brute at all. He was a gifted potter, an artist with a soft heart and compassion for small animals. The brute was only an act.

Beck and I could take the four of them, I thought, if not for the risk it would pose to Meela. They were not above hurting her to enforce our compliance. He and I were of the same mind on that, I knew it when our eyes met.

As we rounded a corner, I saw a large group of people drinking beer outside the alehouse, so I lifted my chin and shouted very loudly, "See how your princess is treated! Bound and captured by the pharaoh's own soldiers!"

The people fell silent and turned our way.

"Pay her no mind!" the leader shouted, then more softly, to my captor. "Silence your prisoner."

"I am Rhianikki!" I shouted while the soldier searched for something to cover my mouth, "firstborn of Pharaoh, priestess of Isis. I saved the queen's sons from an assassin, even knowing they will one day take the throne that rightfully belongs to mfffff...."

My soldier had finally torn a scrap of cloth from his own tunic to stuff into my mouth. But the people were muttering, and others were coming out of their homes to see what all the fuss was about.

The soldier shoved me forward, but I lifted my bound hands and yanked the rag out. "The goddess herself saved me from a killer's bolt in the parade to Osiris!"

They were muttering and nodding. Then I was clubbed upside the head so hard I fell to my knees and saw stars. There had been a gasp, and the muttering had grown louder, I was sure of it.

"Harm the girl again and I'll do the same to you!" Beck lunged and his soldier gripped his arms and struggled to hold him. I swore his voice had gone a full level deeper.

My captor lifted my head, shoved the rag into my mouth so deep I near choked, then untied my hands and retied them behind my back. He pulled me to my feet by one arm and it wrenched my shoulder socket.

"Here, now!" a local woman cried.

Others joined in a chorus.

"She's a crazy girl, caught sneaking about the workers' camp, no princess," the leader said. His calm, confident tone carried the ring of authority. "She's dirty and her clothes are ragged."

I spat the rag from my mouth. "I am Rhianikki, daughter of phar—"

The blow knocked me out this time.

I woke in darkness. A soft hand was stroking my hair, Meela's hand, and I lifted my head and tried to look around. "Where...?"

"A tomb, I think," Meela whispered. Her hands were not bound, and I realized mine were not, either.

"Not a tomb," her father corrected. "Just a pit in the ground. It's lined in mud-brick. There's a water vessel in the corner, full to the brim." I looked where he pointed. The vessel was short with a big belly and narrow spout. "Nothing else," he went on. "Not a blanket nor a crumb of food. The only exit is up there." He pointed up at our ceiling, the starry sky.

As if summoned by our attention, there was movement, a person silhouetted against the night, who was then shoved forward until he fell into our pit with us. The distance was about the height of two grown men, and it wouldn't have been so hard a fall, except that his hands were bound just as ours had been, so he could not catch himself.

He landed hard, with a loud grunt, and lay there for a moment, a slightly built male with a headful of gleaming black curls.

"Kiko!" Meela cried, and she ran to him, falling to her knees and wrapping her arms around him.

She untied his wrists and then helped him sit up, and he stared into her face in the darkness for a moment, then hugged her. "Meela, what are you doing here?" He looked beyond her at me and the man who stood beside me. "Father!"

It was dark, but not so dark I could not see him. He was only slightly taller than I. I'd been told I was tall, for a girl of my age. He had deep brown eyes and thick lashes and darker skin than his father or sister. Their mother must have come from the southern lands.

"What has happened? Why are you here?" Kiko asked.

Neither of them spoke, so I did. "We came to get you out of here, which we will do as soon as THESE IDIOTS FIGURE OUT WHO I AM!" I shouted the final words up at the opening in the earth.

"Who are you?" Kiko asked.

"I am RHIANIKKI!"

The other two joined in for the rest of my speech, adding volume to the declaration that floated out into the night. "Daughter of Pharaoh, priestess of Isis!" we all shouted as one.

And then I tacked on a little more. "And woe to the soldier who would put his own princess into the ground!"

There was more movement. A couple of soldiers peered down at us. I could not see their faces, but I was certain they were not those who'd brought us here. I presumed they had been sent back to their regular duties, and their leader was probably consulting with his general to determine our fates.

They were muttering, but I could hear them.

"Do you think she's *really* the princess?"

"If she is, we'll be executed along with those who captured her."

I tipped my head back and called up to them. "Why not find one of my personal guards, Luca, or the other one, Marin? Ask them if I am your princess."

"I know Luca," one of them said. "He's away, with the king."

"I know Marin," said the other. "But he's not here, either. He's assigned to the Temple of Isis in the village of Terne for..." He stopped speaking, then.

"Yes, you understand now, do you not? How did I know the names of Princess Rhianikki's guards?"

"Could've heard them somewhere."

"Find someone who would know me and bring them here. I lived in the palace for the first five years of my life. I've been gone only four. Surely someone here still knows my face."

"I know!" one man said with a snap of his fingers. "The nurse."

"My nurse was murdered by the assassin who came after my father's sons a year ago. Whoever is nurse now is likely new and would not know me."

"We could summon the queen—"

"The queen wants me dead so her spawn can take my father's throne."

They looked at each other, wide-eyed. One said, "That's heresy."

"It's factual." I was growing tired of arguing with idiots, but I had to keep trying. Given time I could wear them down. "Assume, for a moment, that I am right and you are wrong. Perhaps it would go easier on you if you had at least provided your princess with some small comforts. The girl with me is sick. We are all cold and hungry. And we could do with some light."

"Wait...." One of them fumbled around and then dropped something through the opening, a small something. I picked it up and found a short tallow candle.

"Idiot," said the other guard. "How will she light it?"

"By the Power of Isis," I replied, then I gazed at the candle and opened myself to allow the power of Isis to beam through me. I directed all of it at the candle's wick. A thin spiral of smoke emerged, and then its tip turned cherry red, then brighter. I focused my will gently upon it. With a soft *pop*, a flame burst to life.

The men watching from above gasped and looked at each other. So did Beck and young Kiko. Meela, however, only smiled.

I looked up again and the terror in those men's eyes told me I'd made the right decision, to use magic. "You should probably inform the general of what you have seen here," I said. "Tell him that I am one of only two in the entire Temple of Isis who can command fire, and the other is my teacher. Go on and tell him, hurry now."

As soon as they left, I turned to the o—to Beck. "Quick now, before they come back, boost me up."

Beck didn't even take time to argue or dispute it with me. He bent a knee. I stepped onto it and pushed off as he helped lift me upward. I sprang straight through the opening, catching the edge with my hands and pulling upward until I was out. I stood in an open area, upon bare earth trod down by the soldiers who trained there. Behind the training yard was a long building, pristine with sharp angles and bricks bleached white by the sun. Part of it was the barracks where soldiers slept. Part was a dining hall where they ate. An entire section made up the general's quarters, despite that he had a house near the palace and rooms inside, should they be needed. I remembered all of it very well.

They were in there, our captors, discussing our fate with the general. A stone wall surrounded the entire place, and the gate was guarded. We had to get over that wall.

"Rhianikki!" Beck called up to me, his voice a harsh whisper.

I looked down to see him holding Meela up. She smiled at me and stretched her arms upward, so I leaned way over, grabbed her wrists and helped to pull her up, with her father pushing on the soles of her feet from below.

I set her in a safe spot on the ground, but I did not like that we were in the open. "You next," I said to Kiko.

He let his father boost him up and climbed out easily. Then he looked back down. "What about you, Father?"

"You cannot pull me up. Not even all three of you."

"I know," I said. I'd been looking for a way out and

spotted that same donkey cart I'd seen earlier. Two of the three wine casks remained, and the donkey stood waiting, hitched to the cart and awaiting his owner.

I heard voices raised in merriment coming from inside the barracks. The men were enjoying the wine. The driver was no doubt serving it, currying favor as one does.

I hoped there would be enough time. "Take Meela and hide near the wall," I said to Kiko, and I pointed to a spot where the shadows were darkest, near the gate, where a guard stood.

He scooped his sister up as if she were one of Bast's kittens and moved quickly away. I leaned down. "I need to find something you can stand on, so you can get out of there."

"Yes, yes. Something waist-high or so."

"My waist or yours?" I asked.

He winked and said, "Whatever you can find."

I moved toward the barracks and that cart, praying there would be something I could use. I'd considered the water jug in the hole, but it was too fragile. Beck's weight would crush it. I kept to the shadows, and stopped every few steps to listen, but only for a moment. The soldiers would finish their wine and send the driver out for another cask, at some point.

I reached the cart, and keeping low, moved to the very rear of it. When I climbed inside, it jiggled and the donkey gave a single bray that made me freeze in place and hold my breath.

But no one came. I was still safe.

There were the two wine casks and an oiled tarp covering something near the front of the cart, so I crept closer and pulled away the cover. There was wooden box, square, knee high—on me, but waist-high if one stood it on end. It was filled with smaller jugs and jars with varying amounts of liquids in them. I took the vessels out one by one, and set them carefully in the cart, holding each one by the neck to be sure it wouldn't tip over before releasing it. I was careful and quiet. Then I snatched up the empty wooden crate, jumped off the cart, went fast as I could back to the hole.

"Stand back," I whispered down, and then I dropped box.

"Ow!"

"I told you to stand back."

"You didn't give a pause in between." Beck rubbed his head. "You're supposed to give a pause in between."

"Stop whining and get up here."

He set the box onto its end, and stepped up onto it, but he was still far below the opening. To my surprise, he jumped, pushing off the box so hard it broke behind him, and somehow, he managed to get a hand on the edges of the opening. He pulled himself higher by the sheer strength of his arms. It was a most impressive feat. He got hip-high, pushing his arms up straight, his entire face pulled taut with the strain of it, and then he twisted around and slid his backside onto solid ground. After a moment, he got up and brushed himself off. "I don't know what good you think this will do."

"It gets us out of a hole in the ground, is what good it does. And you're welcome." I lowered my head. "And thank you."

"And thank you, young priestess."

"*Princess* Priestess."

He smiled, then I took his hand and led him toward the wagon, for I had a plan. We'd gone only a few steps when I heard the laughter grow louder, and I pulled Beck with me against the side of the building. We crouched low and waited.

Footsteps came, and the donkey brayed. The cart driver, stooped and old, reached into the wagon and rolled a tall, slender cask of wine toward the back, then into his arms. His knees bent and I thought they would buckle with the weight of all that wine, but he caught himself, straightened, and staggered away carrying the tall pottery cask toward the barracks.

"Forty stout men in there, and they let that old one struggle," I said, shaking my head. "Come on. We'll have plenty of time now. He won't come out again until that cask is empty. Get into the back of the wagon and cover yourself with the tarp. Go on."

He climbed in, then threw something at me. His tattered brown cloak. Perfect.

I wrapped it around me and over my head, then bent over, the way the old man had been when he'd emerged. I led the donkey around and started toward the gate. As we neared, we passed Kiko and Meela crouching near the wall. "Get in the cart and cover up," I whispered. Then I stopped and crouched down, pretending to check the donkey's hoof.

I felt the cart move with their weight. It jostled far too much to suit me. The donkey opened his lips to bray and I covered his nose with my hand, and said, "Shush. There now. Be a good donkey."

He did not bray, and the cart had gone still again. Someone rapped on the wood to tell me to move on, so I did.

I led the donkey and cart to the gate, keeping my head down. The guard opened it to let us pass and never spoke a word. The cart rolled through the open gate, and onto the sandstone road that led up to it. When I heard the gate close behind us, I nearly sagged in relief.

"We did it," I said softly. "We did it, we're free."

"Not quite, free," said a deep voice I recognized.

It was my father's voice, and it quivered with anger. Then the darkness gave way to his imposing silhouette. He stood in the road, blocking our escape, flanked by two guards who held their spears poised for attack, with their tips aimed at our hearts.

## CHAPTER 10
# THE RETURN

I could scarcely believe that we had cleverly escaped our prison and made it past the gates in a borrowed donkey cart, only to find the pharaoh's guard awaiting us on the road. My father, the pharaoh himself, stood in front of us, his hands on his hips, and anger on his face as his men hauled my friends from beneath the tarp.

"Hold them here while I have a word with my daughter," he said. His voice was like thunder in the night, and his men muttered amongst themselves that I really *was* the princess after all.

"Have one of the men return the ass and cart," he told them. "Rhianikki, come." He beckoned me, palm up, fingers folding inward three times.

I looked from him to the soldiers who held my friends and pointed my finger. "Do not harm them. Not in the slightest way, do you hear me?"

They bowed to me, those men. They didn't even ask my father first but bowed and obeyed.

I liked it.

My father saw me liking it, and his eyes were troubled.

He turned and walked away, so I got down from the cart and followed. He led me back along the road far enough for privacy, then off onto the roadside, where boulders provided sitting spots. I waited for him to sit first, lest I give him cause to arrest me, too.

"I was told you'd been abducted from the temple by a brute. And here you are, with a brute. And his brood."

I looked back along the road. The man father called "the brute" stood talking with one of the soldiers. His children stood nearby. Kiko, who was twelve and male, looked frightened while Meela, who was just my age and half my size, wore a fierce expression on her face.

"Well? Have you no explanation?"

I faced him again and said, "Beck did not abduct me." It was a lie. I didn't hesitate to tell it. If it was wrong to lie to my father in order to save the lives of my friends, then I would be wrong and happily so. "He rescued me from the one who did. He took me to his home, fed me, gave me a place to rest until he could take me home. It was only when I saw how his little girl suffered that I opted to stay longer, to help her heal."

He'd watched me, listening intently, his expression unchanging except for the raising of a brow when I mentioned Meela's illness.

"The child is ill?"

"She was. She's better now."

"How?" He studied me. "Magic?"

"If healing by means of herbs, teas, and common sense are magic, then I suppose so. You sent me to the temple to learn these things, did you not?"

"I sent you to the temple to get you away from your brothers."

"Such a danger to them that I saved their lives and

knifed the criminal who meant them harm. I can see why you'd be concerned."

"We're discussing that family over there, not our own."

"Just as well, since *we* are not a family at all."

"*Rhianikki.*" His tone held a warning.

"They were living on nothing but fish! Which is why her older brother stole a loaf of your precious bread when you visited his village. For his sick, dying little sister, he risked his life and his freedom. He has more courage, more honor, than any soldier in your army."

He looked away from me, unable to hold my accusing eyes.

"For this, your men arrested him. A twelve-year-old who stole a single loaf from among fifty, now serves a man's sentence doing a man's work building a monument to his *fair* and *just* pharaoh, who—"

"All right! By the eyes of Ra, girl, you grow more like your mother every day."

I lowered my eyes then, for I had never known my mother. "I am... like her?"

"In all the worst ways." He took a deep breath. "So you're saying this man saved you."

"I am saying so, yes. He is a good man and a gifted potter. His work is finer than anything I saw when I lived in the palace."

He studied my face for a long time. I studied his, as well. It was sun-darkened and beautiful and older than I remembered. If anything, the lines on his forehead and at the center of his brow were even more cruel than before. At length, he said, "I will have the boy released. But I will not reward my daughter's abductor." I opened my mouth to argue, and he said, "I am more than your father. I am your god and your king. You cannot lie to me."

"I believe, my father, that there is more of Isis in me than there is of Ra in you."

"That's blasphemy."

"Isis would agree with me, I think. I want them all released. Furthermore, I wish for them to have a house in the village of Terne. There's an empty one just at the end of town, with a shed for a fine pottery wheel. It's near enough the temple that I can check in on them."

He jumped to his feet. "You are in no position to make demands."

I jumped to mine, sliding down from the large boulder on which I'd sat. "You are in no position to deny me. I am a princess of Egypt with more claim to the throne than either of your two brats. However, if you grant my requests, I will return quietly to the temple and trouble you no further. Ever."

"And if I do not?"

"I will shout to my people from the very rooftops and tell them it was their own queen who hired my would-be assassin two years ago. And the people will believe me. They love me, you know."

He was furious... and stunned. I saw in his eyes that I was right, that she *had* done it and that he had known it. "How would you, a child of nine, even begin to know—"

"Isis told me," I whispered. "And she told me, too, why you sent me away. Because I have power and your queen fears it, fears me." Then I stood up. "She is *right* to fear me. And so are you."

He grabbed my arm and jerked me toward him, "You dare—"

"Have me killed then!" I shouted it so loudly that the guards standing with my friends looked our way. And off in the opposite direction, I saw some locals gathering on the

122

road, who had heard me, as well. "Have your only daughter executed if you want to be rid of me so badly!" I shouted the words with depth and even greater volume.

There was muttering. Even one of his guards took a step toward us.

"Or do what I've asked," I said much more quietly. "Anything else and I swear by Isis that I will hound you to your very grave. I will stand in the public square of every city of Egypt telling the tale of how my father punished a young boy for trying to save his sister and put his own daughter out of his palace because he was afraid of her. Grant my request and I'll leave you alone forever. I will never set foot in Luxor again, nor will your name ever again cross my lips. For it is not worthy of being spoken by my voice."

He held me, his fingers digging into my shoulder, and glared down into my eyes for a long moment, and then, his jaw clenched, he said, "Done. And worth it."

Tears burned. I told myself they were from anger, not pain. Not the white-hot blade of rejection sliding straight through my heart.

He let go of me.

"It shall be done," he said again. "No more slander from your petulant lips."

"By the next full moon," I said. "Or my lips will slander you throughout the kingdom."

He lifted a hand to slap my face, but I ducked and he hit the stone instead. As he cursed me to the gods, I walked away, gathered my friends and began the journey home.

At the temple, my homecoming was celebrated with sweet cakes and wine. and I regaled dear Betta with tales of my adventure all the night through. And then I slept like the dead for a day and a half. I'd lost weight, inhaled river water, and my hair took days to untangle. Beyond all that, my heart had been broken; that had been the biggest blow of all. How relieved my father had been to be rid of me forever.

A few weeks later, when I was fully recovered and mostly rested, I packed up a basket of the finest fruits and breads from our breakfast and a small cask of lung root tea. I put it all into a small, two-wheeled cart, and pulled it behind me along the packed-earth road that wound through our village. All the way to the outermost edge, I went, where a neat little house stood beside its matching pottery shed. I'd seen it, before, of course. It had seemed empty and cold, but now it was warm and full of life.

Meela saw me on the path, shouted my name and came running, while Kiko waved from the doorway with the mother cat twining around his ankles. The girl hugged me. I did not feel the bones sticking out of her back like before, and her eyes were bright and clear.

Beck came out of the shed, wiping his hands and wearing a genuine smile on his lips. "Hello, Princess Priest-ess. Welcome!"

"I would've come sooner," I said. "But I had much to catch up on. It's a wonderful home, isn't it?"

"There are fruit trees and a garden plot in the back!" Meela cried. "And look at Father's workshop." She took my hand and led me right into the shed, where the shelves were lined with vessels in his decorative style. His work-bench and a pottery wheel stood in the center.

"Oh, and the house! Come, come see the house!" I could hardly keep up with her as she pulled me out of the shed and into the house.

They had actual beds in the sleeping room, newly woven blankets, and a thick and beautiful curtain hung in the doorway, keeping the heat outside. There were chairs, there were lamps, there was a table.

"I am so very happy for all of you. Even you, oaf."

He smiled when I said it, and I realized it had become a friendly nickname rather than an insult, as it had been when I'd met him.

"Kidnapping you was the best thing I ever did," he said. "I have a gift for you. We've been waiting for you to come."

Meela giggled, and Kiko went outside, tapping a pot with a wooden spoon.

When he returned, the cat and her three kittens followed. Meela scooped up the largest of the three, and turning, passed it to me. "She is the bossiest one," she declared.

I gathered the creature into my arms. She was sleek and soft, jet black with striking green eyes. Her regal ears stabbed up off her head like the crown of a goddess. I scratched her right between them, and she closed her eyes, and began to make a soft, rumbling sound. I could feel her small body vibrating with it.

"Won't she miss her mates?"

"Miss them?" Beck said, his voice booming in the small house. "She beats them daily—has drawn blood from the runt! And she's even started swatting her mother, now. No, I think she belongs in a one-cat family."

"Or a one-cat temple," I said, gazing at the kitten. She relaxed in my arms as if she knew she belonged with me. She was to cats, I thought, as I was to the other students.

She opened her green eyes and gazed into mine, and it was as if she knew it. When her eyes closed again, I managed to look past her at the family who'd gathered round me. "Thank you is not enough for such a precious gift."

"A cat is not enough to thank you," Kiko said, "for all you've done for our family."

"Do you think the high priestess will allow you to keep her at the temple?" Meela asked.

"Do you think I would allow her to prevent it?" I replied.

Several nights later, Betta and the kitten and I walked together outside the walls after everyone else slept. In an open, barren place, Betta built a small fire using precious sticks of sacred wood.

"That cat has not left your side since you brought her back," Betta said, nodding at the feline who trotted along at my side. "Have you given her a name?"

"I call her Secret, because her eyes hold so many."

"It's a good name." She looked at the cat, then at me as we came to a place we'd come before. "Aren't you afraid she'll run off?"

"She is free to stay with me or go as she pleases. I told her I would never confine her."

Her gray brows rose. "Do you think she understands you?"

"I know she does," I replied.

"Does she come around when you do magic?"

"She comes around when I do anything. Except when she goes hunting. Sometimes she leaves her kills on my pillow."

"An offering to you. A way of expressing her affection and care."

"I give her tastes of my meals in return, but she does not appreciate our meatless diet."

Betta laughed. "You did well, Rhianikki. You stood up to your father and took care of your friends. Even that oaf who knocked me over the head."

"I will never forgive him for that," I said. "Not even knowing there's a soft-hearted artist inside him."

"I've forgiven him," Betta said. "You might as well join me. He was trying to save his little girl's life."

"I know." I shook my head. "The oaf."

Betta put an arm around my shoulder and we laughed, then sat contemplating the flames for a long time. The cat walked nearer the fire, chose a spot, and began digging at the earth with her claws. Eventually, she lay down in the spot she'd made perfect.

I opened a pouch of herbs that were sacred to Isis and Betta opened one, as well. We'd each made our own blends and charged them with the energy of our gratitude for my safe return, for Kiko's reunion with his family, for Meela's thriving health, for Beck having discovered his vocation.

As I sprinkled my herbs into the dancing flames, I said, "And thank you, Isis, for the companionship of this cat. I wish she could be with me always."

The cat made a purring mewl, and in the clear sky, lightning flashed.

## CHAPTER II
# THE TAKEN

In the winter of my eleventh year, I was awakened in the night by a terrible wailing. I woke, of course, as did the other student priestesses. We all slept in the same room, but there were fewer of us by then. One by one, my fellow students had left us for one reason or another. Some of them had no talent for serving the goddess. Some didn't have the intellect, others lacked the skill, and a few lacked the will. They did not wish to live the life of a priestess. Still others were reclaimed by families who missed them too much to leave them at the temple any longer. I could not imagine having a family like that, with people who loved and wanted me.

Yes, my father's rejection still stung. Especially at this time of the year.

For three days each year, the sun would be invisible to us, never rising above the horizon. But on the fourth day, Ra would rise again, reborn. There was always feasting and revelry throughout our 12-day celebration. It was a time for families and friends to celebrate their bonds and the inevitable triumph of light over darkness. And yet I was not welcome in my father's palace.

I pretended not to care, but sometimes, at night, I wept. And sometimes, the scent of the always-green date-palm fronds decorating every window and doorway, caused an answering ache in my heart.

My cat, awakened either by the noise or by my distress, hopped up onto my bed and tapped my face with her head. She had grown long and tall, and she moved like the Nile. I pet her because she would not relent until I did. She had become the only person who could order me around. From Secret alone, I allowed it.

Five student priestesses remained in the Temple of Isis, two from the younger group, two from the group of older girls, and me. We'd graduated from straw mats on the floor to raised beds with thick mattresses stuffed in cattail fluff. That had been my idea, or perhaps it had come from Isis. I'd dreamed it one autumn night and told the others about it the next day. So we'd raided the banks of the Nile, gathering mature cat tail heads and bringing them home. We trimmed the stems and laid the soft brown heads out on the floor to dry in the sun, and as they dried, they expanded into lengths of fluff. We'd brushed the fluffy white seeds into large sacks we'd sewn for this purpose. We'd stuffed them full of cattail fluff, then sewn up the end. They were not very thick yet, our mattresses, but they were incredibly soft. We'd agreed that every autumn we would add more fluff, until our beds were the most luxurious in all Egypt.

We slept soundly, all snug and warm in our soft beds, the scent of those always-green boughs and that from mountains of freshly harvested dates tickling our senses and inspiring our dreams. But that night, a piercing wail cut through our rest and woke us all so suddenly we sat up, blinking in the darkness.

Kayt shouted, "What's happening?" and she sounded afraid.

"Jackals!" Surra declared, diving from her bed and racing to the window to push the curtain aside and look out. She seemed more eager than frightened, however.

I arrived at the window right beside her with Secret in my arms. She'd been curled beside me in my bed, and I'd scooped her up automatically. "It is a woman's cry," I said, straining my eyes to see through the darkness.

The wail came once more and told me we were looking in the wrong direction.

"She's below, at the garden entrance! Come on!" I put Secret on the floor, pulled a wrap around my night dress, and stepped into my bamboo sandals.

"We're not supposed to go out at night," Kayt said. She was a timid and obedient little thing, with short, straight hair she wore always in braids. She was forever reminding the rest of us about the rules, as if we might forget them.

"If we don't go out, then how will we learn what's happening?" I asked, quite logically, I thought.

She pressed her mouth into a pout and got back into her bed, lying down hard and pulling her blanket over her as if that were her answer. The other two, Taresha and Min, remained in their beds, quiet and watching us. They were always quiet and watchful, and usually up to something that would make others look bad and themselves appear better by comparison. They'd had little success in those efforts with me, however.

Surra looked at me and shrugged. "I'll go with you."

She was bravest of them all, besides me, of course. But with her it was a more sullen sort of feeling. I sensed she didn't fear anything because she didn't care whether she lived or died. She was a sad girl, who had the happiest brown curls I'd ever seen. I wished she would find her joy again.

I left our bedchamber, the doorway of which was covered by a heavy curtain, as was the window, both to keep out the chill and to afford us some privacy. Surra kept pace as I hurried through the corridors with Secret running so close to my feet it was as if she were trying to trip me. I'd got used to that behavior, though, and danced around her easily, down a set of stairs, and through a wide, curtained doorway into the temple garden.

The fountain of Isis bubbled beneath a starry sky. Surra and I had decorated it with palm fronds we'd braided into a garland with fresh flowers, dried fruits, and golden trinkets of all sorts for the holiday. I was sure Isis approved. We crossed the cool floor toward the gate in the stone wall that bordered our space, beyond which the woman was pounding and shouting. But before we made it all the way, other footsteps whispered along the halls we'd only just traversed.

I grabbed Surra's arm and pulled her into the shadows between plants, statues, and trees. Secret stood in the open, looking at us as if she was above cowering and hiding.

I wiggled my fingers, making kissy sounds with my tongue to call her, but she only sat down, as still as the sphinx. There we crouched while Priestess Elana hurried to the gate, walking right past the cat and not even seeing her.

I wondered if Secret had mastered the art of invisibility. She'd been frequent witness to me, trying to learn the skill.

The shrubs had grown so full that we'd had to trim them to keep the opening passable. We'd left an arch of greenery over the top, that grew small white blossoms throughout much of the year. I was only just realizing its lush beauty had a blemish—it made it difficult see past it, unless you were at just the right angle. We couldn't see Elana once she'd passed through it, but we heard her when she said, "Stop your howling, woman, you'll wake the entire temple!" She led the woman through the opening into the garden. "What is—"

She broke off when the woman fell to her knees, grabbed Elana around her legs, and pressed her face into her garments. Her words, muffled by cloth, were barely audible, but I made out "child" and "gone," and felt Surra squeeze my hand.

"Come, now," Elana said. "Rise up and speak to me. If you have a petition for the gods, I must at least hear what it is before I can intercede on your behalf. And I cannot discern a thing past all your crying. Come."

Elana pulled the woman upright. She was pretty, with dark hair like mine, but cropped short, so it flared wide above her shoulders. Her dress was white, her wrap, the soft brown color of undyed wool. She was neither poor nor wealthy, I thought. Her clothes were clean and new, but simple, and she wore no jewelry at all.

Elana led her across the garden, but she didn't go back into the temple proper, as I had feared she would. It would have been too hard to eavesdrop indoors. Fortunately, Elana took her to one of the stone benches near the fountain, instead. "I can get you a tea, or some wine."

"I've brought some," Betta said. She was just coming out of the temple, with a cloth sack over her arm. The items in the sack were tapping against each other. Pottery, I guessed from the sound. "I vow, I thought at first Rhianik-ki's cat had come under attack. But when I realized a human was making those sounds, I surmised some wine might be in order. And I see I was right." As she spoke, she removed a large pottery urn and three drinking cups from the sack. She lined up the cups and then poured from the vessel, filling each one. Her hair was wild, all frizzy and white and sticking up all over. She usually tamed it with a wrap, but not tonight.

I loved Betta's hair that way. Loose and natural. It spoke of her power, I thought.

The woman took her cup in both hands and sipped as if doing so might help her somehow. Then she wiped the back of her hand across her lips and said, "My child has gone missing. My husband has roused the neighbors already, and a search is underway. He believes she wandered off on her own, but I fear she was taken. I need divine intercession."

I heard, far in the distance, the voices of people calling for the child, whose name was apparently Cora, and it relieved me to know there were already searchers out looking for her.

"Details will help," Elana said. "Her name, her age—"

"Where she was last seen, and who was last with her," Betta added.

"Her name is Cora," the woman said. She took another gulp of her wine and hurried on. "She was born in the summer, two years ago. She was asleep beside us, but when I woke, she was gone. I searched our house and outside, but I could not find her. And the river is so close!"

"The river is not *that* close," Elana said. "And surely that is the first place your husband and the citizens he's roused will go."

"Do you have anything of hers with you?" Betta asked.

"I... yes, yes, her blanket. I grabbed it as I left the house because it's so cold outside tonight and I... " She dissolved into tears.

I felt my own eyes begin to burn. Secret came to me then. Of course, now that I was no longer beckoning her. She was a contrary beast.

"Give me the blanket," Betta said, taking it when the woman handed it to her, and grabbing her wine cup in her free hand as she rose from the table. She headed for the inner temple, but as she passed our hiding place, without even turning her head our way, she said, "Surra, you will assist Priestess Elana. Rhianikki, you will come with me."

"Yes, Betta," we said in unison, rising and heading in opposite directions. But Surra caught my eyes before she turned to go, and I whispered, "We will find her," and then I decided to say it louder. "You have nothing to fear, woman. We will find your Cora with help from Isis, who sees all and who loves children, as you know."

The bereft mother and the priestess Elana were both surprised to see us there. Not Betta. She had probably known the whole time.

"Come, Secret," I told the cat. Then I followed Betta indoors, and along the hall to the room of magic, the place where I had been studying at Betta's feet all my six years at the temple. The other girls' focus was on religious rites, holiday celebrations, rites of marriage, of birth, of death. And I studied those things too, but my true interest was in magic, and I was good at it. The others learned basic things from Betta, but I, alone, was given the depth and breadth of her magical knowledge. She'd gathered it all her life, she'd told me, from shamans and holy women near and far. And some, she'd said, came to her from the gods themselves.

She held the heavy curtain aside, and I went into the room before her. Secret trotted in behind me, and I was glad she had decided to come along. I never forced her. Betta tossed the baby's blanket onto our work table, and went to the fireplace to stir the embers to life. As they glowed, I brought fuel—dried dung from donkeys and cattle—and stacked it nearby. I held a piece of straw to the embers, and when it blazed, I moved with care to the nearest lamp, and touched its wick. From lamp to lamp I moved until three were lighting the room, and then I placed them at intervals on the long table.

The fire was taking hold and it sent warmth into the room while filtering its smoke out through a hole in the wall. It was as cold, and it would get colder. The sun had not breached the horizon today, nor would it tomorrow, nor the day after. But then Ra would return, renewed and empowered, and our holiday celebration that day would be the biggest and best of the entire year.

Betta went to the rack of crisscrossed reeds that formed diamond shaped openings, every one of which held a bundle of scrolls. She picked through them, plucking out the one she wanted, then brought it to the table where she untied its string binding. "Stretch out the child's blanket," she said.

I did so immediately, smoothing the fabric upon the table.

Betta unrolled the parchment atop it, and I saw that it was a map of the village and surrounding area. She took the three lamps I'd lit, and placed them on the top and two sides to hold it flat. On the fourth side, she placed her pottery cup.

"Oh, we're scrying," I said.

"*You're* scrying. Get the pendulum."

I raced to where the pendulum rested in its drawstring bag in a basket of magical tools, and took it out. It was a stone with a naturally occurring hole made by water, Betta had told me. Through the hole, she had strung a length of twine, and of course the tool had been empowered by magical rites.

I had trained with this pendulum, but a missing child was surely too crucial a task to trust to my budding talents.

And, yet, Betta nodded at me to do the work, and I never questioned her.

I took a deep breath and knelt, closing my eyes, raising my arms. "Oh great Isis, I call you. Awaken within me. Look through my eyes and speak through my lips. Work through my body and work through this stone. Show me where the child Cora is. Help me to bring her home."

Then I rose, and holding the end of the twine, I dropped the stone to dangle it above the map, roughly in the center.

"Deep breaths now," Betta said softly, "so your hand remains steady."

I inhaled slowly through my nose, exhaled steadily through my lips, and willed my hand to be as relaxed and still as a mountain. Secret leapt up onto the table, and sat down beside the map, her tail swishing back and forth over its surface. As I held the string, the stone began to move slightly. I remained still and watched it until it had begun moving in a clear back and forth motion.

As the motion continued, I moved slowly and care-fully, shifting the pendulum to the right of center where I paused for a moment. Then I moved it to the left and let it hover there, but its pattern did not change. Nor was there any reaction near the top of the map, but toward the bottom, the back and forth motion changed. I went still, watching and waiting, and soon the straight-line swing had become a circular motion instead. And sunwise, no less. I moved a bit farther and the circle got bigger, and so I moved farther still, and the circle grew even larger.

"This cannot be right," I said. "She is two and a half years old; she can't have gone so far."

"Yours is not to question, Rhianikki, but to see and hear and interpret the signs."

I nodded and the pendulum wobbled from my motion, so I stilled myself once more and, returned to my steady breathing. Figuratively, I opened the top of my head to allow the light of the goddess to stream in from above.

The circle smoothed its motion once more, and it grew larger the further south I moved the stone, until it began to grow smaller again. So I backed up, continuing as the circles widened, then began to grow smaller. I continued this until I was certain of the spot where the pendulum's circles were largest and pressed my finger to the center of that spot, only then realizing I was touching the Nile, three miles south of the city.

"Oh no," I whispered, dropping the pendulum stone. "Cora has fallen into the river and been swept away."

"Swept away, three miles, against the current?" Betta asked. "This is a time to think with your head, Rhianikki, and not your heart. Use logic, not emotion at this moment."

I blinked and looked at the map again. "The Nile flows north," I whispered.

"And so?"

"Little Cora must be on a boat," I said. Then my eyes widened. "Or in the belly of a crocodile!"

"If she were in the belly of a croc, she'd be dead, would she not?" Betta asked, and I nodded. "The dead are much harder to locate, Rhianikki. The circle made by the pendulum would have been small and weak. This one was large and strong. So given that knowledge, what conclusion can you draw?"

"The mother was correct," I said. "The child has been taken." Then I went to the sack Betta had dropped into a chair when we'd entered the room, the one that had previously held wine and cups. I brought it back to the table, then I rolled the map into its heavy, oiled-cloth wrapper, and dropped it in. I put the pendulum into its drawstring pouch, folded the baby's blanket, and dropped them both into my sack as well. Secret stood on the table, watching my every move as if she sensed my excited energy.

"You're going, then?" Betta asked.

"I am. I only need to stop in the sleeping room to pick up that large knife Beck gave to me, in case I catch the cur who would steal a little baby from her mother's bed."

"We do not kill."

"I can fantasize, can I not?" I smiled at her, but I thought my eyes probably still contained the fire of my anger. Such a person did not deserve to live and dispatching him to the afterlife would be a service to humanity.

"I will watch over your cat," Betta said, reaching out to stroke Secret's smooth black coat.

"Oh, no. Secret goes where I go. At least, for as long as she's willing. Don't you, Secret?"

The cat pushed her head up under my chin as if to agree.

CHAPTER 12

# CHILD-THIEVES' LAIR

I got away with more than the other girls studying for the priesthood, and I knew it was because I was the daughter of Pharaoh. Disowned or not, I was by blood a princess and by right, next in line.

I wished there was more to it. I wished it was because I was more mature, more capable, and more skilled than the other girls. I was all those things, but it was as if everyone around me had agreed not to acknowledge it. So, they pretended I was an ordinary girl, and I pretended not to notice them pretending. When deep down we all knew the truth.

I was not like other girls. Was it because of my royal blood? I thought so. I believed I was part-goddess, part Isis herself. There was nothing I could not do, nothing I did not dare.

I returned to our sleeping quarters, where my belongings lay upon my bed. I gathered what I would need, and would borrow more from the rooms below, where water vessels and satchels were stored.

I felt eyes on me. Some of the good, obedient girls,

memorizing my every move to report to the High Priestess, when she came and asked.

"I'm going to visit my father, the king," I said, as if talking to myself. I took the knife, a gift from my friend the oaf, and belted it around my waist. Then I left and went through the temple and gathered what I needed from the larders; a sack of dates, a loaf of bread, a vessel which I would fill with sweet water from the well outside. I took a large woven satchel that hung on the wall, worn for gathering vegetables from our gardens. I put it, across my chest, and fit all my belongings inside. It closed with rope knots.

I did not go through the garden, but by a passage from the kitchen where food was prepared, to the ovens, which were outside, some distance away.

I went out through that passage with my bag. Twenty steps through a long, lightless stone passage. At first I didn't know when I had exited its far end, for the night was as dark as the tunnel had been. But then I felt the absence of the stone walls around me. I felt the expanse of the outdoors, and I tasted the fresh, fragrant air.

It was invigorating. I started off at a brisk pace, along the road toward the outermost edges of town, toward my friend Beck's home there. When I walked up, Kiko stood outside, gazing up at the stars.

He looked down when he saw me, fifteen now and quite beautiful. "Rhianikki. I should not be surprised to see you. You've heard about the child."

"I know where she is," I said. "I need to borrow your father's boat."

"Then I'll take you."

"I will go alone."

"Not in my father's boat." He shrugged. "Sorry,

Princess, but it's how he makes his living. I'm experienced with it. You are not."

I lowered my head, then raised it again and looked into his eyes. "I believe the child has been taken. There might be violence required to get her back."

He tried to show no reaction, but I saw the wave of apprehension and fear that moved through him. He had no taste for violence. He was a tender young man, teaching himself the sacred script, pressing his words into clay tablets. His own words, not copies of stories committed to memory. Beautiful words of praise for the beauty of our green and fertile land and its life-giving river. His words had the rhythm of a song when he recited them aloud. He was learning his father's trade making pottery at his side, and they were thriving. He was, in every way, an artist.

"Your hands are not meant for killing."

"No one's hands are meant for killing, Rhianikki. So we'll try our best not to kill." He turned toward his clay house. "I'll let my father know and gather some things for the journey."

"Take your time," I said. "I'll pray to Isis for guidance while I wait."

"All right." He went inside.

I ran around behind the house and down to the riverbank, where the boat was always moored. With a flick of my wrist, I untied its rope, and leapt into the boat.

My cat sat down on the shore, refusing to leap with me. "Fine," I said. "Have a holiday visit with your relatives, then." I used a paddle to propel the boat into motion, heading downstream, not up, just to throw them off my path. I turned off at the first small tributary, then another and another, cutting my way back the way I had come. I knew the river well, traveled it as often as I could. Eventually, just when I estimated I was near the little girl's location, according to my scrying, I saw the light of a campfire a little ways from the shore, and I angled inward and beached downstream from the spot, so they wouldn't see me passing by.

I took extra care tying off the boat. Kiko was right, his family's livelihood relied on transporting their wares beyond our own village. I would not let anything happen to it.

I covered the boat in reeds to hide it from thieves, then crept inland, toward the place where the firelight danced. I moved in absolute silence, and when I got close enough to see, I crouched among the reeds and peered out at the dancing flames. There were belongings strewn around, but no people. Where had the people gone?

A hand closed on the back of my neck to answer my question.

I closed my eyes, took a breath, told myself that panic was always an enemy, never a friend.

"What have we here?" asked a gruff voice. Then he picked me right up off my feet and turned me to face him. I dangled above the ground. His face looked aged, wrinkled and gray, but he was strong enough to pick me up and hold me in the air with only one hand.

"I am Rhianikki, daughter of Pharaoh, priestess of Isis—"

He leaned in sniffed twice. "Chosen," he said.

"Put her down, Makeet," said a voice that was so familiar I could hardly believe my ears.

As the old man lowered me, I turned and saw him. "Luca!" My guard hadn't changed a bit. I launched myself at him, and he opened his arms and embraced me. His clothing was wool, rough to the touch, and he wore no armor. "I'm so happy to see you," I said, and he let me go so I could step back and look at him.

He held my upper arms and looked me up and down. "You're nearly grown!"

"Children do. You look the same. Except... Where is your breastplate? Where are your cloak and your helm?"

He lowered his head. "I left the king's guard, I'm afraid."

"Oh." His words felt like a blow to my chest, but I was unsure why.

"But I never left you, little one," he said, his voice low. "I've kept track of you."

"Without me catching so much as a glimpse of you," I said, and he must've heard the doubt in my voice.

He ran his hand over my hair and compelled me to meet his eyes. I did. He said, "I was close to killing the one you call the oaf no less than three times. But each time, I felt certain you'd have been furious."

"Beck is my friend. I borrowed his boat tonight."

"And how are the children? Meela and Kiko?"

"They're good. They... " I frowned, searching his eyes.

"And Secret? Did she come with you on this journey?"

"You *have* been watching me."

"I have."

"But why keep it secret? Why not reveal yourself so we could talk, and—"

"I know it seems odd to you, Rhianikki, but I have reasons. Just as I have reasons for watching over you."

"Then you must tell me what these reasons are."

He shook his head. "Why have you come this far from the temple all alone?"

I lifted my chin. "I'm going to rescue a little girl who has been taken from her bed by a child-thief."

The old man said, "Well, isn't *that* interesting?" Then he

went back to sipping from a water sack. "We're looking for Cora too," he said.

Luca made a face as if he wanted to strangle his elder.

"What? This is your princess, right? She's smarter and stronger than anyone you've ever met, isn't that what you keep telling me? Tell her the truth, then. It's her body. Her blood."

"What about my blood?" I swung my eyes from Makeet's to Luca's. "Tell me."

"We are... distantly related," he said, and I knew with everything in me that wasn't the truth to which Makeet had referred. "And so is Cora."

"We are related?"

"In a way, yes. It's some element in the blood that few people possess. And those of us who do possess it can sometimes... sense one another."

"We sense you and we're compelled to protect you," the old man said.

"You mean, you have it, too?"

"I did."

I bent my eyebrows and tipped my head to one side.

"Never mind that," Luca said. "Just know that we can feel the child. She's moved even further."

"Then why have you stopped here? Why aren't you still going?"

"Because it's nearly daylight," the old one said.

Again, Luca blinked slowly.

"My skin reacts badly to the sun," he said. He'd said something about preferring the darkness in the past, but I hadn't thought it was due to a condition.

"As does mine," the old man added.

"Both of you?" I asked, my eyebrows arching high. "Oh? Is it related to the blood as well?"

"Yes."

"Then why don't I have it? The sun doesn't bother me at all."

Luca seemed to search for words, and finally said, "That part of it... doesn't usually begin until you are older," he said.

I studied his face and nodded and said, "You are working very hard to not tell me something, aren't you?"

"Not at all. But for now, the sun approaches, and we must rest."

The old man got up, walked a few yards, then moved a large boulder from in front of a cave. I couldn't believe he could budge a rock so large. He disappeared into the darkness behind it.

Luca stepped into the opening, but then turned to gaze back at me. "I wish I could explain further. When you're older—"

"Sure," I said.

"Will you be here when we come out at sunset?"

"No," I said. "I will not."

"Be careful, then."

I nodded twice. Luca took another backward step, then put his hands on the boulder and rolled it right back into position. It blocked the entrance entirely. I estimated not even a shaft of sunlight could pierce through.

I stood for a moment, gazing at the stone and wondering what type of men slept by day and hid from sunlight.

No matter. I fed a log to the fire, and then found a comfortable spot to sit. I ate some of the bread and several figs, then drank from my water urn. I packed all my things back into my satchel, and removed the map, the blanket, and the pendulum. I used them in just the same way I had before, and found that the child was at least as far away, as the distance I had already traveled. So, I rolled the map and returned to my boat to resume the journey.

An hour later, I came upon a barge, loaded with cargo, being pulled upriver by donkeys all along the shore.

I paddled right up behind it, looped my rope around a protruding fixture, then put down my paddle to enjoy the free ride.

I passed the entire day on the river. When we neared the point where my divinations said I would find her, I repeated my scrying only to find she'd moved still further. This happened over and over again until we traveled through places I had never seen before, and I feared we were leaving the kingdom of my father.

As the sun went down, we reached a port, and the barge edged itself into a widened harbor, dug by hand. I jiggled my rope until it came loose and paddled to a secluded spot of shore. Then I found a place to sit where I could spread out the child's blanket and unroll the map. I found rocks to hold the parchment flat. Then I took my holed stone and used it once again as a pendulum. It started making circles this time at the very spot where I'd landed.

"No need, little princess. She's near. We feel her."

Luca's voice came from the shadows near my spot and startled me so much that I jumped to my feet and had my knife in my hand before I recognized it.

"Reflexes like a cat," his elder companion Makeet said. Then he began dragging refuse together and piling it in a clear spot, as if to make a fire.

"What are you doing?" I demanded.

"Dangerous as they are to me," he said, "I like a nice fire. It gives comfort."

"If she's near, let us go to her. We have no time for comfort. Luca, tell him."

"I think you just did."

"If she were in pain or immediate danger, I'd know it, and I don't," Makeet said. "It's been a long journey,"

"Yes, and I'd love to know how you made it. I traveled most of the day. You said you couldn't bear sunlight on your delicate skin." My tone was irritated and sarcastic.

Luca shrugged. "Perhaps I wrapped myself in heavy cloaks to protect my... delicate skin. It matters not. I am here. And so is the child you seek. We'll go to her now, together, all right?"

"And what of him?"

Makeet was holding his hands over the pile of fuel, and to my surprise a tongue of flame danced to life. I hadn't even seen him strike a flint!

Perhaps he did the trick Betta had taught me, to call the flame to life with the power of Isis.

He looked like no priest I'd ever seen. His robes were tattered and dirty, his beard tangled and long. But his eyes were beautiful, peering out above his haired cheeks and below his bushy brows. They were blue, his eyes. Light blue, like a foreigner.

"I'll take comfort with the fire. Luca, call if you need me."

"She's that close?" I asked, whirling to search the horizon in all directions.

"No. She's an hour's walk, this way," Luca said, and he started off without me.

I ran to catch up. "How are you supposed to call him if she's that far distant? What did he mean by that?"

Luca looked back at me and slowed his pace so I could catch up. "Sometimes older people say strange things. It's impolite to point it out. He can't help it."

I studied his face and knew he was lying to me. Luca had never lied to me before, but I could tell he was now. I sensed it somehow. I said, "I've seen the elderly when they become that way. He doesn't seem like that to me. He does not seem confused, but perfectly clear-minded."

"I suppose old age behaves differently in different people."

I did not reply and we kept walking. And then I said, "He's by far the strongest old man I've ever seen."

"You think?"

"Yes. And fast, too. To have kept up with you, at the pace required to make the journey you just did."

"Your barge was slow."

"You saw my barge?"

He looked down at me with mirth in his eyes. "Do you win every argument, Rhianikki?"

"Yes. And I always know when someone is lying to me. You are lying to me, Luca. I thought we were friends."

"We are, we are." He bobbed his head as he walked. "And I've not lied to you, only left out some things you are still too young to understand. But I will tell you every bit of it, in time."

"How much time?"

He shrugged. "I cannot say. But trust me that when you need to know my secrets, you will know them. Secrets known by no other being, Rhianikki, I will share with you. That is just how much I value our friendship."

I blinked because his words were heavy with sincerity. I believed he meant them. "I will be eager to hear these secrets when you think the time is right. However, I will remind you my high priestess says I'm more mature than most of the temple clergy."

"I have no doubt you are." He smiled at me, and then suddenly his smile became a frown, and he said, "Oh, no."

"What? What is it?"

A sound, like a sudden wind, whooshed behind me, and when I spun around it was to see Makeet standing nearby. "The girl's in distress."

"I feel it, too." Luca looked at me and seemed to make a decision all at once. "I'm about to reveal one of my secrets. I trust you to reveal it to no one. Understand?"

"I swear to Isis."

"Climb onto my back." He crouched in front of me. Self-consciously, I wrapped my arms around his neck from behind. He gathered my legs and pulled them 'round his waist, then he said, "Hold on and don't be afraid." And then he launched into a run, and then the run became something else—something no human could do. We sped through the night so fast the world around us became a blur.

"We can run like gazelles. Faster," Luca said.

"*That's* how you caught up to me." I had to keep my head down to block the wind from rushing into my face, otherwise I could not speak. And then suddenly we were slowing to a stop, and Luca crouched again to lower me to the ground. I stood, but wobbled, dizzy from the ride.

"You are not an ordinary man," I said. "You are either a god or a demon, I think."

"Perhaps a little of both." Then he nodded past me so I would turn to look and be distracted from my pursuit of his secrets. There was a settlement nearby, mud-brick houses and lean-tos where animals took shelter. There were twenty goats, and two donkeys. Chickens and pea-fowl roamed freely.

I heard a wail, a child's cry. "I want my mommy!" And I sprang from my crouched position, forgetting all about my dizziness.

"Who's there!" A man shouted, and Luca pulled me low again, but not before I'd seen the large bamboo cage holding several small children. I'd even glimpsed toddlers and infants.

The man was coming to investigate. Luca whispered near my ear. "Sneak over there to the children, do not free them yet, just get close enough to see how many and their condition."

"We'll take care of our friend, here," Makeet said.

I sneaked away, skirting the little gathering of houses as the guard approached Luca and Makeet, and I prayed that Isis would protect them.

As I drew nearer, I saw the children. There were three little girls of the right age that any one of them could've been Cora. There was one babe-in-arms, and three more girls, only a year or two younger than me.

I heard someone coming and dropped to my knees in the shadows behind the cage. The older girls heard the motion, turned, and spotted me, but I put my finger to my lips and they nodded and looked away.

"The babe needs milk," said a small girl of eight or nine years.

And a woman said, "Why anyone brought a babe along is beyond me."

"A babe will fetch a fine price where we're going, across the sea. The younger the better, or so I've been told."

The younger ones started crying again, which was good, as it covered the sound of my movements. I wondered how we would get seven children out of here and back to their families.

I pulled out my knife as I crouched, seeing how easily I might cut through the rough rope that held the bamboo bars together. And so when someone grabbed me by my hair and jerked me to my feet, I was able to drop it, right there against the rear of the cage before she tossed me inside with the others.

# CHAPTER 13
## BLOODBATH

When the guard threw me into the cage, I landed hard on my hands and knees. Then I sprang to my feet, grabbed the bamboo bars and shook them. "Release me at once! How dare you?"

*Do not tell them who you are, Rhianikki!*

"Luca?" His voice came from so near I found myself peering from the cage to locate him.

*You can hear me?* he asked.

I nodded but put a finger to my lips looking around frantically, because if I could hear, Luca, surely the guards could, as well. "I can," I whispered under my breath. "And so can they. Where are you?"

The other girls were creeping closer. One only a bit younger than me asked, "Who are you talking to?"

"Have you come to help us?" asked another.

I met their dark and frightened eyes, then noticed the sharp attention of our guard standing a few steps away from our cage. She was watching us closely, and I didn't want to give myself away, so I said nothing, only moved to the back of the cage. The children followed, huddling around me. I was three years older than the eldest among them.

*I'm speaking to you with my mind.* Luca said, and for the life of me, I believed him, for his voice came from no direction, but from within. *Try to speak back to me in the same way.*

*How?*

I felt him smiling, as odd as that was. *You just did it. How many children are there?*

*Seven, including an infant. Eight now that I'm in here with them.* I realized the children were staring at me. Even the crying infant had been distracted from its wailing by my arrival. "Is one of you Cora?"

The littlest of the toddlers gazed at me. "I want my mommy," she said.

I went to her and hugged her close. "Everything is going to be all right."

The other two little ones came and hugged me, too, while the older girls stood nearby, dashing tears from their dirty faces.

"When are you coming?" I asked in a whisper, forgetting to speak only with my mind. One of the older girls heard. I saw the way her gaze sharpened on me.

*As soon as we escape.*

*They captured you?*

*We were outnumbered. No worries. More help is on the way.* He must've sent word to the closest outpost of my father's armies, I thought. *When the fighting begins, make the children close their eyes. And avert your own, Rhianikki. What happens tonight will be cruel, messy, and violent. Know these child-stealers have brought it upon themselves. Know too, that no more children will be harmed by them.*

I shivered and looked again outside our bamboo cage. Adults, mostly men, went about their night outside. There were huts and tents in between, and I heard snores coming from some of them. But many were up and awake. Several had gathered round a fire. They sat, talking in low voices. The one in charge of guarding us children was the only woman, and I thought she resented being given childcare duty. She stood a dozen steps from our tent, her arms crossed, watching us. Her black hair was pulled straight back from her head and knotted there. She wore a leather breastplate over her tunic. Her shoes were made of animal hide. They covered her calves almost to her knees and were wrapped round and round with laces.

I rose from among the children, went to the front of the cage and looked at her until she came forward. "What do you want, newcomer?"

"The children are cold and hungry. They need blankets and food."

"And who do you think you are, making demands of me?"

"Who do you think you are to deny them?"

"I'm the captor. You are the prisoner."

"Would you like any of your people to sleep tonight?" I asked. And then I screeched at the top of my lungs, the sound high-pitched and sharp enough to make ears bleed. When I ran out of air, I took a breath and did it again.

The children shot to their feet, alarmed, but I looked at them and I smiled without closing my lips, and nodded at them to join in. They understood and began to shriek, as well. We screeched and screeched and screeched. People poured out of their tents, and men came running.

"What is the matter with them?" one shouted at our guard. He had to yell full voice and near her ear, at that.

"They want food and blankets!"

"What?"

"FOOD," she shouted at his ear, "and blankets!"

The second man reached into the cage for me, but I ducked his grasp, and then the first one pulled him away. "Not a mark on them, we were told." Then to me, "Stop!"

I went silent and held up a hand so the children would do the same. When they did, he held my gaze, but spoke to his cohorts. I took him to be the one in charge. He was not Egyptian. His hair was orange, like a lion's mane. "There is nothing to be gained by starving and sickening them, and everything to be lost. Fetch blankets and get them soup and bread." The second man ran off to obey.

I nodded once to him. He narrowed his eyes on me. "Where did you come from?"

"The gods," I said.

"I caught her behind the cage, snooping around," the woman said.

"And you don't know who she is?" He seemed alarmed. I smiled to myself. "Did you not think she might have people with her? Family, even now searching for her? Fool!"

The second man came out of a tent with blankets in his arms and poked the corners through the bars. The little ones grabbed for those corners and tugged the blankets through, and the bigger ones helped wrap them round and tuck and knot them to stay in place before wrapping themselves in their own.

A woman brought food and she was the first female I'd seen besides our guard, but she wasn't the same at all. She walked hunched over, with a limp, and carried a basket. Her hair was wild, dark brown in color, coarse in texture and her clothes were rough and ragged. She carried a basket that held hunks of crusty bread and she sent frightened looks behind her every few seconds as she poked the pieces through and into the grasping hands of hungry children. I waited for the final piece, then sat on my blanket against the rear part of the cage, because I had spotted my knife just outside that spot, right where I'd dropped it. I reached behind me and patted the ground without looking until I felt the blade with my fingertips, got hold of it, and brought it to me, through the bamboo bars. Then I tucked it into my belt, underneath the blanket.

The limping woman made another trip, carrying a large pot, which she placed on the ground near the front of the cage, and then yet another trip, returning with bowls stacked high. She used one bowl to dip soup from the pot and poured it into two other bowls. When they were all filled, she looked to the mean guard. "They will not fit between the bars."

"Fine." The guard came nearer, unfastened the same panel again and shoved the old woman through. She stumbled, and soup sloshed from the two bowls she held, onto her hands.

"It's okay, I'll help." I took the bowls from her and handed them to two of the children, and they went to sit in a corner. The old woman reached outside for the remaining bowls and the pot of soup, bringing them into our cage, and then she began filling the remaining ones from the pot.

"Hurry up," the guard said.

"We need water, as well," I told her.

"I'm not going to fetch water with the cage open," she shot back. "You think I'm an idiot?"

"Yes, I do, actually. Close the cage. Replace the panel and get the water. She's perfectly *safe* in here with us." I squeezed the old woman's arm when I said it.

The old woman met my eyes, and I knew from the curiosity in hers that she heard the cunning in my voice. She slowed her movements, filling each bowl as slowly as she could, and watching the camp, her gaze more alert than before.

I took the fussing infant from the arms of her eight-year-old caregiver, handed her to the old woman, and leaned close. "You're not one of them, are you?"

She met my eyes, shook her head quickly side to side with frequent glances outward to be sure we were alone.

"Good. Stay in here with us if you want to live."

She nodded. "I found this infant vessel earlier," she said, pulling out a pot-bellied cup with a tiny spout halfway up. The spout was small, like a nipple, and its opening was slight. She held it to the baby's lips. "Goat's milk," she said.

The baby drank eagerly.

The guard came back with a vessel of water and removed the panel just long enough to put it inside. Then she looked at the bent woman. "You coming?"

"They're too young to properly care for the babe," she said. "I can feed it and clean its bottom. Put it to sleep. Put all of them to sleep, if you wish."

"I do wish," she said. "An hour of peace and quiet without a screaming infant would be a relief. I was thinking of pitching it into the river." She re-affixed the panel into place, then returned to her position several steps away, crossed her arms, and watched us.

I had no doubt that once the baby was content and at rest, the guard would take the slave from our cage. But once the child was full of milk, she lay it down and unwrapped its bottom. She tore a blanket in two, washing the babe's bottom with one piece, and then setting it out through the bars behind us. She re-wrapped a clean blanket around the babe's bottom, and swaddled it in another. And then she held it upright and patted its back until it belched loudly.

160

We all laughed at the gusto of the burp, and I saw the guard notice.

"The babe is quieted," she said. "Back to your work, slave."

Nodding, she handed the infant to me as the guard began to unfasten the panel of our prison. I whispered, "Sorry, baby," and pinched its pudgy arm. The baby howled, and I said, "She is only quiet for you," and thrust the screaming infant back into her arms. She jostled and jiggled and soothed. The child quieted.

"Stay then. Stay the night for all I care." The guard knotted our prison tight and walked away back to her spot.

*They're coming, Rhianikki. Make the children cover their eyes.*

*The old woman in the cage with us is a captive, too. Tell them.*

*Yes.*

*Seven by the fire. Most inside asleep. One guarding our cage. Cover your eyes.*

*No.*

I gathered the children into the rearmost corner of our cage. "Lie down and pretend to sleep. Face the back and close your eyes and do no open them no matter what you hear." As the children curled on their sides, I tucked their blankets around them again.

The old woman searched my face, but I nodded at her to do the same. She sat behind the children, facing the back, holding the infant that had fallen asleep in her arms.

But not I. I moved to the front, my hand inside my blanket clutching the handle of my knife. I knew something was happening, and yet it was impossible to tell what. Within the distant shadows, darker shadows moved. A whoosh here, a blur of motion there. Our captors vanished with those blurs. And I wondered if Luca could move so fast he would become a blur.

I heard screams then, brief screams, that ended abruptly.

A blur attacked our guard and she vanished. Maybe she'd become a part of the blur. What was happening? I had to know.

I pulled out my razor-sharp blade and sliced the ropes that bound our cage. Soon I had removed two panels, opening a passage we could walk right through. "Children, come. Woman, bring the babe," I said, standing to one side of the opening. They got up slowly, all of them with fear in their eyes.

"It's all right. We're being rescued. Our captors are... gone. They've fled."

"From what?" the old woman asked, gathering the infant a little closer to her chest.

"From my friends, and apparently, their friends. We came here together to rescue you and return you to your families. Now hurry up, or our journey will have been for nothing!" I went out first, and to the right, then right again, to take us into the wilderness behind the cage where at least I'd been before. I was almost afraid to look behind me, but I forced myself, and they were coming, two by two. Each older girl held a little one by the hand, and the old woman with the babe brought up the rear.

I moved them as quickly as I could from one patch of scrubby brush to the next, ever closer to the river.

Something whooshed across in front of us and stopped to the left.

"Down!" I whispered, crouching low near a big patch of brushy wood and using my hand to make a downward motion that swept toward me.

They all crouched low and waddled closer, and I said, "Keep your heads down, look at the ground."

They did. I wondered for a moment why they obeyed me as readily as they did. But then my gaze was drawn in the direction where the whoosh had stopped, and I saw Luca, holding our guard in his arms, kissing her neck. Not kissing, no... She wasn't kissing back. She hung limp, her head cocked to one side while his mouth was affixed to her neck. Her eyes were wide open, and I saw the moment when the light went out of them.

Luca lifted his head, his mouth wide. I saw the blood that coated his lips and glistened from his fangs. His eyes glowed red. And I felt fear such as I had never felt before.

# CHAPTER 14
## VAMPIRES

That night was the first time I had ever seen a vampire feed.

I had escaped the cage where I'd been held, and I'd taken the captive children and the old woman with me as our rescuers had attacked our captors. At least, I thought it was our rescuers. It felt more like death itself was sweeping through the child-thieves' camp that night. Wisps of dark shadow seemed to wipe the criminals from existence. Their screams were even more terrifying when they were cut-off unfinished. But as the children crouched low, hiding from the nightmare behind bushes and fronds, my feet were rooted. I strained to move but was unable. I tried to speak, but only gaped as Luca, my friend, feasted at the throat of our female guard, then dropped her to the ground, dead. Blood glistened from her neck, where his mouth had been.

My eyes followed the motion as Luca wiped the back of his forearm across his lips, smearing blood onto to his cheek. And then he saw me, and his face changed. It went lax, his brows softening.

"Rhianikki, I can explain."

I tried to speak, to tell him I needed no explanation. I'd seen the truth with my own eyes. He was a demon who drank the blood of the living. And his friends, those who'd come to help, must be, as well. For a time, those whooshes of energy and truncated screams had filled the night. But now, all was silent and I sensed death all around us.

"I am not a demon," Luca said. It was as if he'd read my thoughts, and I knew that he probably had. "I am not a monster. I am a vampire. Please, let me explain." He took a step toward me.

"Stay back!" I flung up a hand, palm out. It stopped him, I was sure of it. I felt my will blast from my palm. It vibrated between us, a living wall of power I'd had no idea I possessed.

He stood there staring at me. "These people are child-thieves, Rhianikki. And not just any children, but children like you and like Cora. Children we call the Chosen. Children we are compelled to protect. They've taken many who will never be found. They had to be stopped."

"You drank—" I cut myself off, glancing down at the children huddled around my legs, hidden from his demon eyes by a tangle of weeds and brambles. "I am taking the children to their homes. If you follow—I will..." I tried to think of the most powerful threat I could wield. "I will tell my father what I've seen here tonight. And how many of you there are... " I looked around me, my arms suddenly chilled, for I was aware I might be surrounded. "You will be hunted."

"No vampire will harm you, Rhianikki. Nor any of the children. Nor any innocent being, ever."

"I am taking the children back to their homes," I repeated. "Do not follow—"

"We will do as we wish!" Makeet had come up behind me before I'd sensed the whoosh of motion. He grabbed me by the back of my neck, picking me right up off my feet. "We're gods, and you're nothing but a child!"

I slid my knife from my sash. "I am no ordinary child," I said, as I twisted around and plunged it into his chest.

Luca cried, "Rhianikki, no!"

Makeet released his grip on my neck and I landed on my feet as he staggered backward. Blood spurted from his chest like a fountain, despite that he pressed his palm to the hole. Others gathered round him like shadows taking on form as he fell onto his back on the ground. One, a woman, began packing earth into the wound to stanch the bleeding. "The little bitch needs to die," Makeet growled.

"You shouldn't have put your hands on her," the woman said. She was a pale woman with light hair, like Anya from the North. She was beautiful and strong and fierce.

"Vampires can't hurt the Chosen!" he tried to shout the words, but his voice lacked power.

"And how would she have known that?"

"Luca just told her."

"And she's going to believe a being she just witnessed— there's no use talking to you, Makeet, you stubborn old fool." She turned to Luca. "How long before sunrise?" she asked, looking up at Luca.

"Too long," he said.

And they looked at me, all of them, their eyes full of anger. I still held my knife, wet with Makeet's blood, and I backed away from them, closer to the terrified children. "I am taking them home," I said.

"*We* are taking them home," the female said. And then

inside my mind, I heard her deep voice reverberating like a bell inside my skull. *Drop the knife. Drop it now.*

My hand went lax and my blade fell to the ground with a soft thud.

Luca took hold of my arms from behind me. I twisted and pulled, but he was unnaturally strong. "You said you wouldn't hurt me!"

"If we could hurt you, you'd be dead, Rhianikki."

The pale woman wrenched his hands from me. "Leave the girl alone, Luca."

Others had picked up the man I'd stabbed and carried him back toward the very place we'd only just escaped, leaving only Luca and the pale one.

"You've nothing to fear from us, children," the woman said. "My name is Violet." I knew it was a lie. Violet was not her name. "We came here to rescue you from those evil ones who took you. Rhianikki is confused."

"Confused?" I asked. "Do you know who I am, demon?"

"Rhianikki, don't—"

"I am Rhianikki, firstborn of Pharaoh, daughter of Isis, whose spirit lives within me. Do not presume to think you can exert your will over me, for I know the ways of magic." I wrenched myself from Luca's arms, although I knew he allowed it. "And how *dare* you put your hands on me? Did you not see what I did to Makeet for doing the same?" I bent my knees and picked up my knife while the female vampire who called herself Violet gaped.

"Children, come," I said. "Come with me."

They all crowded around me, and the old woman whose name I still hadn't learned, held her arms around several of them as we moved away.

I felt the vampires watching me go, even felt the female begin to come after me, but Luca stopped her, and then the two of them retreated in the direction of the child-thieves' camp.

They'd better.

I thrust the knife into my sash once again, and took one of the toddlers from the girl who carried her, to give her a rest. After a while, I gave it back and took another, and so on, giving each child-bearer frequent breaks, including the old woman as we walked back toward the river, where my small, borrowed boat was beached. Too small, I realized, having no idea whether it would bear all of us safely downriver.

Yet when we got there, I found a much larger vessel, one big enough for all of us, with a wide plank for boarding. Moreover, the little boat I'd borrowed from Beck and his family was attached to the stern by a length of rope.

I looked around, suspicious. This must've been Luca's doing. Who else? But there was no one near, and no monsters hiding in the boat to attack us when we boarded.

"Get into the boat, children. Quickly, now." I kept watch while the girls and the old woman helped the toddlers and the infant, then got in themselves. I climbed in last of all, pulling the plank in behind me, and gave one last look around at the shoreline.

Luca was near, I knew he was and I wondered if he was alone or had brought his entire demon horde along. I put oar to water, and soon the current swept us into its flow. There was little for me to do but steer as we sped away.

"Do any of you know the names of your villages?"

One girl raised her hand, and hesitantly at that.

"I know them," the old woman said. "I know them all. I always hoped one day I'd have the chance to tell their families what had become of them." I met her eyes. She said, "I am Hestia."

169

"Rhianikki," I replied.

"That, I know." She smiled. "You said you were no ordinary girl and I do not doubt it."

The children were leaning upon each other, the little ones already falling asleep. Even the babe was quiet. "Three are from the same family and the babe is their neighbor," she said. "Their village is just past the rapids."

"We should be there by morning," I said. "Cora belongs in my village, Terne," I said. "What of the other two?"

"Kirsa's family farms the outskirts of Terne."

"And what about you?" I asked her. "Where do you belong?"

She lowered her head, shook it slowly. "My husband is long dead and the gods did not give us children. I have no one, nowhere to belong." She looked at me and tilted her head. "What happened back there, Rhianikki?"

I looked at her brown eyes, large and curious, and knew that whatever I told her would be repeated to others. It was too fantastical not to be. I hadn't even decided yet whether I would share what I had seen with anyone. Perhaps Betta, but maybe not even her.

"I do not know. People came and killed all our captors."

"But you knew they were coming."

"I did. My friend and his friend came to rescue the children. I was with them only moments before I was captured and thrown into the cage. They said others would come to help. I do not know more than that."

Hestia shook her head slowly. "Those were no ordinary people who came," she said. "The child-stealers were struck down by Divine means. Perhaps by the hand of Isis, herself. After all, you are her priestess."

I was only a student priestess, but I did not correct her,

and truly believed myself as much a priestess as Naiya herself. "I believe they were demons," I said.

"Demons wouldn't rescue the innocent and punish the guilty," she said. "No demon I've heard of, at least. I suppose you would know more about all that than I."

"Why would I know?" My reaction was quick and defensive, for I had been recalling Luca's words—that he and I were related in some way, and to Cora as well, and apparently, to all the children currently asleep in the boat. Peaceful, they were. Their bellies were full, and they were warm, still wrapped in their blankets. And they likely felt safe, too, away from their cage and cruel captors.

How could I be related to a demon? How could these innocent children, even the babe, be in any way connected to those murderous, night-dwelling blood-drinkers?

"I only meant because you are a priestess. Priestesses learn about such things, do they not?"

"Oh. I suppose so, yes. But nothing in my studies explains the events of this night." I lowered my head. "It might be best to forget this terrible episode and embrace only its outcome. We are free, the children will be reunited with their families, and the child-snatchers will never hurt another innocent babe."

Luca had committed no crime in my mind. Not morally. His behavior and that of his cohorts had been rather heroic. And yet, the drinking of the blood, the elongated teeth, the ability to speak without words and to move faster than ordinary eyes could follow suggested something dark and powerful. Something that could only be evil.

After beaching our barge just after sunrise, we walked into a small fishing village that had no name, all of us hand in hand. People were moving in and out of their homes, some cooking over a fire pit, some hanging freshly washed clothing to dry. And then suddenly one of the children yelped. It was eight-year-old Mia, and she grabbed two of the two-year-olds by the hands, and cried, "Mamma! Mamma!" as she ran toward a small mud-brick house.

The blanket in the doorway moved and a woman came out just in time for the girls to slam into her, wrapping their arms around her and sobbing. Her eyes were round and wide as she held them, then pried them away enough to kneel amid them. She caught each face between her hands, and her tears flowed. She shouted for her husband, who came from behind the house.

Others were exiting their homes as well, due to the commotion and her shouts, and a young women flew at me to take the babe from my arms. "My child!" she cried. "My baby!"

The three unclaimed children huddled closer, and I told them, "You'll be home too before this day ends. I promise you. Do not feel sad. Feel happy for your friends."

"How is this possible?" someone demanded. "Who are you? How did you—"

"This is Princess Rhianikki," Hestia said. "She found and rescued these children. She is chosen by Isis and wields her power. Why, she rescued me, as well."

There was noise, far too much of it, as locals crowded around to see me, reaching out to touch my arm or pat my shoulder. Hestia and I kept our three charges between us as we were herded into a house and onto chairs 'round a table.

Soon food was being heaped before us, ale and water, fruits and breads.

We were treated as heroes, Hestia and I. The villagers sang my praises and begged to hear the story of how I had rescued the children from their captors again and again. I ate, and only talked in between bites, for I was hungry, and the bread was fresh and delicious, the dates plump and juicy.

"I was traveling when I came upon the children in a cage," I said, deciding not to mention Luca or the late Makeet. "Before I knew it, someone grabbed me and threw me into the pen with them. But then some gang or other attacked the child-thieves. During the melee, I cut open the cage and led the children to freedom. It was not heroic, only wise."

"It is *most* heroic!" said the young mother who was holding her baby and weeping.

Someone draped a swatch of fine fabric across my shoulders, and someone else laid a gold necklace beside the plate in front of me. Another person poured a handful of coins into my lap.

I held up my hands. "Enough. Hestia is the hero. She's been with the children for days, and I, only hours. Without her help, I would not have known where they belonged."

It didn't stop the tributes from piling up, it only re-directed them. And soon the both of us had acquired more loot than we could comfortably carry home. I said, "Thank you for the food. But we cannot stay, nor carry all these generous gifts home. We still have three children to return to their parents."

"We can help!" one of the men, clearly a local leader, exclaimed. "We have ships that will carry you in comfort, Princess."

"I cannot—"

"You must rest. You can bathe in our springs, dress yourself in fine garments. In the morning, when you are refreshed, we will join you in your journey.

"The children may stay the night with us," said the mother of the three. "They needn't be separated so soon after all they've been through together."

I clapped my hands to the table and rose to my feet. "We cannot stay." I raised my voice slightly, to make it clear that this decision was already made and not open for discussion. "I wish to be back within the walls of my own temple by nightfall."

There was a moment of stunned silence. "Then we'd best get the barge ready," the man who seemed to be the leader said at length. "Although even then, Princess, there is no way we can make it to the temple by nightfall. Midnight, perhaps, if all goes well."

I shivered when I thought about being out on the river by night. I'd been feeling confident and safe by day, knowing that, whatever he was, Luca could not bear the touch of the sun, and spent his days hidden from it in complete darkness.

As long as the sun rode in the sky, he would be unable to come near me. But once it went down... I had no idea what would happen then.

And yet I did. I knew to the depths of my soul. Luca would come to me. Perhaps not with his band of demons, but he would come.

I clutched the handle of my blade, and prayed to Isis that I would not have to kill him.

# CHAPTER 15

# THE PURPOSE

We rode in luxury on the journey downriver. Bathed and dressed in clean clothing donated by the villagers, the three children who remained with me seemed entirely transformed. The older girls, cousins it turned out, chattered about returning to their families, and even little Cora smiled, sensing the joy of the others, I thought.

Seeing the children reunited with their grateful families was something I would never forget, nor ever be able to describe to another. Being witness to it was a gift I would hold close to my heart, like a treasure of immeasurable worth.

A young man in a sleek, fast canoe had sped downriver ahead of us, carrying news of our journey to Terne. Knowing that he would arrive far before us filled me with relief. Our messenger would ease the mind of Cora's mother, and his words would reassure Betta, the priestesses, and my fellow students at the temple that I was well and would soon return. Kiko would no longer need to worry. And I would soon return his family's boat in excellent condition. I hadn't so much as scratched it.

Sometimes the people in my life worried about me, despite that I had assured them numerous times I would always be fine. I was a harbinger of Isis, I was convinced of it. No harm would come to me unless it was her will, and if it was her will, it would not matter where I was.

The boat was large, and there were soft, cushioned seats for all. A village elder woman, who kept her gray hair cropped close to her head had come along—to tend to us, she said. She approached me with a bundle of white fabric in one arm. "Come with me, if you would, Princess." I glanced at Hestia, and she nodded at me to go along, so I rose and followed.

"I am Katta," the elder woman said. She'd led me to a three-sided bamboo frame with fabric stretched over it and pulled one of the sides outward. Within, there was a pitcher and a large vessel of water, a vial of scented oil soap, hair combs, a small cloth for washing, and a larger one for drying. She had made for me a private bathing stall.

"You wouldn't leave the children long enough to tend your own needs in the village," Katta said. "Even your servant Hestia bathed."

"She's not a servant," I corrected, but Katta seemed not to hear me and continued on unimpeded.

"Now, you are here, and they are safe, and there is time. Here." She passed the fabric to me, and I held it up so its folds fell free. It was a kalasiris dress, pristine white with a golden sash. As it unfolded a pair of soft slippers of the same gold color fell at my feet.

"Thank you," I said, when I could find my voice again. It wasn't enough, I knew. I extended a hand skyward, and held the other one with my palm at her forehead. "I call down the blessings of Isis upon you, Katta. Your time on this earth will be easy, filled with joy and well-being, abundance and love. By the power of Isis, it shall be so."

She closed her eyes and lowered her head. "Thank you, Princess."

"Thank *you*." And with that I went into the privacy of the space she had created for me. Three walls prevented me from being seen by anyone on the boat, but the fourth side was open to the river. I faced it as I took off my torn clothes. My dress had blood on it from the man I had stabbed. I hoped he had not died. Truly, he should not have grabbed me that way, but my mind would not stop questioning whether he'd deserved to die for it. He might have been there to help, as I believed Luca had been.

I gazed out at the river as I wet my hair, pouring water over it from the pitcher, and catching it in the bowl. Then I worked the sweet-smelling oil-soap through it, then rinsed it. Now the water was scented with oil, and still clean enough to wash the rest of me.

My body was changing. Hair was starting to grow between my legs. My breasts were beginning to swell. I felt as much an adult as any of the grown-ups around me, though Betta told me often that feeling was an illusion common to girls my age.

It might be, for most girls, but for me it was no illusion. No one could convince me otherwise.

I put on the dress, and wrapped the sash around my neck from behind, then crossed it in front and tied it around my waist. Then I combed my long, long hair, and wound it into a thick braid that hung in front of my left shoulder. I cleaned my knife in the remaining water, dried it and thrust into the sash at my side. Lastly, I put the slippers onto my feet and stepped out of the privacy chamber.

"My princess," Katta said as she pressed her palms and bowed to me.

I returned to the children, but they didn't seem to need me. Hestia sat in comfort, gazing out at the passing shoreline, her face at ease.

Two men piloted the vessel and that seemed to be plenty. I found a quiet place to stand alone and watched the river flow with us.

We traveled the whole day, and as evening approached, Katta performed another small miracle, producing a meal of seasoned beans, vegetables, and bread. I ate the delicious meal, not appreciating it as much as it deserved, for the sun was near to setting and we still had a long way to go.

Near midnight, by the stars, we arrived at the shoreline of Terne. Residents crowded around the dock, and the priestesses of the temple in their white kalisaris were at the very front of the throng. The pilots brought the boat expertly alongside the dock. One of them jumped off first, to help position the gangplank, and then they helped us debark. I carried little Cora in my arms, and the other two girls walked behind me, with Hestia behind them. As always, we kept them safe between us.

I set foot on the dock, and heard a shout above the others, then saw Cora's mother shouldering her way between the priestesses. She ran toward us, crying "Cora, Cora, Cora!" and took her from my arms, sobbing.

My chest filled to bursting with overwhelming emotion. Her joy and the child's, I realized, somehow flowed through my heart as well. What a wondrous thing it was!

A cheer went up from those gathered as the woman held and adored her little girl. My priestesses then formed themselves into two lines, creating a corridor in between them for us to walk, sheltered from the crowd. And then

Betta appeared at the end of the corridor of priestesses with a woman on each arm.

"There," she said. But I only knew her words by reading her lips. "There they are." And she pointed at me, or rather, at the two girls who hugged me from either side.

The women beamed like the sun, and they ran to me, just as Cora's mother had. The cheer of the crowd, which had never waned, grew even louder as the women wrapped themselves around their daughters.

I once again experienced the rarest kind of joy there could be. It weakened my knees and brought tears to my eyes.

Betta, still at the end of the column, beckoned me.

I started forward, walking along that narrow opening between two rows of priestesses and my fellow student priestesses, I saw as I moved along. They kept the villagers behind them on either side, but those locals chanted my name and shouted my praises.

"Truly, you are a girl beyond measure, Princess Rhianikki!"

"Our own child-priestess!"

"All hail Rhianikki!"

Some even threw flowers at my feet as I made my way toward the end of the column. As I drew near, Betta came to me, and the priestesses on other side of us turned and began walking along the street, inland, toward the temple, never breaking their formation. It was a midnight parade with me at its center, and everyone straining their necks or holding their children up on their shoulders to catch a glimpse of me.

I felt myself grow taller and held my head so high that my spine seemed to elongate. And yet, part of me wondered if I deserved all their praise. Yes, I had rescued the children

—with help from demons who claimed me as their kin. What did it mean?

Betta wrapped her arm around my shoulders as I looked behind us worriedly. "Do you think Kiko and Beck saw that their boat was tied behind?" I asked. "What became of Hestia, the old woman who was with me? How did the girls' families get here in time? What—"

"There, child," Betta said. "The rescue is complete. You can relax your warrior's stance now. What you have done this night is... is astounding."

I nodded but was still twisting my neck to see behind us.

"Cora's mother invited Hestia to her home," Betta said. "And Beck was already untying the boat before you left the dock. When the first boat arrived with news of your journey, Rhianikki, we sent runners to the girls' village to inform their families, and they made haste back to be here when you arrived."

I nodded, still worried, but about things I could not tell her. Luca was near. I felt him. He was somewhere, no doubt waiting for me to be alone so that he could accost me.

It happened sooner than I expected. I was in my sleeping chambers. The other girls had finally stopped their giddy chattering and questioning of me, and fallen fast asleep in their beds, and I lay awake and wide-eyed.

He appeared with a soft whoosh, pausing only a moment, perhaps so that I could see him, before he scooped me up and sped away again. Had my roommates been looking, they'd have seen only a shadow beside my bed, appearing and vanishing in an instant, leaving my bed empty in its wake. But since I heard no screams, I presumed they had not been looking.

He set me on my feet again in the temple garden, near the fountain of Isis. I gazed at her face, her sparkling gemstone eyes, and I spoke to her from my heart. *Protect me, mighty Isis.*

"You need no protection from me, Rhianikki."

"Nor from me," said another voice, and I turned and saw Makeet, the old man I'd stabbed, standing there upright and strong, looking as well as ever he had. "Much as you deserve it, I'll not harm you. Nor would I have last night."

Nearby stood the pale woman who called herself Violet. Her eyes, when they found mine, were kind. Of them all, I thought, only she was happy to see me.

"How was I to know that you would not harm me, Makeet?" I was defensive. "You had me by the neck."

He lowered his eyes. "I ought not have done that."

"That's the conclusion you've drawn, is it?" My tone was sarcastic. But then I softened it. "I am glad you are not dead."

"As am I. It was a near miss."

"It wasn't. I asked Isis to spare you."

"Oh. Well, in that case—"

Luca sent him a look, and maybe a silent command. Makeet waved at me, then left the garden through the gate, wandering out into the wilds to await his friend.

Luca nodded toward the bench, so I sat down. He remained standing, but Violet came and sat beside me. "You have questions," she said.

"I have no questions for either of you. I want nothing from you except for you to leave me and never return."

"You want to know what we are," Luca said. "You want to know what it means. And most of all, what I meant when I said we were related. It's the blood, you see. The magic resides in the blood. You have it, as do several of the rescued children."

"Not all of them?"

"No, not all. The siblings were bycatch, taken because it was easier than to leave them shouting out and alerting the families.

I nodded slowly. It made sense. "What did the child-stealers want with them? Moreover, how could they know of this magic in their blood?"

He paced away from me, shaking his head. "I do not know how they know. That is a question I can't answer. But I do know that vampires sense such children, and—"

"Vampires," I repeated. "That is what you are."

"That is what we are called, yes. And sometimes, we linger near such children, to watch over them."

"Demonic guardians."

"We are not demons."

"What are you then?"

He turned to face me again. "I used to be human, with the special blood, just like you. Humans who have the magic, they do not live into old age. They weaken and die well before they reach forty years, and often before they've even reached thirty."

I jumped from my bench to stand upright. "You came here to tell me I will die before I have lived thirty years?"

"Yes. Unless you are changed before then."

I stood staring at him. The fountain sang its water-song as it always did, as if the world were not tilting out of balance. The wind seemed to whisper my question before I worked up the nerve to ask it myself, but then I repeated it aloud. "Changed... how?"

"A vampire must drink from you until you hover at the brink of death, then restore you by feeding you from his own veins. You will sleep, and then wake, and then you will be as I am."

"And how, exactly, is that? What are you, Luca?"

"Where to begin." He lowered his head so that his chin nearly touched his chest, then took a breath and began in an almost emotionless manner. "I live by night and sleep by day. I will always be as I was the moment I was transformed. If I cut my hair off, it will grow back while I rest. If I am stabbed by a girl with a knife as big as her forearm, it too, will heal while I rest, if I do not die before the sun rises. But I can die by blood loss, by exposure to the sun, by beheading, or by fire."

"And other than that, you are... immortal?"

He met my eyes again and nodded. "And so much more. My senses are heightened beyond anything you can imagine in your current state." He went silent for a moment, closed his eyes. "Listen to the night, Rhianikki, and tell me what you hear."

I listened, mesmerized, perhaps by his words and not at all afraid. I was in my goddess's temple. What had I to fear, even from him?

"I can hear the fountain, and the wind from the desert, and night birds." I smiled. "I can hear Betta snoring."

He nodded. "I can hear all that, and much more. I can hear the Nile. I can hear the footsteps of a desert fox in the sand. I can hear Cora's mother speaking to Hestia in the village. She's asking her to stay, to live with them. Cora loves her and doesn't want her to leave." He smiled. "That's a good outcome."

"You can hear all that?"

"And more. But nothing quite as beautiful as the happy tears and joyous voices of those mothers when you returned their children to them. That was something I'm most glad to have witnessed. Such joy as that is a rare gift."

I blinked at him, standing in the temple garden before the Isis fountain, admitting he was a monster while celebrating the reunions of mothers with their children. "What kind of a monster are you?"

"I am not a monster. As least, I don't think I am. I am good. I strive to do no harm, except to those most deserving of it. And while it's true, I must drink blood to survive—"

"Human blood?" I asked, my eyes wide. "You have to do that?"

"Animal blood will work," he said. "But it has to be living blood."

"So you must kill in order to live."

"No, Rhianikki. I can sip from a person without even waking them from their rest. I need not take enough to cause harm. And I almost never do. What you saw at that camp—that was different."

I thought about that for a moment.

"The child-thieves target the very children vampires are compelled, beyond reason, to protect. Also—and this will sound like an excuse to you, but it's only the truth—like our senses, our emotions are heightened. We feel things more powerfully than when we were mortal. Including, I'm afraid, anger."

"I see."

"And now you know everything," he said.

"That can hardly be everything, Luca. How long have you been a... vampire?"

"There is only one older. I knew survivors of the Great Flood, though I was born some time later, they walked in my time. They knew me as Iskur."

My eyes widened and swept over him from head to toe, again and again.

"That's enough, I think, for your young mind just now, Rhianikki. I intended to tell you all this much later, when you had become a woman grown. Because while we do not offer the dark gift to most, you, girl, are most worthy. Possibly the most worthy I've ever come across. And we need leaders like you among us."

I blinked, stunned. "You want me to become a vampire? A leader of vampires?" I blinked up at him, then looking at the sky said, "And if I do not, I will die?"

"You have much time before such a decision will need to be made. But now you know. And I must ask you, Rhianikki, to promise that you will not repeat this knowledge to anyone. Not even to wise Betta."

"Betta already knows," I said softly.

He brought up his head, his eyes going wide. "You have told her?"

"I have not."

"Then—"

"She told me once that she was teaching the other girls as a matter of form. That she was really here for me. That she had been sent. And not by my father, that is sure. A woman of magic, not of the priestly caste would sooner wind up in his work camps than teaching the mystic arts to his firstborn. Rejected or not." I gazed at the temple walls before us, my eyes straying to Betta's window, and for an instant, I thought something moved just behind it. "She knows there is something special about me. Something unique."

"Anyone who ever met you knows that, young princess."

"No. It's more than my boisterous nature, more than my

father's lineage. She knows about this other thing, this thing in my blood that makes me a vampire."

"Not a vampire, Rhianikki. Not unless you one day choose to be."

I dragged my gaze from Betta's window to meet Luca's eyes. "Is there any doubt in your mind that I will?" I asked. "If there is, then you do not know me at all."

He smiled at me. "I will stay away from you if that is your wish. I will return only when your life is nearing its end and your decision must be made. And then I will change you, if that is your desire."

I gaped at him. "You cannot go away! We must find out who is behind this plot to steal the children with the magic in their blood. What were they doing with them? How many more are missing? How can they tell these special ones from ordinary children? Who—"

He placed a hand on the top of my head, a gesture meant to settle me, but it was also loving, as if he were a parent and I, his child.

"Little sister," Violet said, and that was enough to silence the flow of my words. "Our desire to protect those children is even greater than yours."

"Is it?"

"We could not do otherwise, even if we tried. We will find the answers to all those questions. Even now, vampires are searching for the missing children. And we can sense them, when they are near, so we will not fail."

I stared at her for a long moment, then turned to Luca. "I want to help."

Luca said, "I know you do. But—"

"Are you really going to tell me that I'm too young? Too weak? Too inexperienced? That I must leave it to the *adult* vampires?"

"You are not yet a vampire. And yes, I would tell you all that and more. I would tell you that it is too dangerous, and that you have a purpose in life that will go unfulfilled if you get yourself killed before you even reach maturity."

"My purpose in life is to wield the power of Isis for just cause," I said. "If *she* doesn't require me to grow up first, then what makes you think you can?"

He looked at me as if I'd punched him in the nose, then he turned toward Violet as if seeking her help.

She shrugged and said, "Do not look here for assistance. I am on her side." She winked at me, and I thought I might love her a little bit.

"What is your real name?" I asked her. "I know it is not Violet."

"It is Violet now," she said, and I sensed she would say no more.

Only hours ago, I'd been fearing this encounter, thinking of them as angry monsters coming to vent their fury at me. But instead, they were kind. They were informative. They were, I thought, honest. I had not sensed deception the entire time we had talked, and when they left, I wished they'd stayed longer.

# CHAPTER 16
## THE BETRAYAL

After the children were settled back into their homes and I was safely returned to the temple, Luca left me again. He didn't say goodbye or give me any information about where he was going or when he would return. That conversation in the garden, in the dead of night, with him telling me I was too young and it was too dangerous to try to find out who was behind the child-thieves, had been our last.

He, Makeet, and Violet had left as suddenly as they'd appeared that night. I'd stayed on the garden bench for a little while, because their departure had been so abrupt I was certain they were coming back. But they did not. And I was tired to my very bones. So I returned to my bed and slept like a vampire by day.

It had been weeks since that time, and I had not heard from them again, nor had they been seen by anyone in the temple or the village. They'd just... gone. And even though Luca had told me he would return if I should ever need him, that he would know if I were in trouble, I still grieved his absence. I had more questions than there were stars in the sky, and though I was

189

still unsure whether he qualified as a demon or a monster... I loved him. He treated me the way I'd longed for my father to treat me. And there was no one else to do so. I thought I could come to love Violet, too. I might even learn to tolerate Makeet.

But since there was nothing I could do about that, I had to let it go.

A moon cycle after my return, just after sunset when the purple darkness spread like a blanket over the village, I took a basket of fruit and breads from the garden and left through the lush shrubbery wall's arched opening. Secret came shooting out like a shadow just behind me.

"Secret! You'll behead yourself, you foolish creature."

She rubbed my calf, and I bent down to scratch her head. She purred, loving the attention. "All right, then, you may come with me. I think you miss your siblings more than you let on. But I fear you'll be disappointed. We are not visiting Beck and his family this night. We are questioning witnesses."

I walked into the village with the cat trotting along at my side, and I swung the basket as I went. I had questioned Hestia already, of course, about her time with the child-thieves. But I hoped that in the days since then, she might have recalled more. She must have heard names mentioned among the criminals. They must have called each other something. Maybe one had mentioned his family, former profession, or hometown. Anything at all might be a clue that I could use to take my query one step further.

The home of little Cora's family was in the main part of the village, and not a very long walk at all. I thought Secret might keep going to visit her siblings at Kiko's house, but she stayed close beside me.

"Princess Rhianikki!" Cora's mother called when she

saw me. She'd been outside, gathering clean, dry clothing from the tree limbs and large rocks where she had spread it to dry. She bowed, clothes all draped over one arm. "Come inside. The family will be so happy to see you. I'll fix you food."

"No need, no need. How is little Cora doing? Still having nightmares?"

She lowered her head. "Yes, but not as often."

I took a small pouch from my robes and handed it to her. "Tuck this beneath her sleeping pad, near her heart. Betta and I made it together. She says the ingredients have a naturally soothing and relaxing affect. We added our own magic and asked Isis to add hers, to boost it.

"What is it?" She brought the pouch to her face, sniffed it. "Mmm. Smells wonderful."

"Herbs from the earth, empowered by the sigil of Isis. It will soothe her."

"Thank you."

I nodded. "I was hoping to speak with Hestia."

"Oh, dear, you've missed her, I'm afraid. She's leaving, going to stay with friends of hers who are meeting her at the docks. You might still catch her, she only just left."

"Thank you," I said. Then I gathered up my cat and hurried away. Secret did not like to be carried, but I was afraid she could not keep up, especially the way I went. I left the well-worn dirt tracks of the village, instead cutting through both tended ground and scrubby lots, a shorter route to the river.

In no time, the scrub turned to reeds and the ground beneath my feet softened. The scent of the Nile was in every breath, moist and fertile, like fish and mud and algae. It was a scent I loved. The moon was full, and its beams danced upon the surface of the river, frolicking with every swoop and ripple of its current.

I emerged near the base of the nearest dock and saw Hestia with a group of women standing upon it near a boat. There was a gangplank extended, and a boatman waiting aboard the small vessel.

The women wore dark cloaks with hoods. One of them was patterned with the outline of an owl upon its back. Its two onyx eyes winked in the moonlight.

"We've missed you, dear sister," they said, each woman in her own way as they greeted and embraced Hestia. There were five of them, altogether.

"Did they harm you?" asked one.

"No. But the vampires wiped out the entire camp before the mission could be completed," she said.

*What mission? The mission of sending the children off to their fates? Was she involved with the child-thieves, after all?*

No, she couldn't be. She'd cared for the children, soothed them.

She seemed different from the Hestia I'd known, I realized once I got past the shock of her words. She sounded... educated. Before, she had been poor-spoken, halting in cadence, gruff in tone. Also, her stance was different. She'd stooped, before, hobbled instead of walking. Her posture now was straighter, stronger, younger, and her words were smarter.

"How did you survive?" one of the women asked. I could see three of them, and Hestia. The fourth woman stood with her back toward the moonlight and wore the hood of her cloak pulled up over her head.

"I convinced them to leave me in the cage with the children, told them I could win their trust and make them cooperate more easily. Not to mention, care for the infant properly. None of the crew wanted to hear its incessant crying. And apparently, I did win the children's trust, because when the vampires came, the princess told them not to kill me."

"And they listened?" The others seemed stunned.

I was stunned that Hestia knew our rescuers had been vampires!

"Oh, they listened, all right," she said. "I think she *killed* one of them when he grabbed her by her neck." The others gasped, riveted by her story. "She's one of the Chosen," Hestia went on, using a term I'd only heard from the lips of vampires themselves. "They can't hurt her. The poor creature couldn't even defend himself."

"Well, how was she to know?" another said. "A young girl, face to face with a pack of murderous vampires on the rampage."

"She didn't seem the least bit afraid of them," Hestia went on. "She ordered them as if she were Isis herself. So what else could they do? They had no choice but to let her take the children and go."

She was aware of my connection to the blood drinkers, as well! I needed to question her. I needed more time with her to make her tell me everything!

"I only made it back here alive because I was in the right place at the right time." Hestia shook her head slowly and then said, "And because of her. That princess of yours is something."

She spoke directly to the woman whose face was shadowed. But then she raised her head, and her hood fell backwards, revealing her wild gray and silver hair, and the shape of her face, so familiar to me, and so very dear. She was my very own Betta. The person I trusted more than any other in my life.

"That she is," Betta said. "And she will not let this go, you mark my words. That's why it's best for you to return to the sisterhood, Hestia."

I could not believe it. Betta, in league with—child-thieves! And she knew about vampires, and knew, too, of my bond with them, for she'd expressed no surprise at anything Hestia had told her.

She'd kept the truth from me. All these years, she'd been deceiving me. And why? To what purpose?

"We can't have her digging into this." Hestia looked around them, scanning the shadows and darkness as if she suddenly feared I was somewhere near. She was afraid of me, I realized. And she ought to be. "She's too intelligent by far. What if she discovers—?"

"Leave Rhianikki to me," Betta said, interrupting her before she could work herself into a full panic, I thought.

Hestia clasped Betta's arm through cloak she wore. "She must never know about us, Betta."

"I've been her watcher all these years. I know how to manage her, I tell you. Stop worrying."

Manage me? She was managing me? She'd been lying to me all this time, and was, instead, spying on me for this league of females? But why? And what could she have to do with the child-stealers?

The other women exchanged looks and eventually nodded. "The boatman awaits," Betta said, nodding toward the far end of the dock where a barge moved in rhythm with the current, scraping its sides and scarring its wood. "Go."

The other four women, Hestia among them, went to the boat and helped each other aboard. They wobbled, clasping onto one another for balance, before setting themselves down within the vessel. The boatman dipped his oar, then, and pushed them away from the dock. As the prow turned outward, I saw the image engraved upon its side. An owl. Then the Nile took hold of the boat and swept it away.

Betta stood there watching until the boat carrying her "sisters" had vanished from sight, and then she turned, pulling her hood back up and walking away. She took the road toward the village and the temple beyond.

My friend had lied to me. She had deceived me. She was watching me on behalf of this sisterhood, by all appearances, and perhaps even reporting my actions back to them. I should confront her. I should demand answers to my questions. I should inform the palace guards of her involvement with the child-thieves. I should—I should not let Betta know I'd discovered her secrets this night. She must not even suspect that I had witnessed her clandestine meeting.

Which meant I must get back to the temple before her!

I hugged Secret closer and ran through orchard and garden, through dooryard and goat yard, leaping small barriers as I came to them. I approached the temple from behind, since Betta would likely approach from the front, dashed through the gate into the garden, then headed to the fountain there.

Secret shot away the instant I released her, leaping to the ground with a little growl, as if she was angry for all the rough handling she'd suffered. She darted amid the lush plants and vanished from sight. I would not see her again before morning, no question.

My cheeks were hot from my run, so I laid my face down upon the stone bench, first one side, then the other, and I dipped my hands full of water from the fountain and splashed it onto my cheeks. Patting my face dry with the hem of my kalasiris, I tried to assume an innocent position upon the bench to await Betta's return. She might not enter by the front doors if she wished to keep her nocturnal wanderings to herself.

I closed my eyes, and spoke inside my mind, to Isis.

*Explain it away, if you can, mighty Isis. Let me discover a reason for all this that means my dear Beta is not a liar and a spy and perhaps even a child-thief. But above all else, let me discover the truth, and grant me the power to put an end to those who would steal and harm innocent children. Empower me to wield your justice like a sword and bring the criminals to their rightful end, no matter who they are.*

I heard the bushes move, and the soft padding sounds of bamboo soles on a stone path. I turned as Betta moved along the stone walk, toward the temple.

"Betta?" I said, feigning a tone of surprise.

She turned her head toward me sharply, and I saw suspicion flash in her eyes before she hid it. "Rhianikki? What are you doing out here at this hour?"

"Secret woke me, mewling as if something was wrong, but when I came for her, she darted in there, where she's still hiding." I shook my head. "Temperamental beast. Where have you been this night?" I asked.

"Only out for a walk. You should be in bed, asleep, Rhianikki."

"I'd have returned to my warm nest already, but since I was already here, I decided to have a word with Isis, first," I said. "I feel closer to her here than anywhere else."

She came nearer, smiling at me as she sat down upon the bench beside me. "What did you speak to her about?"

"She's empowering me to catch the child-thieves," I said.

"The child-thieves?" She looked at me in surprise. "But Rhianikki, you told me yourself that they were all dead.

Attacked in the night by some enemy or other that vanished as fast as it had arrived."

"Yes. Yes, it appeared that they were all killed. Those holding the children and I in that camp are dead, and they deserved it, don't you agree?"

"I'm not sure anyone deserves death, Princess."

"But if anyone, then surely a child-thief," I said quickly.

She lowered her head.

"Maybe they knew," I said. "Whoever the night-raiders were, maybe they knew it was a den of baby thieves they were raiding. Perhaps that's why they didn't kill us with everyone else."

She nodded slowly. "Maybe."

"Maybe they'll hunt down the others in just the same way," I said.

"Others?" She searched my face in the moonlit garden.

"Surely you know the child-thieves were not acting on their own. Someone else must have sent them out to steal children. Particular children." I looked into her eyes when I said that, and I saw her brows bend as she gazed into mine, so I hurried on. I didn't want to reveal how much I knew, but I did want to shake her. *Manage me*, indeed.

"I will never let this go," I said, repeating her own words back to her. "I will find the truth. I will learn where they were going to take the children, what would have become of them and why, and who is behind it all."

"I have no doubt you will," Betta said. "But there is no word of any more missing children since those abductors were killed."

"How do you know?"

"The tale of those stolen babes and your rescue of them, and the violent end those baby-thieves faced, has spread throughout the kingdom. Word of another missing child would reach us just as quickly. You know how gossip spreads up and down the Nile."

I said nothing, but only watched her face. It was true enough there had been no further word of missing children. I, too, had been paying close attention to the gossip of travelers, merchants, and boatmen. And I'd had Kiko and his family seeking out information, too, for they traveled frequently. Beck was a skilled potter, and regularly filled his small boat with his wares to sell in nearby villages.

"Perhaps," I said. "The tale of the rescue is the only reason the child-abductions have halted. The babe-thieves cannot continue their evil plans if everyone knows about them. And so they bide their time, and wait for us to forget. But sooner or later, they will strike again."

"Let us hope that is untrue," Betta said.

"Even if it is, there are still children missing. Children who were taken before the ones I rescued."

She met my eyes. "I hope and pray they are safe."

"They are not safe," I said. "They are stolen from their parents, held against their will. There is no one to protect them. How can that be safe?"

Betta tipped her head sideways. "Are you angry with me for some reason, Rhianikki?"

"Of course not." But I averted my eyes when I said it.

Again, I was tempted to tell her I'd seen her at the river with her co-conspirators, with Hestia and her "sisterhood." I wanted to lash out and tell her I'd heard her admit she was only here to watch me, to *manage* me.

But I could not tell her any of that, for if I did, she would be on guard around me, and I would not be able to watch her every move. And that was precisely what I planned to do from then on.

That very night, I began.

I walked with her to the bed chambers on the upper floors. We came to hers first, so I bade her good night, and kept walking toward my own, but then I ducked around a corner and waited. She moved around in her room. It was private, not shared as ours was. Once I was initiated as a priestess, I too would have a room of my own.

I heard Betta when she lay down and pulled a cover over her, and I waited still longer. So much time passed that my legs grew tired, and I sat down on the cold floor with my back against the stone wall. After a bit longer, I began to nod off, my head dropping suddenly, only to snap up again as I started awake.

I've no idea how much time I spent there, but eventually, I heard Betta snoring. It was not false. She was not pretending. It had been far too long for her to suspect I still lingered. So I tiptoed back downstairs, to the large room where we held our lessons, and I drew the curtains over its doorway tight to block out the light of the oil lamp I would use. Once inside, I ignited the lamp without a match, using the method Betta herself had taught me. I thought of that day when I'd inadvertently set another girl's hair on fire, and tears dampened my eyes. Even then, Betta had been lying. She had given me magic in the name of deception.

Wrong. The magic came from Isis herself and had been inside me from birth. Betta had only helped me access it.

With the lamp lit, moving slowly and silently, I began to search the lesson room. I looked inside every pot and every vessel. I unrolled every scroll, perused it, and rolled it up again. I thrust my hand deep into every vessel, those that held dried herbs and those that held tinctures, oils, or infusions, as well, wiping my hands dry on a spare piece of cloth from the basket of scraps in the corner, intended for that very purpose.

When I'd searched everywhere else, I ran my hands along the stone walls in search of any niche or secret compartment where she might have hidden anything at all. I even searched through the large basket of gemstones that had yet to be sorted according to each one's magical properties. And that was when I felt it. A shape that was different from the other stones, with points and engravings in its face.

I closed my hand around it, and pulled it from the basket of crystals, turning my hand and opening my fingers to see what it was—an onyx stone carved into the shape of an owl. It had a ring through its top, so that it might be attached to a necklace or other piece of jewelry, or even a belt, I supposed.

Its reverse was engraved with hieroglyphs. I ran my fingers over them as I interpreted their meaning aloud.

"Sisterhood of the Owl," I whispered.

The owl. I had seen it on one of the women's cloaks, and also on the boat that had carried them away. I could have kicked myself for not following them! I'd considered it. There had been other boats, tied to the docks and unattended. I could have taken one and followed them to learn where this Sisterhood of the Owl called home, how many there were, and what their purpose was.

I had decided to question Betta instead. And I prayed there would be another opportunity to learn more about this group. I would bide my time. I hoped the stealing of children had ended for good, as Betta had suggested. I hoped my actions had made the children of my kingdom safer.

But even if they never stole another babe, I would find who was behind this. Betta was involved, somehow. Sooner or later, she would contact the members of this sisterhood again, and when she did, I would be there, lurking in the shadows, seeing and hearing and witnessing every bit of her duplicity, and learning of their ultimate scheme.

Betta had told me once that she'd been sent to the temple *for me*. Sent by this sisterhood, I wondered? Sent for what purpose? What did they care about me? It seemed that already, they knew as much about me as I knew about myself. For most of my life, they had known more.

How could Betta keep so much from me?

I put the amulet back into the basket of stones, burying it deeply. Then I took a final look around the room, ensuring myself that everything was exactly the way Betta had left it. After that, I went to my own room, passing Betta's on the way, holding my breath as I did.

No soft snoring came from within. But that didn't mean she wasn't still fast asleep. I was tempted to pull back her chamber curtain and peer inside to be sure she was there. But though I paused, and even reached out, I couldn't convince myself to do it. What if she saw?

No, I must keep my suspicions to myself until the time came to reveal them.

I moved past her chamber quickly and went to my own, creeping in on tiptoe so as not to wake the other girls. I got into my bed in silence, moving as little as possible, pulling the covers up over me.

And then at last, I lay there, realizing that nothing I had believed about Betta had ever been true. I had considered her my friend, and closest ally in this place. But now it turned out she had lied to me and might very well be my enemy.

By the gods, I wished Luca were here!

He'd told me he would know if I needed him. And before, that horrible night of the bloodbath in the child-thieves' camp, we had spoken to one another without words. Only with the power of our minds, had we done it.

I wondered if it could work even now. I wondered how far away he was, and whether the bond between us could reach that far. I had to try, for I felt alone, more alone than I ever had. And vulnerable too. Discovering the person closest to me was an adversary shook me to my very core.

I closed my eyes and called Luca's face to my mind. *Luca! I need you to return. Betta has betrayed me. She is my enemy, and I am alone.* I hoped with everything in me that he had heard.

## CHAPTER 17
# DEATH AND REBIRTH

I t was the darkest part of the night when Luca returned to me, and it had been only a day since I had called out to him in my mind. I was in the garden, sitting on the lowest branch of a fig tree. Betta's sleeping room was on this side of the temple, on the second level, and her window was just above. I could not see her lying down, but if she got up, I would have a full view. I was determined not to let her slip out again without my notice.

I never heard him come in through the gate, nor did I detect a single footstep. Luca moved like a shadow. One moment I was focused intently on Betta's window, and the next, I was startled by his voice whispering my name from directly below. I jumped and nearly fell out of the small tree.

Luca reached out a hand to brace me, though, so I did not fall. I sent him a furious look and climbed down on my own. "You nearly scared the life out of me," I said in a harsh whisper.

He smiled. "Then I've achieved what few others could.

What is wrong, Rhianikki? And what are you doing up an olive tree in the dead of night?"

I brushed my night dress free of bark and angled my head up toward the window. "That's Betta's bedchamber. I've been watching her. She's in league with the child thieves, Luca. She and Hestia both!"

He raised his brows and I saw the alarm in his eyes. "Come with me," he said, and put a hand on my shoulder to lead me out of the garden and into the untended land that surrounded the temple. There were grasses and weeds near our temple walls, but the further one walked, the more the plants gave way to desert. If you curved toward the right just ahead, you could cut through a straw field and straight down to the river bank.

When we had gone what he deemed a safe distance, he took a seat on the boulder I often used myself. I took the smaller one near it, as I did whenever Betta and I walked together.

He pulled something from his pocket, something wrapped in a large leaf, and pressed it into my hand. "I brought a sweet for you. Enjoy it first, and then tell me everything," he said.

I unwrapped the item. It was a gooey sweet bread, tender and sticky. I ate it in three bites, closing my eyes in pleasure. I even licked my fingers. "It's wonderful. Thank you, Luca." And then upon reflection, I tilted my head to one side. "Do you miss it? Eating food?"

He thought for a long moment, then said, "There is a satisfaction beyond anything before in what I imbibe."

I made a face. "I might become the only vampire who refuses to drink blood. Yuck," I said.

He laughed softly. "You have much time to decide. Now tell me what you have discovered about Betta."

"Yes!" I said. "I went to see Hestia, only to learn she was about to leave. Her friends were meeting her at the small dock, south of the village. So I went there, hoping to speak with her once more before she left."

"About the child-thieves."

I nodded. "She was there on the dock with several women and one of them was Betta. They knew each other. They're part of something called the Sisterhood of the Owl. Have you heard of this group?"

"Rumors only," he said. "Women, they are, aware of the existence of vampires and far too interested in us for my peace of mind. I do not know what they want."

"Are they dangerous to you?"

"Anyone who knows of our existence is a danger to us. But so far, I've not heard of them telling tales about us to outsiders. They're keeping the secret to themselves as far as I can tell." He sighed heavily. "I am confiding these things to you as if you are both vampire and adult."

"I am as good as either."

"What did they say, these women? Anything could be a clue to their motives."

I closed my eyes and called up the memory. I had replayed it again and again in my mind, so I would not lose so much as a single word. "Hestia told the others that vampires had wiped out the entire camp before the mission could be accomplished."

"The mission?"

I nodded. "She was different from before. Well-spoken, as if educated, and she no longer limped nor was her back bent. She stood straight and tall and seemed far younger than I had believed her to be."

"Clever."

"She said she knew she'd won my trust, because I'd told

you not to kill her with the others. The women seemed stunned that my word held any weight with you, so perhaps they did not know of my lineage or stature."

He lowered his head to conceal what might have been a smile. I could not tell for sure. When he raised it again, his gaze was serious and steady. "What else?"

"Betta told Hestia that it would be best for her to return home. Said she knew I would not let this go. And then Hestia said I must not be allowed to investigate. Her words, were 'we cannot have her digging into this.' She sounded very afraid of what I might find. And then Betta told her she would manage me. *Manage* me. Can you imagine?"

"What were her exact words, Rhianikki?"

"Her exact words were knives in my heart, Luca. They haunt my dreams. 'I've been her watcher all these years. I know how to manage her.'" My throat tightened, making it hard to swallow, and I wished for a drink of water. "All this time, she's been lying to me. All these years, watching me, *managing* me for this group of evil-doers." My voice held the tears I refused to shed.

"Perhaps her motives aren't evil," he said.

"What else could they be? They know my connection to you. Hestia was on some mission at the child-thieves' camp."

"So were we," he said. "Were we not?"

"She has a stone engraved with the owl hidden deep in a basket of gemstones in the lesson room," I said. "The glyphs for Sisters of the Owl were engraved on the reverse." I looked up at him, straight into his eyes, for I'd been afraid he would not believe me, or would try to make light of my discoveries. But his gaze was not dismissive. It was focused and contemplative.

"What do we do?" I asked. "How do we make her tell us what is going on?"

"If we made her tell us anything, how could we be sure it was the truth?" Luca shook his head. "This is very serious, Rhianikki. If they decide to share knowledge of our kind, every vampire's life will be in danger."

"I think the same."

"You're not going to like the solution." He closed his eyes, shook his head slowly. "You're going to hate it, in fact."

"Tell me," I said.

He drew a breath so deep his shoulders rose with it, then sighed it all back out again. "We watch her. More specifically, you watch her. You are the closest person to her; you are in the best position to do this job. If she leaves, follow her. Keep close watch, and do not trust her."

"That part is already done," I said. "I will never trust her again." I closed my eyes and sighed. "What else?"

"I will track Hestia. Did she leave by boat?"

"Yes, she and three others. They went south."

He nodded. "No doubt Hestia is not her real name, but still, people will remember a boat full of women heading south."

"If anyone saw them. It was dark."

"I'll speak to dock workers and those who live closest to the riverbanks. Someone will have seen them."

"And what else?" I asked.

He shook his head. "All we can do is pay attention. We listen, we hear, we observe, and in those ways, we learn. When we have enough information to act, we will act."

"And when will that be?"

He shrugged and said, "I do not know."

"I am living with a deceiver who has attached herself to

me for her own reasons, Luca. This is not a situation I can bear."

He put a hand on my shoulder. "You are the strongest female in this temple, Rhianikki. Do not forget it. You can bear anything." And then as he gazed upon my face in some sort of wonder, he added, "I wish I could see your future."

There was a man in it, I thought. With dark eyes and dark hair and a foreignness to him. He was not Egyptian. I had glimpsed him once, in the fortune-teller's crystal ball, and his essence had filled my very soul. It was as if I knew him. And I would, someday, I knew that for sure.

"You are immortal," I told Luca. "You will be there to see my future. You must be patient, I suppose."

"As you must be," he said. "Betta will reveal herself in time. You must be as patient as the sphinx."

Secret chose that moment to leap from the tree onto his shoulder. He was startled, but caught her rather than batting her away, his large hand curving around her back. She knocked her head against his chin and began to purr. He stroked her, and she curled up on his shoulder as if choosing it for her new bed.

"Can you do it, do you think?" he asked.

"Of course I can. I am Rhianikki. There is nothing I cannot do."

Time marched on, unstoppable, merciless time. Two years later year, I stood in the uppermost room of the temple, the official room of the gods, as High Priestess Naiya presented me to Isis, a newly initiated priestess. I repeated my vows to her in a strong and steady voice and gave her my offerings of fruit and mead.

It was the summer of my thirteenth year, and while I took the ceremony seriously, and behaved in solemn way, I knew in my heart that I had been a priestess of Isis for a long time already. I had spoken my own vows to her in the garden, in front of her fountain, where I believed she lived. Isis did not wish to be enclosed in a room full of stone statues, choking on incense smoke, watching offerings wither at her feet. Isis was as alive as the trees and plants in the garden. Her power and love flowed like the waters of her fountain. Her sight was as broad and the all-encompassing as the sky. Her strength was as stable and eternal as the ground on which I stood.

I was given a silver cord and a necklace of lapis lazuli and gold with a pendant in the shape of an upturned crescent moon, also called the horns of Isis.

After my initiation we gathered in the garden, where fruits and sweet breads were piled high. I was the first initiate of our group. The other girls had not yet shown their proficiency in all areas, as I had, and were months or years away from earning their silver cord. They could not attend the initiation ceremony, for only those of my rank or higher were permitted. Yet they were happy to celebrate with me afterward.

Everyone brought gifts. Priestess Elana gave me a fine new kalasiris. The High Priestess Naiya gave me a golden bracelet and with it, a sack of coins. "From now on, you will be paid for the work you do here in the temple, tending to the gods, just as we are," she said.

I was stunned. "I need no pay to serve the goddess," I said.

"The goddess insists her priests and priestesses be compensated," Elana said. "She gives blessings to the people in return. It is your right, Priestess Rhianikki."

I took the sack in my hand and felt the satisfying weight of the coins inside.

"Well, if the goddess insists," I said, and everyone laughed.

Betta gave me slippers and a cloak of pure red. I'd never owned anything in such a rich, vibrant color before, and I frankly loved its brilliant hue, even though I no longer trusted her.

I no longer trusted any of the women in the temple, though I had no reason to be suspicious of anyone but Betta. Still, it wasn't as if one could just show up with a change of clothes and a bedroll and move in. High Priestess Naiya, at the very least, must know where Betta had come from, and who'd sent her. I wanted to ask her, but I was afraid to give myself away in case she, too, was a part of this sisterhood.

I had tried to glean what I could. I had searched the High Priestess's sleeping room three separate times, and Betta's six. But I'd found no hint of an owl nor anything else suspicious in either of them. I did not need to follow Betta when she left the temple, for she asked me to accompany her every time. Never again did I catch her slipping out in the dead of night for clandestine meetings.

I was frustrated. But there had been no further children stolen, not in all this time, so the urgency I'd felt had dulled slightly. And yet my questions remained.

And then near the end of the celebration that night, Betta said, "I have to go away for a time." She smiled and took my hand in hers. "It might be two moons before I return."

"I will go with you."

"You have duties now, Priestess Rhianikki," she said. "More than ever before." Her eyes were so warm as they gazed into mine—how could they be hiding lies? "You must tend to the gods, carry to them the petitions of the people, pray for their healing and blessings."

I looked at the high priestess, who would surely give me leave to go with Betta. But she only shook her head no.

"Why are you leaving?" I asked. "Where must you go?"

"To my sister, who is ailing and needs my help. She... she is dying, I fear."

High Priestess Naiya put a hand on Betta's shoulder. "My heart is heavy with this news. I will pray to Isis for your sister's healing." She looked as if her heart really was heavy, I thought.

My heart wasn't heavy because it was a lie. Or nearly a lie. Perhaps Betta *was* going to see a sister—one of her owl sisters, or all of them. And I was going to follow her. My duties could wait. This, I knew, was what Isis wished for me to do. And moreover, it was what *I* wished to do. I'd been waiting a long time for this chance.

When the celebration ended and we all retired to our sleeping chambers, I bundled a handful of things from the basket beside my bed, barely paying attention to what I included. A kalasiris, a comb, some sandals, some fruit. I wrapped it all in a large, heavy cloth that could serve as a wrap by day, a blanket by night, slung it over my shoulder, and raced into the hallway, past Betta's room, certain she was already far ahead of me. But I saw her in there, packing slowly, with care and deliberation. I glanced inside at her, and she looked right back at me, and at the pack I carried. Her eyebrows rose, and she was about to speak, but then there came a scream, echoing through the stone halls of the temple.

Betta's eyes locked with mine. "That sounded like Elana," she said, hurrying toward me.

I nodded, and together we ran back along the corridors. When we passed my sleeping chambers, I slung my pack toward my bed, and it landed perfectly atop my covers. Betta noticed, I saw her notice, but she said nothing.

We raced up the staircase, for the high priestess and Elana, her second, resided on the third level, with only one level higher—the cella, the home of the gods. As soon as we started through the corridor, we saw the other students gathered outside the chamber of the high priestess.

I shouldered through, but even upon entering the room, I could not see her, for the priestesses gathered around her sleeping platform. Elana, who was nearest her head, looked up at me. "I... came to bring her a cup of Betta's healing tea. She said she was feeling poorly before she retired."

I moved closer, and for some reason, I clasped Betta's hand as I did and tugged her along at my side. Finally, bodies parted enough so that I could see Naiya. She lay on her back looking more relaxed than she had ever been. Every wrinkle she'd had in life, had fled in death. Her face was as smooth as my own. Her hands lay upon her chest, one atop the other, the pose of death—as if she had known in time to position herself in just that way.

Elana finally lifted her head and wiped the tears from her cheeks. "Send for the priests of the dead," she said in a voice raw with grief. "She will be tended as well as any queen."

Several of the girls rushed away to obey, and I felt their relief to be gone. None of us knew what to do. My heart ached as if it had been bruised.

To those who remained, Elana said, "the rest of you, please return to your rest. Rhianikki, you must stay with me. We will remain with her until the death priests arrive.

I stood there beside the bed, gazing down at the high

priestess's placid face as everyone else filed out. Betta, beside me, clasped my hand, and I swung my gaze to hers. "Do not leave me. Not now, not with this."

She squeezed my hand. "Of course I will stay. Naiya was my friend."

"And mine," I said. For she had been more to me than a teacher or spiritual guide. She had believed in me, tolerated my outbursts, protected me more times than I could count. More times than I likely even knew.

"I will not leave this temple today, Rhianikki. I promise you this."

I nodded, and clung to Betta's hand even when she turned to go and pulled it free. Why? Why was I so attached to her when I knew she had been deceiving me all this time?

Had High Priestess Naiya known as well? I would never have the chance to ask her now. Or perhaps I would, if I could master the art of necromancy.

Elana was moving around the chamber, gathering jewelry and wraps and pawing through Naiya's belongings. "It's missing," she said, and she sounded frustrated.

"What is?" I dragged my eyes from the face of death to look her way.

"Her best kalasiris. The red one. I've found the gold wrap, but not the dress."

I looked again at the woman in the bed. "She is wearing it, Elana. And look, her necklace and bracelets, too. It's as if—"

"She knew." Elana came closer to the bed, pulling back the covers from beneath Naiya's folded hands. "She knew when she went to bed that she would not wake again." Then she frowned. "What is this?"

There was a scroll, rolled and tied with a ribbon lying

beside her, hidden by the blankets. The outside bore the glyphs that represented my name. Elana took it up and handed it to me. I saw her eyes moving as she sought another, perhaps with her name upon it, but there was only this one. I felt her disappointment.

I untied the knot and unrolled the parchment. Priestess Rhianikki, it said, addressing me by the title I had only possessed for a day. I decided to read the High Priestess's final message aloud, for I thought Elana deserved that much, at least.

"'Priestess Rhianikki,

You have been harbored here and protected here. My power as high priestess has kept you safe, but there are those who would do you harm. When you came to us, we sent for Betta, a wise woman with knowledge even I do not possess, to help keep you safe. And to help us teach you in all the ways of magic and of power. For you, Rhianikki, are unique among women, and among humankind. I do not know from whence your powers come, only that you have possessed them since birth, and that a girl of such power strikes fear into the hearts of men. Even your own father feared you.

Upon my death, Priestess Elana will be elevated to High Priestess of this temple and she will serve for three years. Your work during that time will be difficult and burdensome, but necessary, for upon the eve of your sixteenth year, Elana will step down and you will assume the High Priesthood and the power that seat entails. Power that will help you protect yourself when Elana and Betta and I no longer can. This has been the plan from the beginning. I pray that Isis will grant you a long and satisfying life in her service. May it be so."

I blinked, stunned that the letter had ended without

any more information. I even turned it over in search of more glyphs, but there were none. Lifting my head, I met Elana's eyes across the bed. "You knew all this?"

"Of course."

"And you agreed? It's not fair! You should serve as high priestess for as long as you wish. It is your place, not mine."

"My place is to serve until you are ready, and I am happy to do so," she said softly. She closed her eyes. "I'd hoped I would never have to serve at all, that dear Naiya would still be alive and well at the advent of your sixteenth summer." She put her hand atop the High Priestess's folded ones. "I have loved her as a daughter loves a mother."

I put my hand over hers. "As have I. Oh, Elana, how will we go on without her?"

Tears flooded from my eyes, then. I had questions, so many questions for Elana. Who were the people who wished me harm, and why? And how much did she know about Betta? Was she aware of the Sisterhood of the Owl? What did it have to do with me, that one of its members should be sent to watch over and to teach me?

But just then, only one question was topmost in my mind. How would we get by without High Priestess Naiya's wisdom and guidance? And how would I ever, in my wildest dreams, fill her role as High Priestess of the Temple of Isis?

## CHAPTER 18
# MOMENT OF TRUTH

I walked with the others from our temple in front of Naiya's sarcophagus in the funeral procession. Ahead of us a drummer beat a slow and steady cadence. The funerary box was borne by visiting priests, through the village and out into the desert, where her beautiful tomb awaited. My father the pharaoh had ordered its construction for her years ago. I'd had no idea about that until Elana had told me. I was grateful.

The pharaoh attended her burial rites himself. I saw him along the route, standing alongside watching us pass. He and his entourage would fall in behind, and march with us to the tomb. He was surrounded by soldiers, but had come without his queen or spoiled eight-year-old sons, who were, according to gossip, horrible brats. When he died, I expected they would kill each other fighting to succeed him—unless they changed course as they grew into young men.

My father looked up at me as we approached the spot where he stood. I met his eyes and gave a nod of thanks for the elaborate funeral. Yes, he'd only done it out of gratitude to Naiya for having taken me off his hands. But it was a funeral worthy of her and one she deserved. I was glad of that.

I walked beside High Priestess Elana to the dire drum-beat. And while I'd always pretended to feel superior to everyone around me, the idea of becoming high priestess of the Temple of Isis intimidated me. I did not feel equal to the task. But I felt certain Elana was.

Elana told me that just before she'd gone to bed that final night, Naiya had pressed Elana's hands between her own, and gazed intently into her. She said she felt as if Naiya had passed something to her. And I wondered what it was. Her power? Her position? Her blessing?

Since then, Elana had risen in some undeniable, yet unidentifiable way. Her eyes seemed brighter, and they seemed to see more, somehow. Her gait was more graceful and deliberate, and her attention seemed sharper. She stood taller and seemed to have taken on additional strength in some inner way.

There would be a public ceremony in another moon cycle to name Elana High Priestess of the Temple of Isis. The delay was to show respect for Naiya, and to give us all proper time for mourning her, and for sending up prayers and offerings on her behalf to help her on her way. So one moon cycle, and then the official elevation of Elana.

But the *real* ritual that conveyed the high priestess-hood would be private and would happen tonight. No one was allowed to witness it except other High Priestesses. They had come from temples all over Egypt to honor Naiya and walk in her procession. While here, they would gather in secret to anoint Naiya's successor. I did not know what the secret rite entailed. I did not know if the priests or high priests knew about it. We only had visiting priests at the Temple of Isis, none were in residence, and no male students, of course, so I had no interaction with them. But even among the novice priestesses, the secret rite of the high priesshood was spoken of in whispers and treated as a sacred mystery. We would never discuss it outside the temple. And we knew better than to ask the priestesses.

It was a mystery I would one day discover. I had only three cycles of the sun to prepare. But I would begin as I would begin, and it would be as it would be.

We surrounded the tomb that stood like a small temple in a large pit beneath the blazing sun. Earthen ramps had been formed so we could walk down with her. The bearers followed us down the ramp, carrying the sarcophagus with Naiya's face depicted upon its lid. It did not capture her beauty.

The tomb was two square rooms with a flat roof supported by columns. One section of the roof was open, so that those above could observe. It would be sealed later, as would the entrance, before the entire thing was covered over.

We spread out around the area in front of the tomb, but the bearers continued on and carried Naiaya into the tomb, across the outer chamber, through a narrow opening into the dark and silent inner chamber. They placed her sarcophagus upon a raised platform, then came back outside.

The lyre players began to strum their strings, and the pipers played their pipes, adding melody to that relentless and steady beat of the drums. One by one, we mourners were to enter the outer chamber and leave a gift or offering to Naiya. I expected Elana to go first, but she closed her hand around mine and pulled me in at her side. I heard soft murmurs among those gathered, likely speculating on the symbolism of that.

We entered the tomb, with everyone else waiting respectfully outside. There were already items lining the small, mud-brick room. A basket of scrolls, another that held her best clothing. Large vessels of wine and beer, and platters of fruit and bread had been placed there, along with several oil lamps and bowls of sacred herbs for burning.

I took the kalasiris and wrap that I had made from the finest fabric I could find. It was orange in color, and I'd never seen cloth like it before. It had been a gift, sent to me from Anya, the northern woman I'd helped to have a child so long ago. She'd sent it with a caravan passing through our village, and it had been left for me at the temple. I had embedded the dress with gemstones, rescued from the fountain in the temple gardens; topaz, turquoise, onyx, lapis lazuli. I believed Isis agreed with this decision.

I laid my offering in the outer chamber, draping it across a vacant stone slab, but my eyes were drawn to the dark rectangle that led to the inner room.

Elana placed her offering, a statue of Isis with lapis eyes. It was the length of her forearm and painted beautifully. Then she moved to light one of the pots of herbs, so their smoke could fill the chamber, and two of the oil lamps.

She turned as if to go, but I did not move. I was still gazing at the dark doorway.

"Go in if you must," Elana said.

"I think I must." This was not customary, and yet I could not stop my feet from taking me across the threshold into the private sanctuary of my dead high priestess. I carried no light to disturb her journey. I placed my hands upon the cool, elaborate lid. "I love you, Naiya. I implore Isis to enfold you in her wings and carry you into peace, rest, and renewal." A tear welled in my eye and spilled onto my cheek to roll slowly down. "Care for her, Isis," I said.

I stood with her for a few moments, but soon I sensed the unease outside. Others were waiting for their turn and noticing my unusual behavior. So, I left the tomb, and stepped once more into the outer chamber.

"You are a priestess now, Rhianikki," Elana said. "Step into your new position. Hold up your chin and stiffen your spine. Feel the power of Isis within you, as you have always done. But even stronger now. Become the priestess you wish to be. Do it now. There is no later."

I nodded firmly and understood perfectly. I was under scrutiny this day, and though only thirteen, I was a priestess and next in line for the High Priestesshood. The doorway to the inner chamber would be sealed by mud brick later tonight, as would the missing ceiling panel, and the entrance to the outer chamber. And when everyone had gone away, the workers would fill the pit, burying the tomb and all its treasures.

I joined Elana in exiting Naiaya's tomb. We stepped outside into the darkening sky. I took her advice and followed her example, by standing as straight and tall as possible, and acting as the priestess I now was as we moved back up the ramps and out of the pit.

The music being played was nearly as dire as the solo drumbeat had been all on its own. And it still thrummed on beneath the lyre and harp and pipes, a steady, plodding beat that seemed for all the world like the ceaseless and inevitable approach of death, marching toward us all.

Except for me, of course. I would never have an elaborate tomb or funeral procession. I would become a vampire and live forever.

As I stepped off the top of the final ramp onto the ground, I noticed Betta, just starting to make her way down. She held a gold necklace with lapis beads, her offering. There were tears in her eyes, and she looked right into mine.

I hated feeling this awfulness between us, and knowing Betta had lied to me, while not knowing why or what it all meant. I had loved her. I wanted to love her again.

I put a hand on her shoulder and said, "We must talk before this night is over."

"Yes, child, yes, we will." She patted my hand on her shoulder, then turned away to keep walking downward.

There was feasting and ale in the village that night. People took turns speaking of Naiya's good deeds, telling tales of how she had helped them during some time of need. It seemed there was no one in our village, nor even those surrounding it, who had not been touched by her kindness and wisdom in one way or another.

I heard many such stories, but I did not linger. Instead, I returned to the temple, which was empty and silent. I moved through its halls, my footsteps echoing like ghosts. It had stood for centuries, our temple. Many high priestesses had served and died, had been buried and mourned. I wondered if Naiya would encounter them, and hoped she would. It felt good to think of her being welcomed into the midst of all the high priestesses before her.

I moved up each set of stairs, one level after the next.

As I passed a corner, Secret pounced on my feet with a playful growl, scaring me out of my wits. I had to catch myself on the wall to avoid falling on her. But by then she was already rubbing around my ankles and purring loudly, and that sound was much better than the silence had been. I scooped her up into my arms and held her close. "You ridiculous cat. This is a somber evening, not time for play."

She lifted her head from beneath my chin, then swatted my nose with her paw, wriggled free, and jumped to the floor. She ran ahead of me as if she knew where I was going, and I imagined she did. I had spent a lot of time on the flat roof of this temple, and the events of the day had me wondering if other young priestesses had done the same.

As I emerged onto the roof, the night breeze lifted my hair, carrying to me the sounds of the musicians, still playing in the village below, though their melodies were more upbeat now. I could see the fire the younger ones had built in their usual place, and the shadows that moved 'round it, and the murmur of voices was loud enough to reach me when the breeze was right.

I took a deep breath of the night air and moved toward the cushion where I usually sat, only to see it already occupied. Betta sat cross-legged with her eyes closed, her hands on her knees, her palms upturned and open.

I moved past her to the empty pillow over there, and sank down, folding my legs and calling up the courage of Isis within me. I said, "What is the Sisterhood of the Owl and what does it have to do with me?"

Betta's eyes opened. She blinked, and said, "Where have you heard of such a thing?"

"From your own lips and those of your sisters the night Hestia left. I wanted to see her off. I was in the rushes near the dock when you met with those women. I heard what you said... about *managing* me."

"Ohhh." She was silent for a moment. "I imagine that angered you."

"As it should. I trusted you. I believed in you. And then to find you lying to me—"

"By omission, I suppose." She sighed. "And it took you this long to decide to ask me about it?"

"I kept hoping you would reveal yourself, either by accident, or deliberately. But you have not."

She nodded slowly. "I knew this day would come. You're too smart not to have discovered my secret. I thought it would take longer, but here we are."

"Here we are," I repeated. "And if you lie to me, Betta, I will know. Isis will reveal it as she revealed this."

She met my eyes. "The Sisterhood of the Owl is an organization of women with a passionate interest in... things not of our normal realm. Like vampires, for example."

I widened my eyes, then quickly looked away to hide my surprise.

"I know about vampires, and so do you. Your friend Luca is one."

"That's a very dangerous thing to say about him. If the wrong person heard—"

"Who is there to hear? We're all alone on the temple roof, aside from your cat and the temple's own ghosts."

"And Isis," I said.

"She is wherever you are, young priestess. I wish I could tell you more, but the sisterhood is hidden. It's secret. We tell no one of our existence. Do you understand?"

"Much like the vampires. If they trust me to keep their secrets, can you not trust me to keep yours?"

Betta searched my eyes as if she could see whether I

was telling the truth in them. "A little more, then. We consider ourselves protectors of the natural order as well as the supernatural order—that is, the world beyond the one we know. The world where vampires exist."

"You protect them."

"We observe, we study, we learn, and we record. We keep others from interfering with them. I think that's a more accurate depiction. And sometimes we intervene when it looks like someone is about to do that. That's why Hestia was at the camp of the child-thieves. Her mission was to find where they were taking the children so that we could rescue them all."

"She was there to rescue them?"

Betta nodded. "I did not know until you brought her home to Terne, but yes. She told me that was her mission. But she could not free them until they got where they were going, so we could locate the others."

"So, you don't *just* observe."

She shrugged. "They were interfering with the supernatural order by stealing the children known as the Chosen."

I gaped. "You know about that, too?" My voice emerged as a hoarse squeak.

"Yes, and I know that you are one of them. That is why I came here, you see. To watch over you. To observe. You were—you are *my* mission."

"But you interfered, too. You taught me magic."

"I taught you to manage the magic you already possess, which is far better for the natural order than a novice child winging it wildly about." She smiled, and I knew she was trying to change the subject.

"The truth," I said softly. And I held her gaze until her smile died.

She lowered her head a little. "The sisterhood is unaware I've been teaching you magic, and healing and divination. They would probably agree that I am interfering. So, I chose not to tell them. I've been eager to begin teaching you the methods of physical combat every woman in the sisterhood must master, lest it made you ask more questions. But now I can do that, even though it's forbidden." She moved her gaze over my face. "They would probably agree that loving you is an equally bad idea. So, I don't tell them that, either."

I searched her eyes as thoroughly as she had searched mine. Secret padded across the roof and directly into her lap, where she pawed, laid down, and began to purr.

"How many of you are there? Where are they located? Is there a temple, or—"

"No. All of this is oathbound. Even our existence is oathbound."

"Will you promise to tell me the truth now, no matter what I ask?"

"If I can. If I can't, I'll say so."

I nodded. "Am I going to die young because I am one of the Chosen?"

"Yes," she said. "And in your case, younger than most." She reached across the space between us and closed her hands around mine. "You will not see twenty years, according to my divinations."

I felt the words like blades in my heart. "What if I become... one of them?"

She looked into my eyes very deeply. "How could a priestess of Isis also be a vampire?"

"Same as anyone else, I would think."

"You'd have to drink living blood."

"I am told it becomes most appealing once the transformation has taken place, and not disgusting at all."

"Priestesses do not even eat meat," Betta said as if I needed reminding.

"Nor will I," I said, tipping my head to one side and studying her face as she argued against my decision. I tugged my hands from hers and asked, "Surely you can't prefer that I die at nineteen."

"Of course I don't want you to die! But to live without ever seeing another sunrise, to live shunned by the gods—"

"Who says I would be?" I demanded. "In what tablet is it written that vampires are not as beloved of the gods as humans are?"

"I do not know. I only suppose—"

"Isis will continue to adore me, bless me, and flow through me, even if I become a vampire," I said. "I am convinced of this." Betta averted her eyes, but not before I'd seen her troubled expression. "What is it?" I asked. "Would you try to stop me?"

"I do not think I have it in me to watch you die at nineteen. Not while knowing there exists a way you might live."

My eyebrows bunched. I sensed there was more to her answer, words that she was not saying. I strained to see what they were in her face, and then I spoke a question as if someone else were speaking through me.

"Would *they* try to stop me?" I asked. And she knew exactly who I meant.

She met my eyes briefly, then looked at the floor. "They might."

# CHAPTER 19
# THE HIGH PRIEST

It was the springtime of my sixteenth year when the high priestesses of the kingdom gathered once more at the Temple of Isis. High Priestess Elana had invited them to "help me prepare" for my new role. They filled every room in the temple. Elana hired extra villagers to cook for and clean up after so many guests.

I observed them keenly, because I was in sheer wonder at the unique power thrumming from each of them. I had felt it the last time but hadn't been in such close proximity to them as I was now. Now, I walked among them, dined with them, talked with them.

I was to be named High Priestess of the Temple of Isis in three days' time, in a public ceremony. But my mind was filled with anticipation of the *other* rite, the one spoken of in whispers. Was it only a rumor, that had taken on momentum until it became a sort of legend? Or was it real?

I could only wonder—until, in the deepest part of the night, they came to my bed while I lay sleeping. I felt their approach and came awake to a soft hand covering my mouth, and soft lips near my ear, whispering, "It is time for the *true* rite of the high priestesshood, which is a secret rite. Do you vow to keep it as such?"

My eyes adjusted to the darkness and I saw High Priestess Lara of the Temple of Bast, kneeling before me with her cat's eyes and sheer kalasiris, draped with scarves. Beyond her, the other high priestesses had crowded into my sleeping chamber. I saw the shape of Elana's face among the others, if not its features.

I met the kohl-lined eyes of High Priestess Lara and nodded. She took her hand away from my mouth. "Bathe, dress, and meet us above. Tell no one. Make no sound. Now close your eyes and count to three."

I closed my eyes. I counted to three and opened them again. Naturally, they were gone. I looked around my room as if it would tell me what to do. But there were only my clothes and my pitcher and basin for washing. Urns of water stood nearby.

It was my own room. I'd had no girls sleeping in bunks around me since I'd been initiated as a priestess.

I paced, and my mind raced with excitement. I would wear my red, yes my red kalasiris, and the purple to wrap round my shoulders. And my moonstone, the one Betta had given me last week, on the anniversary of my birth. And...

My racing thoughts came to a sudden halt as something deep within me whispered that this was happening. The secret rite was actually happening. Tonight. To me!

Never had my heart beat so hard or fast! I lit a lamp, cleaned my teeth, and washed my hair and body, using every drop of water from every vessel. I used the sandalwood soap I'd purchased from the local soap maker, and its scent wove a spell of enchantment around me. I tried to leave my apprehension behind in the water.

I combed my long hair. The desert air coming in through the unclothed window drank every drop of moisture from my hair and skin, kissing me dry. I put the moonstone's chain around my neck and donned my red dress. I draped the purple wrap over one shoulder and made a knot that looked like a desert rose. On my feet, I put gold-colored slippers.

When I was fully ready, I closed my eyes. "Be with me, Isis. Walk with me." I felt her, I swore I did. There was a tingling in my backbone that made it straighten. I extended my neck, and stood taller. I felt the goddess beaming from my eyes.

It was time. I called to Secret, and she fell into step beside me as we moved silently through the corridors and up the stairs to the cella—where the gods lived, and where ceremonies were held.

And yet when I entered, no one was there.

A whisper echoed from the walls. "Keep going, young priestess."

So I kept going, up the final set of stairs and out onto the roof, my favorite place in all the world. As I stepped out of the temple into the night, they stood there, forming a circle. Beyond them, the dessert unrolled like a lumpy brown carpet, and the sky went on forever. There were a million stars and a waxing crescent moon lying on its back —a sign of blessings to come.

The women were young and old, short and tall, dark and light, thick and thin. But they all had a glow about them. Elana had it. She'd been just Elana before, and then after, she'd been... more, somehow.

Two of the high priestesses parted to make way for me to enter their circle, and so I did.

The High Priestess Melikka from the Temple of Ra

awaited me in the circle's center. She held a staff with a citrine sphere on the top. "Who are you?" she demanded.

I had not expected the question, and had to clear my throat and gather my wits to answer. "I am Rhianikki, priestess of the temple of Isis."

"And why have you come?"

"I was summoned."

She thumped her staff to the floor. I had no doubt I'd answered incorrectly. "Why have you come?" she repeated.

I stood there, searching my brain, but then I felt that tingle in my spine, and I lifted my chin, and words came to my lips. "I have come to receive the rite of high priestesshood."

High Priestess Lara smiled, pleased with my answer. "And are you worthy?"

"I am *most* worthy," I said. "Isis lives in me."

A few of them gasped and many sets of eyes widened. I supposed a simple "I am" had been expected.

Lara restrained a smile, but it twinkled in her eyes all the same. "Do you vow to serve the gods, and to exercise the will of the gods even when it is in conflict with the will of man, even the will of Pharaoh?"

That was borderline treason. I loved it. "Yes. I do."

"And do you vow to the keep the secrets of the High Priesthesshood?"

"I do."

"And do you vow to protect and defend your sister high priestesses, even at the cost of your life?"

I didn't know about the cost of my *life*.

Lara tapped the floor with her staff.

"Yes, I do," I said.

"Hmm." She stepped away from me, back into the circle of women. I stood in the center, their hub. They leaned close to each other by twos and threes, whispered, and their eyes were frequently upon me. Eventually the whispering stopped, and they all looked at Lara.

She locked eyes with each of them in turn, then nodded and came forward once again, to stand beside me in the center of the circle. "We find you... *most* worthy, Priestess Rhianikki. Kneel."

I knelt, and immediately they all surged forward, crowding around me, and each of them put a hand on me. There were hands all up and down my back, covering my arms and shoulders, and pressing to my head. I lifted my eyes, tipping my head up as much as I could, and saw they each had one hand on me and the other in the air, palms open, fingers all pressed tight, forming a slight cup.

One of them began to hum. It was not a melody, it was a single note, but then as others brought their own notes, it became a harmony of voices. It went on and on, layer upon layer. I knew they must stop for breath one by one, but I did not detect it. It was the song of the gods, I thought. It had to be.

*Open to receive it.* The thought came clearly to my mind, and I closed my eyes and opened all my senses. And I felt it! There was light beaming into me from all those hands. Each beam was slightly different, and they suffused me with warmth and power.

The hum faded and then stopped, and the women straightened away from me.

"Rise, High Priestess Rhianikki," High Priestess Melikka said.

I was stunned, and it took a moment for me to unfold and rise to my feet again. And then they were all smiling and hugging me, and High Priestess Lara said, "To all those gathered here to witness this sacred sharing of power, we are pleased and proud to introduce, Rhianikki, High Priestess of the Temple of Isis."

They gave a cheer, then quickly shushed each other with laughter erupting past the shushes. Someone poured wine into cups that were passed around to one and all. Lara muttered and moved her hands around to end the rite, then joined the rest of us in celebration.

Elana came and hugged me. Then she placed a chaplet of precious stones on my head. "For you, High Priestess of Isis."

"Thank you, High Priestess of Isis," I said.

"Painless, wasn't it? Not even any bloodletting," she smiled. That was one of the rumors I'd heard, that the new high priestess would be ritually bled as an offering to the gods. I was glad it hadn't been like that.

"It was different from anything I might've expected. Them putting their hands on me like that, sharing their power, beaming it right into me—"

"What did it feel like to you, Rhianikki?" Elana asked.

"Like... unity. Like I was part of something bigger than myself. Like I was shown the secret passage to all the power of heaven and earth." There was no question in my mind that *something* had been given to me.

"Yes. Yes, that was how it felt to me, too."

We walked to a cushion and sat to drink our wine. The others were chatting and drinking, and seemed in no hurry to leave. Someone came tiptoeing up with a platter of fruit and breads, giggling and shushing herself. She must have swiped them from the kitchen.

One of the high priestesses brought me a plate she had filled from there. "Sister," she said, with a slight nod.

"Thank you, Sister," I replied.

My heart swelled in my chest, and I could not keep the

smile from my face. The high priestesses of my father's kingdom had embraced me as one of their own and shared their power with me. It was a gift I would treasure for all my life. No matter how long.

"**D**o I look as different as I feel?" I asked Elana three days later, as she helped me dress for my public elevation ceremony in my traditional white kalasiris, with the red sash crossing my body from one shoulder. We would emerge from the chamber where we now stood, which had been Naiya's and would now be mine. It had been empty since Naiya's death. Elana had never moved in, knowing she only held the role for me.

Outside this room was a large balcony designed specifically for the purpose of addressing the public.

"You do seem different, Rhianikki. You seem older... or perhaps ageless is the word. Your smooth skin says you are sixteen, but the wisdom in your eyes says you might be sixty."

"I saw a change in you, too," I told her. "It shone from you somehow. Made you seem stronger, surer, and yes, older in some indefinable way."

"I see all the same in you." She straightened my hair beneath the chaplet I wore. "The sharing of the power is already done, Rhianikki. It can never be broken or reversed. It is yours for always."

A throat cleared, and we both turned to look at the high priest of Ra from the capital city entering the room. He was a bald man with intense eyes that were always lined in kohl, all the way round. It made for a bone-chilling glare, which he sent our way. He wore black and red and his weight in gold ornaments. Each cord round his waist represented some spiritual achievement or station, and there were many, in every color of the rainbow.

He told us of his impatience with his eyes just before he stepped out onto the balcony.

Below, the villagers would have gathered to witness my elevation.

Elana leaned close. "Don't look so sullen, Rhianikki. Po, the High Priest of Ra from the temple in Luxor, has come to personally bestow your new rank and title. It's an honor."

"It feels more like a slap. I'd have rather it come from a high priestess, from you, Elana."

"It already did, and not from one high priestess, but from us all." She squeezed my hand. "Come, your destiny awaits."

I walked with her out onto the balcony, then caught my breath as a vast, living sea of people began to cheer. They filled the yard, and the road, and the fields alongside it. As far as my eyes could see, there were people, and their shouts and cheers were a roar.

"What... How?"

"Your name is *widely* known, Rhianikki," Po said. His tone conveyed disapproval. "You have a tendency toward heroics that garner praise and public attention. That is one of the things you'll have to cease, now."

He held up his hands to quiet the crowd, but the cheers went on and on. An adult man in white priest's robes came out onto the balcony, then. His hair was cropped close on one side, but long on the other. No gray nor silver touched its raven length, but his face conveyed maturity. There were frown lines etched deep in his brow.

"Who are you?" I asked. And when he looked at Po, I did as well. "Who is he?"

"Rhianikki, come forward!" Po shouted the words, a useless attempt to be heard above the crowd. When I stepped up beside him, the cheers grew even louder.

Po did not wait for them to quiet, but held his hand over my head, and said an incantation in a language I did not know. One of the ancient tongues, I supposed. Then he said, "By the might of Ra and the authority of our king, I name you, Rhianikki, daughter of Pharaoh, high priestess of the Temple of Isis."

I bowed my head toward him as he wrapped a gold cord shot through with silver strands around my waist and tied a knot to seal his decree. The cheers became deafening. I looked out again and the people were wild, even wilder than before.

"And for the first time in the history of this temple," Po went on, though no one below could hear him, "there will also be a high priest.

I gasped, and swung my eyes toward Po only to see him pulling the newcomer forward. "By the might of Ra and the authority of our king—"

"No," I whispered as Elana clasped my arm.

But Po went right on all the same. "—I name you, Ron-du, high priest of the Temple of Isis."

As he tied the cord around Ron-du, a blanket of silence spread across the crowd. People looked up at them, confusion etched on their faces.

Ron-du looked at me and smiled as if he'd just defeated me to win some very important prize. I had not even known there was a contest.

# CHAPTER 20
# THE "ACCIDENT"

Elana came into my chamber, where I was striding back and forth, cursing Ron-du and Po and priests in general. She stood in the doorway, just inside the thick curtain I frequently wished was a slab of stone. She was my older sister in every way that mattered. I had no need to stifle my emotions with her. I barely broke my stride as I ranted.

"How can this be? How can they do this, Elana, and why?" I strode to the balcony but did not step out. Our temple had become a place of great interest among the locals. Every time I gazed down, there were revelers standing around, talking and laughing, eating and drinking good local beer, and looking frequently toward the temple in case they might see their furious young high priestess lose her mind.

"It was your father, Rhianikki," Elana said. Her voice was deeper than normal and gruff. She had been crying, I realized. I'd been so deep in my own feelings that I'd failed to notice hers. She was distressed. Her eyes were wet and wounded.

239

I went to her. "My father sent Ron-du here? How do you know?" I pushed her hair away from her face, and left a hand on her shoulder, as if I could lend her my strength and outrage to bolster her wavering spirit.

"High Priest Po decided to tell me when I threatened to speak out in the village square that the priests of the Temple of Ra had launched a coup against the priestesses of the Temple of Isis."

"Mmm," I said, but it had a growl to it.

"I've talked to the high priestesses about Ron-du, Rhianikki. You must take care with this man. He is known as a cruel and exacting priest. No one wishes to study under him at the temple of Ra. He is spoken of with hatred and fear by the priestesses who've suffered his presence, and the students are terrified of him. Those who serve with him have an unspoken rule that no female should ever be alone with him."

I blinked. "Why would my father send such a man here?"

"Po said that his underlings' fear of him was the very reason he was chosen. He's been sent here to subdue you. To control you and put you in your place."

"Oh." I lifted my brows and looked toward the door.

"And I'm being sent to Luxor," she said.

I whirled around to face her and felt her words like a blade through my heart. "No!"

"I won't be here to help you, Rhianikki." Fresh tears spilled over her cheeks and I pulled her closer and hugged her to me.

"Speak the truth, Elana. Do you *wish* to go to Luxor?"

"No! I wish to stay here. It's what Naiya intended. I've been here since I was little girl. I know no other home. You, and the others, you're my family."

"Perhaps if you go, you could become high priestess of some other temple."

She pulled free of my embrace to look me in the eyes, and lifted her hand to stroke my hair away from my face.

"I want to stay with you, Rhianikki, and help you be the best high priestess Isis ever had." Then she hugged me again.

"Well, I'm *already* that," I said, but my voice was muffled by her hair. "If you truly want to stay, then I will take care of this. Have arrangements yet been made for your journey?" I extricated myself from the hug as she answered.

"I am to travel back by caravan with the high priest Po tomorrow, late afternoon, so they can travel by the cool of the night. Everyone will sleep late in the morning with all the revelry tonight, celebrating your elevation."

"And that of our new high priest," I said, not kindly.

"No," she said. "The people of this village love you, Rhianikki. You've been among them since childhood. You saved their children. You are a hero to them." She sighed. "I will miss you so much—"

"Don't be ridiculous, Elana, you're not going anywhere." I held her eyes to make sure she believed me. "Pretend you are compliant. You might even pack, to be convincing, but you will not be leaving with that caravan tomorrow."

She looked relieved, then doubtful. "Po and Ron-du are men of great power and influence. They have the favor of your father. Be careful."

"Soak in a hot bath," I said. "Close your curtains to keep out the noise and sleep easy tonight, my dear friend. Good night."

"Good night," she said, and looked relieved as she turned to return to her own room.

I was still in the beautiful white kalasiris and red sash. I now had a gold sash that crossed my body from the other shoulder. The gold cord of my station remained at my waist and the chaplet of precious stones from Elana upon my head. I removed the chaplet, and I removed the cord-of station. I had intended to change clothes and join in the celebration of feasting and music and beer. But I would not be celebrating this night. I had to figure out how to fix this mess.

I had long believed that if I accepted my father passing the throne to one of his sons, instead of claiming my right as firstborn, he would leave me alone.

But this felt like a declaration of war.

"High Priestess Rhianikki?" Ron-du's deep voice came from outside the drawn curtain in my doorway.

"What is it?"

He parted the curtain and entered my room, though I had not invited him to come in. He met my eyes and said, "I would like you to meet me in the cella. There are going to be changes in this temple, and as high priestess, you ought to be informed."

"Informed? You need my *consent* to make any changes, newcomer."

He lowered his head to hide the smile on his face. "You see, this is one of the changes. I am the authority here. From now on, you serve me."

"I serve Isis.

He came closer in two strides, gripped my forearm, and squeezed hard. "You serve *me*. On the authority of Pharaoh." He leaned over me, his face close to mine, and I could smell the beer heavy on his breath.

I did not turn away, but said, "We shall see."

"Yes, we shall. I will show you your place, priestess."

"*High* priestess," I corrected.

He let me go and strode out of the room. "Come to the cella. The longer you make me wait, the harder this will go for you."

I waited only until his footsteps faded from the hall to dash out of my chamber and run in the opposite direction, down a flight of stairs and along the corridor to Betta's chambers and inside. "Betta!" I looked around, but the room was empty, so I ran to the window opening to gaze down at the crowd in search of her.

People still lingered in the street below. They would stay until the last crumb and drop of the food and ale were gone. All of it had been provided by the pharaoh in fake celebration of his daughter's elevation. Maybe his real cause for celebration was this plan to finally put an end to the rebellious ways of his oldest daughter.

At least the palace hadn't sent an assassin this time.

I could not see Betta down there.

"Damn, Betta, I need you!" I turned and placed my back to the wall just as a Betta crossed the threshold into her room. I lunged to her, gripped her hands. "Betta! Betta, thank goodness you're here. Po is sending Elana to Luxor, and Ron-du has demanded I meet him in the cella. He's here to control and subdue me, Betta. The priestesses refuse to be alone with him. My father sent him to... to break me."

"Oh, child." She wrapped her arms round me and held me to her. For a long time, I stood there and let her hold me, thinking that there had been far too much hugging for me this day. Eventually, stroking my hair, she said, "Do you not know who you are?"

"I know who I am. But I'm afraid of that man, Betta. He's powerful. Strong. Did you see his arms? His chest? He's more warrior than priest. And I don't know what he wants of me, but it feels... predatory."

"Who are you?" she demanded.

"Betta, I— He's waiting, and I—"

"Who are you?" She put her hands on my shoulders and held me away from her, gazing into my eyes. "Tell me."

I lifted my chin, met her eyes, called up Isis within me. "I am Rhianikki, high priestess of Isis and firstborn of Pharaoh. I am rightful queen of Egypt. I am protected by hordes of dark demons, the vampires who call me family." With every word my spine felt a little stiffer, and my chin rose higher.

"I have taught you all I learned from the Sisterhood about physical combat, and all I've learned about magic as well. You are not a girl who can be broken."

"No," I said. "I am not."

She nodded. "Have you called for Luca?"

"Yes. He's far away but coming as fast as he can."

"I will go to the cella with you."

"Only to have him send you away, too? No, no I can handle him. You've taught me much, Betta."

"I have betrayed my oath to the Sisterhood of the Owl to teach you to fight."

"I want to teach it to all our students, all our priestesses, all our servants. Every woman should know these things."

"What a wonderful high priestess you will be," she said softly. "Well, if I cannot come with you, perhaps I'll seek out the high priestesses amid the festivities and bring them up for a demonstration of my magic in the cella," she said. "That way it appears accidental when we interrupt."

I nodded hard, because my bravado was largely forced. "Be as quick as you can, Betta."

"I will. You be smart, child. Keep him at bay until help arrives."

I nodded and hurried back to my chamber to fetch my precious knife, and strapped its sheath to my thigh under my dress. Then I pulled my long hair back and twisted it into a knot. Betta said they were taught to do this before battle, if they had enough warning, so an enemy combatant couldn't use one's hair against them.

I walked slowly, knowing he would be angry that I'd made him wait even the short time that I had. On the fourth level, I entered the dark cella where he'd lit only a single oil lamp on a tall stand. He stood near its light. The dancing flames on his face made him look like some evil sorcerer. But I knew better. He was just a man.

I disliked the feeling of his energy in this sacred place. It seemed to befoul the very air. I reminded myself that Isis did not live here. She need not abide where some human temple-builder might think she should. The garden was her place in this temple, and the fountain there. I'd sensed these things from my very first day.

And in me. Isis also abided in me. I called her up, and immediately my fear was overshadowed by anger. Who did this man think he was, summoning my presence?

I stopped midway across the large room. Statues of Isis and Osiris surrounded me. They lined the walls, carved of black onyx, and painted with gold. Wherever the lamplight touched them, they gleamed. Their shadows stretched and danced as if the gods had brought their images to life.

"I am here. What do you want?"

"First, I want you to come closer. There is no need for me to shout across the room."

"There is no need, you are correct. My hearing is excellent." I moved not a single step closer.

He came to me instead, his gait aggressive and fast. I started to back away, but he grabbed my arms when he reached me. His fingers dug deep, and he pulled me across the room toward where he'd been standing before. Then he let go.

My fury blazed from my eyes. "You *dare* put your hands on me?"

"I am your master, Rhianikki." His breath stank more than it had before, and I saw a large vessel lying empty on the floor beside a clay cup. "I outrank you," he said, "and you are under my—"

"Our rank is equal. High priestess and high priest of the same temple, according to Po."

His slapped my face. My head snapped sideways under the force of it, and my skin burned. "You'll address him as High Priest Po," he corrected. "And I outrank you by virtue of being a man, and I will subdue you in every way a man can subdue a woman. I will break you."

"I outrank you by virtue of being a goddess. I am the firstborn of Pharaoh!"

"Pharaoh is the one who sent me." He held my eyes, refusing to break under my steady gaze. And then he said, "Kneel, wench, and make that smart mouth useful."

What escaped my throat was close to a snort.

"I *will* break you. And it begins here, where you will serve me before the gods as a slave serves a master. Now kneel."

"Never." I spun away from him, but he grabbed me and pulled me back around. He was very strong, but I was quick and graceful, and when he threw me to the floor, I rolled and sprang upright again. I raced past him by the only possible route, up the stairs to the rooftop. The first rule of combat, Betta had said, was to avoid it.

He followed on my heels. "Better yet," he said. "Let the revelers who celebrate your elevation in the streets below see their mighty high priestess on her knees, worshipping the new high priest," he said that as he chased me up the stairs. And then he lunged and grabbed me, gripping my arm as hard as he could, I was sure. I relaxed, twisted and hit his arm with my free hand. His grip came free, but tore my kalasiris and his nails raked my skin. I ran, and he lunged and grabbed for me again, but this time, I dodged.

I emerged onto the rooftop. The night wind was warm and angry. It set strands of my hair free from its bundle. A storm was coming. I felt it to my very toes. Where was Luca? Where was Betta with the high priestesses?

He came at me again, and I backed up until my legs touched the short stone rail that surrounded the roof. It was only knee high. There were four stories to the temple, and I stood atop it. There was nothing between me, the ground below, and the people gathered there, all of them looking up now, some were pointing. A woman screamed.

Ron-du took one step toward me, then another. I had nowhere to go. Then he spotted the people below and smiled. "Witness your wild and arrogant high priestess brought to heel! Kneel before me, Rhianikki! Kneel and take my—"

"Make me," I said. I said it quietly.

He put his hands on my shoulders, pushing me downward, trying to force me to kneel. People below gasped. I stiffened my knees and refused to let them bend. He leaned over me, for he was much taller, and he pushed down even harder.

I stopped resisting all at once, dropping from beneath him so suddenly that he pitched forward, and as I ducked between his legs, I surged to my feet, adding momentum to his launch. He went headfirst over the side. His scream ended in a dull thud with some crunch to it, and with people shouting in alarm.

I turned and looked down over the side. There was a crowd of locals down there, all gathered around the place where the new high priest had landed, with more coming from all directions to see the cause of the commotion.

I felt Luca, looked up, and found him immediately, racing toward the temple. But he was brought up short when he saw the crowd, and then he looked up and met my eyes.

*Never mind*, I told him with my mind.

"Here, now, move aside, move aside," someone on the ground below said. Oh mighty Isis, it was one of Po's men. As the crowd parted I pulled my gaze from Luca's to look down at where Ron-du lay on the ground. His head was turned entirely backwards. Luca was looking too, and when he looked back at me again, his eyes were wide. I shrugged.

Hurried footsteps came behind me so I had to turn away from him.

Betta led the High Priestesses. They were still dressed in their finest. Some wore elaborate head wraps, jeweled belts, elaborate jewelry, and all of them wore bright colored kalasiris and wraps.

They stood there gazing at me. "Where is the high priest?" Betta asked. "I understood he was up here."

I nodded my head over the railing, toward the ground. There were gasps and hurried footsteps and then they were all looking down over the wall.

"Is he dead?" asked one of the high priestesses.

"Thoroughly," Betta said. "I can see from here that his neck is broken."

"Praise Isis," someone muttered, and then everyone looked around to see who had said it, but no one owned up.

"What happened?" Betta asked. "Did he... Did you...?"

"We all saw what happened," said Lara the high priestess of Bast. "High Priest Ron-du had too much to drink at the festivities. I saw him staggering around behind the temple only a short time ago."

"He did stink of beer," I said.

"Of course he did. He came to the roof, likely with the notion he might make a drunken speech to the villagers, and he fell over the side. Such a tragedy. But we all saw it, did we not?"

The priestesses looked at her, and then one by one, their gazes all turned to High Priestess Melikka of the Temple of Ra, Ron-du's home temple. She was High Priest Po's counterpart.

She looked at me, and her eyes fell upon my shoulder. I looked down and saw the bloody scratches he'd torn into my skin, the bruising handprint just below it, and my torn kalasiris. I knew she saw them too. They all did.

She met High Priestess Lara's eyes and said, "Ron-du has always been a bit too fond of his beer. We all witnessed his... *tragic* accident."

As soon as she spoke, the others all nodded, agreeing wholeheartedly.

"There were people on the ground who saw the... accident, too," I said. It would not do for them to lie to protect me, if the witnesses below said differently. They were still down there, muttering among themselves while Po's man shouted for assistance to move the body.

High Priestess Melikka walked up beside me. She put her arm around my shoulders, a visible sign of her support that would not go unnoticed. She called down, "You, villagers below. Yes, you there. Did any of you see what happened to High Priest Ron-du?"

Every set of eyes shifted my way, where I stood at the railing. Then as one, they looked back at High Priestess Melikka, and one of them said, "He fell."

"Yeah, looked like he fell," said another.

"That's what it looked like to me," a third chimed in.

Others nodded and voices tripped over voices with similar words. *He fell. It was an accident. Looked a little drunk to me. We didn't need a high priest anyway.*

Then they all turned and walked away, not wanting any further involvement in such intrigue. But several glanced back to meet my eyes. Some gave a nod, others a smile, and a several turned fully and thumped their fist to their heart, a gesture of respect.

They had seen me, I knew they had. They had seen me resisting Ron-du's hands pushing me down, and they'd seen me drop away beneath him. They might not know what had happened after that. Indeed, from below it might've looked like he'd just fallen once I'd moved. They couldn't know for sure I'd given him an extra boost, and indeed, he might've gone over anyway, even if I hadn't. Those villagers knew I had been involved, though.

And yet not one of them spoke against me.

Some would say that the celebration of my ascension to the high priesthood had been overshadowed by the death of Ron-du. For me, it was the highlight of the week, for it seemed like validation of my power, and of the might of Isis flowing through me.

His body was gathered up within the hour, under High

Priest Po's watchful eye. They wrapped it in cloth for the journey back to Luxor and carried it to a local building used by the death priests.

As soon as the body was gone, High Priest Po turned and strode back into the temple, and I knew he would be looking for me. I was not ready to talk to him just then, however, so I sent word that I too upset by Ron-du's death to carry on a coherent conversation and would speak with him before his caravan departed the next evening.

I had bathed and slept like a newborn babe with my cat ever at my side. I wore as much gold as I possessed, including a headpiece clearly crafted for a royal. It was shaped like the horns of Isis. I'd found it upon rising, on the balcony outside my window, a gift from Luca. I knew he'd visit when he could, but he wouldn't risk it with so much excitement going on.

I kept to myself for much of the day, meditating and speaking to the goddess. I emerged feeling unsure whether it had been more she or I who had given Ron-du that extra push on his way over the side. I knew for sure she was not displeased.

In the afternoon, as people rose and the temple came back to life, I went down to the garden to face Po in front of everyone. Secret walked beside me, but leapt up onto my shoulder as soon as she saw how many people were around. This was where all the dignitaries who had attended my elevation had gathered to feast before they journeyed home. I joined them there and was greeted by the high priestesses as a friend and an equal. Each of them embraced me as I came into the garden. I walked taller than I had before, held myself with more dignity. Later, Elana would tell me that there was a new fire in my eyes and that it seemed to say, "Don't test me."

Po was already there and he saw the way I was received. He noticed it. He was paying very close attention. He said, "High Priestess Rhianikki, we will speak."

"And afterward," said High Priestess Melikk, "come and eat with me near the fountain." She walked away, stroking my black cat as she passed. She was Po's equal and perhaps, his adversary. And she had made it clear she stood by me in this matter. Perhaps in all matters.

Secret jumped off my shoulder and followed her.

Po cleared his throat. "You have gained nothing by Ron-du's death. Your father will send another high priest."

I shrugged. "Eventually, he will run out of high priests to send, don't you think? I wonder when it will be your turn?"

He blinked at me in absolute shock, opened his mouth, closed it again, and puffed out his cheeks. "Are you threatening to—"

"This is the temple of Isis," I said, loudly enough so that those nearest us could hear and spread my words far and wide. "Isis wants women tending to her temple. Not men. She will not tolerate her hand-chosen high priestess being supplanted by one of Ra's cast-offs, nor by anyone else. If my father sends another high priest, they might very well meet with the same fate as Ron-du. Isis, you see, is not a goddess to be tested."

Po blinked at me, and I knew that he knew I'd had something to do with Ron-du's death. And yet he feared me just as my father had feared me. His paralyzing fear of his five-year-old child was why the great and powerful pharaoh had sent me here.

I turned and walked away from Po, joining Melikka and Lara at the bench near the fountain of Isis. Seeing jewelry upon the goddess that had not been there before, I felt my heart lighten and glow. The bangles and scarves I provided and changed and tended, had apparently been noticed by the visiting high priestesses. They had each added something of their own the collection of offerings. There were beads, precious stones, and lengths of satin. Never had Isis beamed so brightly. I could feel her approval of us all.

"When you see my father," I said to High Priestess Melikka, "will you give him a message for me?"

"Of course. I will repeat your words precisely. I have an excellent memory. What is the message?"

"I will leave him in peace only so long as he leaves me in peace, but Isis and I will tolerate no further interference in the running of this temple."

"Very good. I shall repeat it back to you. 'Rhianikki will leave you in peace as long as you leave her in peace. Neither she nor Isis will tolerate further interference in the running of the temple."

"Perhaps... of *my* temple," I corrected.

"Neither she nor Isis will tolerate further interference in the running of *her* temple," she said. And she nodded hard. "Perfect. I have committed it to memory."

"Do you think it will work?" I asked, a little of my bravado fading.

"I think the whispers of your power and Ron-du's fate will reach him long before our caravan does. I think those who saw what truly happened, now believe their priestess is even more powerful than they already thought. Yes, Rhianikki. I think it will work."

After the meal, we stood in front of the temple and watched the caravan depart. Some of the priestesses were leaving by barge, but most journeyed by land. Elana stood on one side of me, and Betta on the other. High Priest Po had approached her once, probably to ask her why she wasn't preparing to leave with the rest, but the look in my eyes, and the palm I held toward him were enough to back him away.

Each of the women had an arm round my waist, and as soon as the caravan began to move away from us, Elana sighed, "Thank goodness. It will be good to have our peaceful temple back again."

"Peaceful?" Betta asked. "Peaceful might be a stretch, considering the new leadership."

"Oh no, you are wrong, Betta. My time as high priestess will be the quietest and most uneventful ever."

Betta and Elana exchanged a look, and then they both burst out laughing as we turned to go back into our temple.

## CHAPTER 21
# CATASTROPHE

O n this sunny morning, the students and priestesses had lined up in the temple garden to practice the techniques of physical combat that I had learned from Betta, and Betta had learned from the Sisterhood of the Owl, and the sisterhood had learned from one of its branches in faraway lands. This was the new routine, one I had instituted during my very first week. At first, there had been much grumbling and complaining. Now, nearly four years later, it had become normal. No one complained anymore. The girls loved the classes. My young novice priestesses would never be defenseless against any aggressor, no matter how big or strong, and that felt very good to me.

On this particular day, I stood in the front of the girls, moving my strong arms and legs from one position to the next as the students followed along. I felt wonderful. I thought Betta's prophecy that I would not see twenty years had to be wrong. Or perhaps my fate had changed. I was feeling none of the symptoms I'd been warned would signal my impending death. I was feeling better than I ever had, in truth.

The younger girls were awkward, but some of the older girls moved with power and grace. Betta sat beside me in a large chair with great, soft cushions of purple and gold, her ever-present crooked staff in one hand.

As I extended my arm, she whacked it with the staff. "Higher. And tighter, too. That's it."

I sent her a mock scowl and the girls tittered. "Thank you, Betta." I corrected my arm position and noted the girls correcting theirs.

"If I'm stupid enough to risk my neck sharing the secrets of the sisterhood, I might as well teach them *right.*" She muttered those oft' repeated words so that only I could hear, and perhaps one or two of the most attentive and closest girls. I was sure it was a tremendous exaggeration. The sisterhood couldn't be all that bad, or Betta would have cut ties with them long ago. They were learned women, with a burning curiosity about all things. They studied the supernatural world, observed, but rarely interfered, and I'd been told they would keep the secrets of the vampires, for they feared the revelation of them could cause harm to both worlds. I could see the attraction of such a fellowship based on the insatiable hunger of the mind. I felt a sisterhood with the other high priestesses, so I understood the need for kindship and purpose.

Elana was usually in the very front row, and had mastered the moves as well as I. But this morning we'd had visitors at the front entrance before the sun had even risen, and she'd offered to deal with them and whatever it was they needed, so the morning class would unfold on time.

I executed the final move, then pressed my palms and bowed, and the students returned the gesture. "Well done.

Now you may eat," I said, and they raced to the tables where food was already piled high awaiting them; dates and pomegranates and sweet breads.

I watched them go with a smile, then fetched plates for Betta and me, filled them both, took a piece of fruit from each plate to the goddess, and then returned to Betta's side. She stayed where she was. I did not know Betta's age. I had never known it, nor had I asked, but these days she walked slowly and stiffly, with a pronounced limp, and she put more weight on her staff than she used to. Her back was bent. More wrinkles marred her face, and her wild gray and silver hair no longer had a single dark strand woven through.

I loved her, and she loved me too, though she was not supposed to. She had been sent to me to observe and record, not to teach or enlighten or protect, but she'd done those things, too.

She took the plate I offered, with thanks, then looked at the food upon it and pressed her lips.

"Is your belly still unsettled?"

Betta nodded. "Third day now. And my eye is twitching, and my sleep is restless. Something is coming."

My brows rose. "I feared you were unwell."

"Oh no, girl, this isn't illness. This is something else."

"What?"

She shrugged one shoulder. "I only know this is how it will make me feel when it happens. Sick. Sleepless."

"And twitchy," I said, but it did not lighten the expression on her face in any way.

I sighed and ate one of my dates. And then I said, "I apologize things under my reign haven't been as... serene as I promised."

"You're reign? You are high priestess of the temple, not queen."

"Not yet," I said, but I said it with a smile. Truly, if I still desired it, I could succeed my father as king. I had been a good steward of the temple. Then, too, I'd had a lot of help.

"You could be queen, you know," she said softly, grabbing hold of my eyes with hers. "You are beloved by the people."

"The people of one small village," I said. But it was false, my modesty. I went into the village daily and visited families there one by one until I'd seen them all. Sometimes I went further into the outskirts, where those who liked their privacy lived. I talked to them, and I listened. And then I spent the rest of the day solving their biggest problems. I'd helped many discover their gifts and talents, the way I had done for Beck. And so many crafters and artisans and bakers and brewers had started up, that our village had become a regular stop for every boat on the Nile. My people were thriving.

"One small village, yes. But a village where people from all over the kingdom stop to trade, thanks to you. And while they are trading, people talk. I have it on very good authority that the name of Rhianikki, true firstborn of Pharaoh, is spoken throughout the kingdom with reverence and pride. And there have been rumblings of dissent against the queen's whelps. Many question why the first-born should not be the next pharaoh."

I shrugged and the golden wrap I wore over my white kalasiris fell lower, exposing my shoulders to the glorious sun and warming me through and through. "The business of running the temple bores me, which is why Elana has kindly carried on doing most of it. The business of running an entire kingdom would kill me, I think."

She smiled at me. "You could have an Elana in the palace, too, Rhianikki. You could have as many Elanas as you might need, tending to the mundane while you do as you wish."

"I do as I wish now," I said. "Goal achieved."

She should've slapped her thigh and laughed. Would have, I thought, if she'd been herself, but she was truly out of sorts, and only continued to gaze at me as if she could read the future in my eyes.

Then Elana called my name softly, and I looked behind us to see her standing in the doorway from the main part of the temple. There were urns spilling over with flowers on either side of her, a pair of bumblebees were wobbling around on pink blossoms, drinking nectar. I smiled at their antics and shifted my gaze to Elana's. And then my stomach twisted because she looked stricken.

"What is it?" I set my plate on a nearby bench and took a step nearer.

"It's your father, Rhianikki. He... has died. The pharaoh has died."

I was so stunned that my knees turned to water. Elana grabbed my shoulders, and even Betta lurched to her feet to help, but I held up a hand. "I'm all right." And then I sat down on the bench beside my nearly untouched food. "How?" I asked. "He was strong and well, last time I—"

"I was told no one knows," Elana said. "They say he died in his sleep. But there is a rumor there were scorpions found in his bed, beneath the covers with him."

Betta rubbed a chill from her arms.

"Scorpions?" I asked. "More than one?" Because one might be accidental. Or the act of an angry god. But more than one...

"Six, or so the gossips are saying. Officially, he died in

his sleep and the cause is unknown." Elana looked from me to Betta.

Betta moved closer, so that the three of us stood in a huddle. The students and other priestesses were beginning to look our way curiously. "Go pack a bag, Rhianikki. We are leaving immediately. Elana, will you pack us up some provisions?"

"I can't just leave!" I was looking from one of them to the other in disbelief, but Elana went straight to work gathering food into an empty basket. "I am not going. Betta, I am the high priestess of this temple. I have responsibilities."

"Elana can handle it," Betta said.

"I can and will," she said, returning with a basket of food. "Betta is right, Rhianikki. You should be in hiding until we see how—"

There came, all at once, the sound of many, heavy footsteps taken in unison, a rhythmic thunder. Every woman and girl turned to look and see what was happening as soldiers marched around the temple from both sides, and I understood that they were surrounding it.

I pulled free of my friends' restraining hands, stepped into the opening in the garden's greenery, and looked at one of them, holding my head high. "What is the meaning of this? This is the Temple of Isis. The king's guard has no business here."

The man stared straight ahead, not looking at me, but over my head at some invisible spot in the distance. From behind him another man said, "The queen's guard, now, Princess. It's on her orders we've come." He shouldered between two men and set foot within the entrance to our garden. I did not back away, and I did not blink. "It's for your protection," he said.

"Do not insult my intelligence. It's for my containment."

"We have orders to let no one in or out."

"Well, that will be difficult since my personal guard Luca will be arriving at any time now."

"Luca is imprisoned, by order of the queen for suspected treason."

"Imprisoned how? Where?"

He smiled. "I was told that you would likely attempt a rescue if you knew that."

"Not attempt," I said. "He's in the rock quarry to the east, isn't he? The one so far out in the dessert that no one dares escape, lest they die of thirst in the burning sun trying to make their way to the nearest water."

His eyes acknowledged I was correct before he averted them. "I don't know where he is. They did not tell me."

But I knew. It was not as if we had a number of places to keep prisoners. When a crime was committed, the perpetrator was punished by flogging or by execution. There was very little call to keep criminals for very long.

I pictured the quarry in my mind, for I had seen it once. It was mostly exposed to the sun but there were places of shade where large rocks had been cut out and removed. At least there had been, all those years ago. The shape of the places changed constantly as rock was cut out for building statues and palaces and temples.

I hoped that Luca had shelter from the sun. My stomach knotted at the thought of him bursting into flames at Ra's fiery kiss. I closed my eyes and tried to project my thoughts the way I had been able to do with him. *If any vampire can hear me, please help the vampire Luca. He is in the quarry ten days' walk east of Luxor. Please help him.*

"For how long will you stay?" I asked the man—the

general, I corrected, finally placing his face. I'd seen him before. He had aged well.

"We stay until the queen orders us to leave," he said.

"The next order she gives you," I said, "will be to kill me." I drew a deep breath, turned, and saw that most of the students had gone inside and were probably cowering in fear. The priestesses however, which included all the girls who had been with me from the beginning, stood behind me in the ready-to-fight stance Betta and I had taught them in this very garden.

Then I turned back to the man who seemed to be in charge. "How many are you?"

"Seventy-two, Princess."

"Seventy-two large, armed, well-trained men to contain one small high priestess. The queen must fear me very much. But I warn you, Isis will protect me. She protected me when the queen tried to kill me as a little girl, and her assassin paid a dear price. You should fear Isis. Even more than you fear the villagers who adore me—and you should fear them a lot—you should fear my goddess. And me. You should fear me."

His smirk faded, as if he was no longer so sure I was bluffing. I knew my reputation had spread wide, and it was filled with whispers of my powers, my skill in magic, my fearlessness, and my temper.

"You will move your men farther away from the temple walls," I told the soldier. I pointed. "No nearer than that dying tree there in the back and an equal distance all the way 'round. There will be consequences if you do not comply."

I turned then and nodded at my priestesses. "With me." And then I went inside and started up the stairs. "Where are the students?" I asked.

"In the lesson room," Priestess Surra replied. "No windows. It seemed best."

"Go to them, Teresha," I said, addressing a priestess who was too timid to be much help in battle. "They're terrified. Tell them all is well and then distract them with a new lesson. Something fun."

She nodded and hurried away.

"Is the cook still here?"

Elana nodded.

"And the kitchen fire, is it still burning?"

"The bread was baked this morning. There would still be coals."

"Excellent. Tell the cook to stoke the fire hot. Tell her to fill every pot with water and heat them all to boiling. We'll need pails, to carry the hot water up here." Elana and Betta gaped at each other, but then with a shrug, Elana rushed off to deliver my message to the cook. I turned to the priestesses. "Who among you is strongest?"

Surra and Min raised their hands and I nodded at them. "When cook heats the water to boiling, pour it into pails and carry it up here. Fill the pails only partway, so the hot water doesn't splash and scald you. Use thick fabric to protect your hands. Move with care, but the quicker the better."

They obeyed immediately. I imagined it occurred to them what I was up to by the time they reached the cella.

I walked to the edge of the roof and gazed down over. The soldiers were still gathered so near the temple that I had to extend my head over the side to see them. They'd taken off their helmets in deference to the day's heat. One of the newest priestesses, whose name escaped me, gasped, and I felt a tug on my waist. She'd grabbed hold of my sash, so I wouldn't fall off the roof.

"Careful!" she said. "Remember what happened to that high priest who came here that time. It's dangerous up here."

It is dangerous up here, I thought, especially when I am up here.

While I awaited the hot water, I paced the rooftop. The priestesses watched me but did not approach. I saw their love and concern for me in their eyes. They knew what was happening as well as I. I was a threat to the queen and her sons. The throne should be mine, both ethically and legally. And I was more beloved by the people than any of them.

The queen was known to be arrogant—because she was. She set herself apart from the people and looked down on them. Her sons were spoiled, entitled fourteen-year-old criminals. From all accounts, and I heard many, they bullied and abused, took what they wanted from merchants without paying, and had sex with any beautiful girl they desired, sometimes at the same time. And it need not matter whether the girl returned their affections. She needn't even be willing.

And yet, I did not want the throne. I loved the temple. I loved my life within its walls. And if I were to die before twenty, I wished to do it here.

Betta stepped into the path of my pacing, closed her hand around my wrist and said, "You must leave the temple. As long as you are here, you put them all in danger."

"They only want me," I said.

"They want you, yes. They want you dead," Betta said, and I could not deny it was the truth. "Every woman and girl here will try to protect you. With their lives, they'll try. As will any villager who's given the chance. As will I, my beautiful girl."

I closed my eyes. My time in this place, my home, was

coming to an end. And I felt sure that if I left, I would never see this place, nor these women, again.

Surra and Min returned with the water, and I directed them, one to the left wall and one to the right. Behind them, Elana came with stacks of clay vessels.

"Everyone take a smaller vessel and fill it with hot water, then spread yourselves all around the edge of the roof. Take care not to burn yourselves."

I took a vessel myself and went to the nearest pail. Surra was using a long-handled dipper to dispense the hot water. I set my vessel down as the others had done, moved my hands clear to let Elana fill it, then took it up again, using my wrap to hold its hot sides.

It took only seconds for each of us to be in place with a full vessel. "I told you to move your men away," I called down, for I had spotted their leader and stationed myself right over his head. "And I also told you there would be consequences." I dumped my water, and while he was yelping, the others dumped theirs.

Soon the men below were all yipping and howling and moving away from my temple. I watched only for a moment, for there was much to be done. The sooner I got away from these women, the better.

"Proceed with your day as far as you can while indoors," I told them.

They all left smiling and clasping one another's hands in celebration of a battle won. I turned to Betta, who had stayed behind. "You're right. I need to leave, or they'll be in danger. I have so loved it here."

"Pack the things most meaningful to you," she said. "I know a place where you'll be safe."

# CHAPTER 22
## EXODUS

"Our cook has to leave." I stood at the garden's entrance shortly after the evening meal, with Betta beside me. The captain of the guard was in the front of the temple. This young man in his service, was in the rear, at the exact distance I had demanded. As a result there was more space between the soldiers. His comrades were out of earshot. "She's a village woman with a family at home awaiting her. She's no threat to anyone. And you can clearly see, I am not going anywhere. I am right here. And I'm one the queen wants... contained."

The young soldier flinched when I said that, and I sensed a weakness and decided to widen it. "She's going to order you to kill me," I whispered. "She thinks I'm a threat to one of her sons becoming pharaoh. But she's wrong. I don't want it. I even attested to that in front of witnesses when my father was alive, just to reassure him." I pressed a finger to the corner of my eye and said, "I am so afraid."

Betta elbowed me.

I cleared my throat. "Please, sire, may my cook pass?"

"Yes, yes, of course." The guard nodded and turned to one side, indicating with his whole body that she could go."

Betta limped forward, leaning heavily on her staff. "Thank you, young man," she said as she passed him. Her limp was not as bad as she was making it seem right then. She played it up until the guard turned to face me once again. And then she picked up the pace, hobbling like mad out into the shadows.

She would give the soldiers a wide berth and head to Beck's home to beg his assistance with my escape.

In the deepest hours of the night, I waited just inside the archway threshold between garden and temple. I'd decided to leave Secret behind, for my plan was treacherous. I was as dangerous to my cat as to everyone else I loved.

I'd entrusted her to Elana. She'd sworn to keep Secret with her the night through, so she wouldn't try to follow me.

It broke my heart to leave the cat behind. But it was best for her. It was odd, though. That long ago night when I'd wished Secret could be with me for as long as I lived, I had felt something. There had been a surge of energy, a spark inside my brain. And Secret had reacted as if she'd felt it, too.

Nothing made sense. Leaving here didn't make sense. And yet our plan was in place. Help would soon arrive. I'd still come up with no better options.

Being further from the temple caused a gulf of space in between the soldiers. It also made what was about to happen a bit easier, I thought. And I was gratified that most of them were bare-headed. No hats, no helms.

One by one, villagers emerged from the shadows behind the guards. They moved silently until they were very close. A bird call was the signal, and they sprang as one, wrapping drawstring sacks lined in sticky tree sap over the heads of the queen's guard. The soldiers yanked at the bags, then at the drawstrings, then at the bags again as the villagers raced away. I ran from my hiding spot to join them, running past the guards who were struggling to free their hair from the sticky sap. They grunted and swore, but I was running like the wind.

I veered right and cut through the grain fields, the shortest route to the riverbanks, and when I reached it, Betta was already in a small boat, awaiting me. I did not hesitate but jumped in, and we were off.

I took the paddle from Betta and took over propelling us upstream, south along the Nile.

"I pray no one is punished for my crime."

"There was no crime," Betta said. "Besides, who can they punish? They did not see a single face. Earlier, I had Beck whisper to the captain that there had been strangers in town. Men with weapons. Mercenaries, perhaps."

"That was smart. One of the rumors about me is that I have a secret army at my disposal."

"You do, don't you?" Betta asked.

"I have been trying to keep my distress to myself. I don't want them to risk exposing themselves because of me." I leaned into the paddling, and kept looking back, but it was quiet on the water. There was only the soft dip and swish of the paddle, and the sounds of insects buzzing and whirring. There a fish jumped, and here an owl hooted.

"Why aren't they after us yet?"

"They'll search the temple first to make sure you aren't there. There are a few among the guards who admire you, Rhianikki."

"The one at the gate."

"And others. They know each other. They will catch a glimpse of you inside, and then realize it was a priestess who is like you."

"There is no priestess who is like me."

"It will delay them long enough. No doubt you left a path behind you clear to the river, when you came through the straw field. Some of the soldiers will commandeer boats, and others will take to the road north and south of the village. A messenger will be sent to Luxor to inform the queen. But by then we'll be well hidden."

"But if they're coming onto the river after us—"

"They won't find us. Ahead, over there." She pointed to the opposite bank of the Nile. I saw a man waiting there with two camels.

"Are those camels for us?"

"You tread the grasses and weeds all the way to the riverbank."

"That's the way you said I should come!"

"For good reason. They will be searching for you on the water. But you will be crossing the desert on a camel."

I glanced behind us once more and saw nothing, but I thought I heard them and I was certain I felt them. The water was uneasy. And then, I saw a light as someone lit a lamp to help them navigate the Nile by night.

"They're coming!" I paddled faster. When the bottom ran aground, someone leaned out over the water for us. I extended the paddle as far as I could reach, and he grabbed hold and pulled us in. Kiko!

He was a grown man now, with a wife and a child on

the way. Meela was there, too, with food sacks and water flasks. She had remained tiny, but she was healthy and happy now.

Kiko and I helped Betta out of the boat and he scooped her right up into his arms and carried her up the riverbank, not stopping until he'd settled her into a luxuriously padded saddle on the back of a camel.

Kiko said, "You have to hold here, and put your feet—"

"I've been riding these beasts since before you were born," she told him.

I had taken the little boat and was about to drag it up the bank when Kiko said, "No. Don't drag. It will leave marks in the mud. Carry it." He picked up an end, so I waded into the water to pick up the other. We carried the boat up the river bank. I could hear the muttering of soldiers in the distance. They would be near enough to see us soon.

"You must go," Beck said. "Now."

Meela draped the shoulder bags and water flasks over my shoulders, then she hugged me. "I love you, Rhianikki. Please be safe."

Then Kiko hugged me, too. "Go with Isis, my sister."

And finally Beck himself, the big lug who'd just arrived with a donkey and cart, hugged his arms around me, then picked me up and put me right onto the camel. "Go! Have a long and happy life!"

"This way, Betta said, turning the camel and starting off. My camel followed hers without me having to do anything at all.

I turned and looked back to see Kiko and Beck putting the boat onto the donkey cart. They covered it with tanned hides, then started off walking back toward the village, not by road, but by a path known only to locals, which veered inland from the river.

"Watch over them, Isis. Watch over them all, and your temple, and all who serve there. And Secret, my perfect cat. Protect them as I would."

The camel took to running, and I nearly fell off, it took me so by surprise.

"Always look ahead, young priestess," Betta said. "Never back."

I nodded, and followed for a while, until she dropped her dromedary back to an easier pace. And then I nudged mine up beside her. "I'm glad we are going east," I said. "It's where Luca is held captive, east and then north."

"Days north," Betta said. "If the sun were going to cook him, he would be ash by the time we could reach him. We are going east, then south to Ta-Seti, the Land of the Bow."

I pulled the reins and brought my beast to a halt. "I will not leave him to die. He is... family."

Betta scratched the back of her neck, bending her head to do so. While she pondered, I closed my eyes, and thought as hard as I could at Luca. I had tried many times, but as before, there was no response. He must be too far away to hear. We continued east. I did not argue. Luca was east, then north. I would not turn southward with Betta. We need not argue about it all the way there.

We rode the night through, then stopped at an oasis for a meal and nap in the shade, but we kept to its very outer edges and avoided the other travelers, and the residents and merchants who made the place their home. No one bothered us. A local woman brought a basket of grains and grasses and placed it in front of our camels. Then she bowed and scurried away.

As soon as the sun reached the horizon again, we rose,

we ate, we made sure the camels had a chance to do the same, and then we were once again heading out. And as soon as it was dark, my head was filled with Luca. He was calling out to me, searching for me, worried about me. *Thank goodness! I feared you were dead*, I told him with my mind.

*And I feared you were. I went to the temple, but you were not there. They said you escaped and the queen is furious.*

*She'll kill me this time.*

*She is occupied now with your father's funeral. There are still some soldiers seeking you, but most have been called back to Luxor.*

*Thank goodness.*

*Where are you?*

*I am with Betta. She is taking me to the headquarters of the Sisterhood of the Owl, I think. She says it's a safe place, just across the border of Ta-Seti. A full day's ride east then south, she says.*

*I will find you.*

*How did you escape the quarry? That is where they kept you, yes? I was coming for you, you know. I would not have turned south with Betta, but north to come to you.*

*If you were worried for me, you did not give it enough thought. I can jump as high as any pit they might throw me into, and I can run fast enough to escape the desert before the dawn, even from that far out. And as you know, I never drink... water.*

I smiled to myself, relieved beyond measure. *Do you know if everyone at the temple is all right?*

There was a long pause before he replied, *Yes, I saw Elana and the students, I saw the other priestess. I noticed no one missing. I will see you soon. Perhaps together we can learn the secrets of this sisterhood that knows so much about my kind, and whether they are a threat to us.*

*Anyone who knows about us is a threat to us*, I said, repeating his long ago words back o him. And it felt right including myself among them, for we shared the same blood.

"You're awfully quiet," Betta said, looking over at me.

"I am concerned about Elana and the others at the temple."

She nodded. "Staying would not have prevented their harm. Leaving might have. You made the wise decision."

"I hope that is true." Then I put on a more cheerful expression and asked, "You're taking me to the sisterhood, aren't you? They have a palace or a temple, don't they?"

She glanced sideways at me. "Yes, but you mustn't tell your vampire about it. I presume you've heard from him, yes?"

"How can you tell?"

"The darkness has left your eyes."

I smiled, but I said, "I am only relieved that we are far from our pursuers. And I think the queen will be occupied with my father's burial rites for a few days. Maybe too occupied to bother with me."

"She won't call them all off. Do not relax your guard," Betta said.

And we rode on for a while in silence

Riding a camel across a nighttime desert is an experience difficult to describe. The air was dry and cool, and every breath of wind carried sand with it, dropping it as it passed. Betta had wrapped her entire head, except her eyes. It had taken the first blast of wind to convince me to do the same, and still the stuff burrowed into my hair and clung to my skin. The camel's long easy gait rocked me like a cradle. I'd no idea where Beck had come by these magnificent beasts, but they were fine, and the saddles, of the highest quality. Fit for royalty, I thought. The animals moved at what seemed a lazy pace, but their legs were so long we ate up the distance.

"We're no longer in your father's kingdom," Betta said on the second night. "And our goal is just beyond that rise. You see?"

"It's greener off that way."

"We are going into the green lands, but only just. The Sisterhood of the Owl has an agreement with the king of this land. I don't know anything about those parts of things, though. Not what it is, nor who made it. I only know they leave us alone here."

We rounded a barren mound of desert-dry earth, and soon our camels were stepping among patches of gnarly grass. And the further we journeyed, the more there were, and up ahead, trees like I'd never seen, short with wide tops. In the shade of their wide boughs, the grasses and other plants grew in great abundance, and far ahead, two hills distant, I saw the thatched rooftops of a village.

"Is that village where we're going?"

"No, well this side of it," she said. "It's not far now. You could see it from here, if they didn't keep the building well concealed, so as not to invite the curious."

"Oh." I took a moment to call out to Luca. *We're nearly there. There's a village south of the border, and she says the place is this side of it, but well concealed.*

*That's only helpful if I know where you are now.*

His immediate reply reassured me. It was a long journey across the desert between where he'd been, and where I now was. I knew he had to find shelter by day, and that could not be an easy task, in the desert.

*It's the place where the village first becomes visible. To a mortal. Which probably tells you nothing.* I felt his laughter. I also felt his weakness. *You're pushing yourself too hard. You feel exhausted.*

*Tired, not exhausted. I'll have to stop again soon. Damn the daylight. But tomorrow night, I'll make it to you.*

*What part of tomorrow night?* I was eager to see my friend again. He'd kept his distance, he said for my protection. He didn't want anyone to connect him to me in case his secret were ever discovered. So we seldom saw each other.

Luca was one of the few people I trusted. I could count the others on the fingers of one hand. I trusted Beck, and Kiko, and Meela. I trusted Elana. I even trusted Betta, despite that she had kept things from me for a large part of our relationship. She'd made up for it. She'd saved my life and helped me escape the queen's reach. I began to relax for the first time since the soldiers had surrounded the temple. We had left Egypt behind. We were safe, and our haven was just ahead.

We rode around the base of large mound of still barren ground that rose higher than our heads. There was one other I trusted, I thought. The beautiful man whose face I'd seen in the fortune teller's scrying crystal. The one who had so struck me when first his image had appeared. I'd learned that I could conjure that image again in my own scrying mirror, or a pool of still water, or sometimes in a candle's flame. But with it came a sense of great distance and an even greater gulf of time. I sensed so much time between us that I wondered how I would ever catch up to him.

I started to ask Betta about it when something from

atop the earthen mound hit me, knocking me off my camel. My back hit the ground, and the thing that had hit me was on top of me—a soldier, raising his dagger over his head.

I heard Betta's wild cry, high pitched and warbling. Her camel charging toward us was just beyond the blade speeding downward. I could not believe it when the blade sank into my chest as Betta's camel hit the man full-on. The descending blade wrenched inside me and I screamed from the very root of me. The sound emerged low and deep, driven as if from the depths of my chest by that blade.

I felt Luca's shock, knew he was reaching out in fear and worry.

I turned my head to see the soldier rolling to his feet, lunging after the camel, grabbing Betta's ankle to pull her from its back.

I got up with the knife still in my chest, and staggered after him as he tugged on her leg, and Betta tried to kick free. I pulled my own blade from the cord at my waist, and with one more lunge, sank it deep into his neck from behind. Everything in him stopped. He went limp where he was, and dropped to the ground, dead before he landed

I sank to my knees, and wondered if I were dead as well. Betta climbed down from the camel's back, fell when she landed, then pushed herself up on all fours and crawled to me. She clasped my face between her soft hands.

"Rhianikki. My Rhianikki, you must hold on. You must not die."

# CHAPTER 23
# ESCAPE

I looked down at my chest, where the pain had faded. My mind, I thought, could not process so much of it. The ornate blade was the kind carried by my father's army. My step-mother's army. The handle was tilted toward the center of my chest. Twisting my head to the left, I lifted my left arm, and saw the blade's tip sticking out there.

"Get this thing out of me."

"You'll bleed out if I do," Betta said. "I'll catch the camel. We need to get you to—"

She stopped and I realized why as the sounds of plodding hooves and something that creaked came our way. We both saw it, a beast such as I'd never seen before, with a woman riding on its back. It pulled a cart toward us. The animal was rather like a donkey, but far larger and more powerful, with longer legs and smaller ears. It was the most beautiful creature I'd ever seen, besides my cat.

It stopped beside us, and the woman lowered the wrap from around her solemn face.

"Mathilde, thank goodness!" Betta said. "She needs our help."

"We saw. Let's get her onto the cart, yes?"

Betta took hold of my feet, and the other woman, who was far younger with dark brown skin, tightly braided hair, and eyes that held the world inside them, took my arms. They lifted me onto the cart, and the pain returned and emerged as another deep cry. I felt my own blood soaking my shirt.

"We have to stop the bleeding," I said. "I have... a condition."

"A bleeding condition, we know." The woman nodded to Betta. "Ride on the cart with her. Use her wrap. Wad it tight and press both sides where the blade goes in. Press hard."

Then Betta was leaning over me, tearing strips from my wrap, and winding them up. "What is this animal?" I asked, though our rescuer was no longer within my sight.

"It's called a horse," she said.

And then the cart jerked into motion and I screamed, and then Betta pressed those wads of cloth to either side of the blade in my chest, and I screamed again.

When I next awoke, I was lying in a bed with a mattress so soft, I thought I was home, in my own room, where the other girls and I had stitched cloth together and stuffed it with cattail fluff.

I opened my eyes, expecting to see my room and my cat. But instead, I found myself gazing at a window that was not my own. It was square, not arched. And the stone walls were of a dark gray, not the sandy reddish rock of Egypt. And there was whispering.

I turned my head so I could locate the source of the whispers, and saw Betta, thank goodness, nd that woman who'd ridden the strange animal. I tried to recall what she'd called it. Horse, yes. And there had been a cart.

I recalled all at once the blade sinking into my flesh, and angled my head to see it, but it was gone. My chest was swathed in thick bandages that wrapped all the way around my upper body, including the wound underneath my left arm. It seemed the pain came awake just then. It hurt more now than it had before.

At least I was alive.

"I do not expect her to survive the night," the woman said.

"I fully expect her to, Mathilde. She's strong. Her will is like none I've known, and her bond with Isis—it's real. And powerful. If it is not her time, trust me, Isis will not let her die."

It was an odd proclamation, I thought, from one who had predicted I wouldn't live to see twenty.

The other woman nodded slowly. "Perhaps she will pull through. But either way, it must happen on its own. It must follow the natural order. No intervention can be permitted. Do you understand?"

"I'm not sure I agree," Betta said softly.

"You've just told me her connection to the goddess is both genuine and potent. Her abilities frightened the very pharaoh so much that he sent her far away from his sons to protect them."

"And yet she saved their lives," Betta said.

"As one of them, she would be unstoppable," Mathilde said. "I know you care for the girl—"

"She's not a girl. I don't think she ever has been."

"Perhaps she will pull through on her own," Mathilde said at length. "But there will be no vampiric intervention. We cannot permit it."

"It's not our mission to permit it. We do not get to decide which humans change and which don't. That has never been our position."

"They are propagating faster than you know," she said. And then she took a breath, and went on. "You've been away. You need time to adjust to being home."

"Yes. I am tired." Betta paused, then said, "I don't think you could stop the vampires, though, should they decide to come for her."

Betta knew Luca would make it here tonight. I had told her as much.

"Flaming arrows will stop them," Mathilde said. "We have archers lining the rooftop on all sides. And we're placing torches around the perimeter to illuminate the entire area. The vampires will not get in. I need to know, Betta, where do your loyalties lie? With us, or with the undead who wish to claim the princess?"

"How dare you ask me that?" Betta snapped. Then there was a long moment when nothing was said at all. Then at last, she went on. "Have I not spent thirteen years away from home on behalf of the sisterhood? That you question my devotion after I've lived my life for this organization offends me deeply, Mathilde. And on my first day back."

Mathilde looked at her, then slanted her gaze my way and I didn't close my eyes in time. "She's awake."

I was, once again, feeling unsure about Betta. Surely, she would not try to keep me here. The two women came to the bedside. As scrambled as my thoughts were, I knew better than to reveal what I'd heard.

"How are you feeling?" Mathilde asked from my right, while Betta pulled back a blanket to examine the bandages on my chest.

"Grateful," I said. It would not do to reveal the anger rising inside me. She had revealed herself to be my enemy. "You saved my life. I'll see to it you are rewarded in equal measure." I pushed myself upright in the bed, though it hurt my chest terribly and my head swam.

Mathilde put a hand to my shoulder before I rose very far, though. "You've lost a great deal of blood. You're weak. You must rest."

What I must do, I decided, was speak to Betta alone.

Or maybe not. Could I even trust her?

"I'm thirsty," I said, since I didn't see any water around.

Betta turned as if she would go, but I grabbed her hand. "Don't go. I'm... afraid."

It was not a lie. I was afraid I might have to hurt someone to get out of this place. But if that was what it took, I would find the strength. I was not willing to die this night. I had barely even begun to live. And I had yet to meet the man in the crystal ball, whose eyes haunted my soul.

"I'll get water," Mathilde said. "And food, too. Do you feel you could eat?"

"I could try," I said.

Nodding, she turned and left the room. I sat up, pushed back the covers, and had my legs over the side before Betta could try to stop me.

"You're too weak, Rhianikki."

"Because I am dying," I snapped. "Are you going to stand by and let me go, or help me get out of this place?"

She pressed a finger to her lips and glanced nervously

toward the curtained doorway, and I understood that someone might be listening. I lowered my voice. "They're going to try to kill any vampire who comes to help me, Betta. Including Luca. All to ensure my death." My eyes widened. "They might be in league with the queen!"

"The Sisterhood of the Owl is not in league with your step-mother. They only care about preserving the natural order."

"The Chosen become vampires," I said. "If they desire it, and if the vampires deem them worthy, I suppose. *That* is the natural order."

"There's never been a vampire like you would be," she said slowly. I had the feeling she was having this argument internally, as well. "They fear you."

I held her eyes and let my anger show in mine. "They should."

I heard footsteps in the hall, and she swallowed hard, crossed the room to gather a vessel from a stand near the window. She brought it to me. "Drink this water. Quickly. What Mathilde brings might contain a sleeping powder. She does not intend to let you leave this place tonight."

I brought the vessel to my lips and tipped it up, took a long drink, then returned it to her and wiped my mouth with the back of my hand. "Thank you, Betta. I... I love you, you know."

She smiled at me, and her eyes were watery.

Betta left the room, and I laid down to feign weakness while I awaited the food I must not eat. I did not feel hunger. I would not need to fake that. I glanced toward the window, as the sun touched the horizon, and as it lowered, so did my eyelids. They fell as if weighted, and a wave of something washed over my brain.

And then I flashed my eyes wider. The water! Betta had given me drugged water. I lurched from the bed, fell to my knees from the stabbing pain in my chest, then thrust a finger deep into my throat. I gagged myself enough to bring the water up. My stomach was otherwise empty, so the mess was minimal. There was an extra blanket folded on the foot of the bed, and I kicked it over the puddle, then poured the remaining water from the jug into the pile it made. I fell into the bed again just as the door opened.

I kicked at the covers and moaned, hoping it would explain my position in the bed and the blanket on the floor. But I kept my eyes closed, and my vocalizations incoherent. Inwardly, I was chanting to Isis for power against the drug. I'd only taken a single draught and I thought I'd got most of it up. I must be stronger than the small amount that had made its way further into my body.

"By Isis, is she feverish?" Betta asked, hurrying closer.

Mathilde came right on her heels, but I noted no smells of food, no trays clattering on the stand. She must've known I'd be asleep upon her return. She hadn't even bothered to bring a meal as a ruse.

Had Betta known the water was drugged? Had they planned this together, the two of them?

I felt Betta's soft hand on my face, and then she said. "No fever, praise the gods. Must be the pain making her thrash in her bed."

285

She pulled my blanket back over me. I willed her not to go pick up the one on the floor.

Mathilde said, "She'll sleep now. And she needs it if she's to have any hope of healing."

But Betta stayed near the bed when Mathilde walked away. I dared not peer out, but I felt her movements. I heard her picking up the water vessel on the stand, upright and empty.

We'll leave someone outside the room—in case she needs anything. Come with me, Betta. We need everyone to help keep watch. If the vampires come for her—"

"*When* they come," Betta said. "For they will. They are compelled to help the ones like her. I'm not sure they can help themselves."

Mathilde was silent for a moment. Then she said, "This is not sisterhood knowledge. Where did you come upon it?"

"I heard it from someone who heard it from a vampire."

For a moment I felt them both looking at me, and then Mathilde said, "Come, I need you with me. She will sleep now, I think."

"You won't stop her from doing as she wishes, Mathilde. To attempt it is the act of a fool."

"She's an ordinary girl, not a god, Betta."

"I think perhaps she is, a little bit."

"I'll leave someone outside, to watch over her. Come, the sun is nearly gone. They could be on us in moments."

I heard Betta's sigh as she followed her sister from my room, and just as quickly as their footsteps faded, I poured myself out of the bed, onto the floor, dragging my pillow with me. And then I made my way across the floor, pulling with my hands and sliding. My eyes wanted to close, and my head was spinning.

*Luca!* I thought with all my might. *Do not come to me. They...*

The room spun so wildly I had to close my eyes and press my hands to the sides of my head. The sensation was sickening and debilitating.

I sat very still. I willed it away. It passed.

*They have archers on the roof and flaming arrows. I'll make my way out to a safe meeting place.*

*Rhianikki?*

I opened my eyes and looked up toward the window. It was dark beyond its square opening, but only just. The night was a newborn. He'd only just awakened.

*Do not come to me,* I told him. *They've lined the rooftop with archers and lit the area all around. They're waiting for you, Luca.*

*Why does your energy feel so strange? Are you injured? Drugged?*

*Both. Stay away. I'm coming out.* I pushed myself to the wall, then reached up to grab the lowest edge of the window. It took everything I had to pull myself to my feet. I took up the pillow, hugged it to my aching chest.

*You're coming out, how?*

*The window,* I told him, and then I hauled myself over the edge. *I'm only on the second level."* The pain was beyond endurance, and yet I endured. I looked down. No one below me, but there were people in the distance here and there; women, walking in the night, watching for vampires. They were brave, I'd give them that.

I looked up, but from this angle I could not see the rooftop archers. Which meant they could not see me. And directly beneath me there was only the earth, with those thick bunches of grass that were everywhere out here.

I pulled myself up, and then over the window's stone

sill. Halfway out I tried to turn sideways, moving my lower half out over the edge. I would dangle from my fingers to make the drop shorter. But as soon as my body weight shifted, over the side I went. There wasn't even time to put the pillow between myself and the ground before I hit it, and the impact drove the air from my lungs. That was fortunate, for the pain was so bad, I'd have screamed the place down, otherwise.

## CHAPTER 24

# REDEMPTION

I landed on my left side, the same side as the knife wound that was killing me. I'd lost too much blood, they said. I was dehydrated from my long journey, thirsty as hell. I spotted the well only a few feet from the dark stone building, and I longed to drink as much water from it as I could hold. It was made of stacked stones of that same dark color as the building, in a large square shape, waist high or so. It cast a dark shadow, like a path from it to me.

I moved a few steps away from the building, keeping to the shadow thrown by the well that was my goal. I saw a water pail beside it and licked my dry lips. I took another step, but then wobbled and nearly lost my balance, I was so weak.

I crouched low, my hands on the ground to help me balance, and looked around and then up. I saw the archers. Their gazes, however, were fixed unflinchingly outward, toward the very farthest edge of light cast by the torches. They would not look down at me unless I made a sudden movement or sound.

Farther than the immediate yard, out near the torches, women passed back and forth every couple of minutes. They must be circling the building, I realized, evenly spaced. There was a brief span of time between them passing. I started to count. I got to fifteen.

When the passing guard stepped out of sight, I hobbled forward, keeping to that shadow-path and counting in my head. Halfway to the well, dizziness swamped me. I toppled, but caught myself on my hands, and managed to land soundlessly. I was still counting. Twelve, thirteen... I pushed up and forward, graceless and clumsy, and I when I reached the well, I fell against it. My hands hit the uppermost stones and they gave way. I panicked, grabbed hold and kept from tumbling in—just barely. Then I sort of hung there, holding the loose stones while they held me.

I took a few breaths, looked around to make sure I had not been seen. Not one gaze was focused my way. And then I moved silently to the pail and picked it up. Water sloshed inside it, and I was glad, for I couldn't see water in the well. It was a long way down, if it hadn't dried up entirely. I took the pail and sank to the ground, my back against the stacked stones, my body in the well's shadow, the pail between my legs. I tipped it up and drank. And then I drank some more.

Then I let my head fall back against the stone and wiped the back of my hand across my mouth.

Luca's energy came across the distance, his message reaching me as if he were speaking it into my ears. *I'll be there soon, Rhianikki. I'm only an hour away now.*

*You seem as drained as I feel,* I said, though it wasn't quite true. He felt tired. I felt... as if I were fading away, bit by bit. *Does moving so fast for so long sap a vampire's strength?*

*We do better with shorter bursts of speed, it's true. But I'll manage.*

*You should rest,* I told him. *You should... you know... feed.*

*I can sense your energy too, you know, Rhianikki.*

If he could feel how very impermanent I felt, he would charge in here even if fire rained from the heavens.

*There are others gathering near. Your distress is felt by all. And while we are not many, we are loyal. We take care of our own.*

My head had dropped upon my shoulder. I no longer possessed the strength to hold it upright. *Am, I that? Your own?*

*Tales of Rhianikki, firstborn of pharaoh, favored by Isis, one of the Chosen, Priestess of her temple—*

*High priestess.*

I realized I had let my guard down when I felt alarm ripple through him. And if he were that alarmed, I must be nearer death than I had thought.

*Do not expend any more energy than you must. Do you hear? Be still. Count your breaths. Relax your mind. Stay alive. Help will be there soon.*

"Warn them," I whispered, accidentally aloud, "about the archers."

"Warn who about the archers?" The voice was that of a woman I did not know. She was foreign, light skinned with eyebrows so fair they seemed absent and vivid copper hair. She stood over me looking down at me with cold, unfeeling eyes. "We're not going to let you become one of them," she said. "We're doing what's best for you. For all of you."

"I know... what's best... for me," I said.

"You aren't in your right mind."

"My mind is... clearer than it has ever been. I want to come back inside. But I'm... too weak. I don't want to die on the ground. Please, help me." I raised up my arms and reached for her. She hesitated. I braced my feet flat on the ground and bent my knees slow, so she wouldn't notice. My breaths were more and more shallow. I tried to breathe deeper by will, and I wiggled my fingers at her. "I can't get up on my own."

She reached down. She went to take my hands, but I clasped her wrists instead, and then I called the very might of Isis through me, and I pulled her as hard as I could. Her head smashed into the stacked stones, which gave way and tumbled into the deep well with her right behind them. She did not have time to scream. I heard one distant splash and then no more.

The splash had been distant and muted, but it still might have been heard. I looked up, and my eyes fell upon Betta's. She stood nearer the building, close to where I'd landed below my window. She held my eyes, and I held hers.

Then she cupped her hand to her mouth and shouted, "The girl has escaped." And as my heart broke, she spoke the rest. "She's heading northward from the front!"

I heard the commotion as every woman on the ground ran around the building, and everyone on the roof headed that way, too.

I grabbed onto the crumbling stone well to pull myself up to my feet. But the stone gave way, and I stumbled.

Betta ran to me, clutched my shoulders and lifted me upright. "I'm sorry I brought you here. I did not know... Things have changed. Things here... something is not right. But I did not know. Please, Rhianikki, please forgive me."

I put my palm to her cheek, and said, "I want to believe you." But she'd handed me right over to them. And she did not fight to free me. I turned away from her and started walking, dragging my feet with each painful step, in the opposite direction from where she had sent her precious sisterhood.

I'd gone not far at all, when a blur became a woman. A vampire. Violet. I was so happy to see her, I could barely contain it.

She looked behind me, and said, "I'll kill her for you."

"No, don't kill her. She let me go, in the end. And I've learned much from her. But... but... I don't think I'm going to..."

My world went black. The last thing I felt was the vampire's arms closing around me.

## CHAPTER 25

# THE DARK GIFT

I opened my eyes, and they widened in wonder, for I was seeing as I had never seen. Colors I'd have called green or red or blue before, were myriad shades now, and I could see the waves of energy that rippled from them. And there were so many colors to see. I was surrounded in lush, green plants and towering trees, and I heard the word *jungle* in my mind. It felt as if the jungle itself had said it.

I had once eaten a mushroom to induce a journey into the spiritual realms as part of my training with Betta. I saw now, as I had seen then. I saw that everything around me was a living being, and all of them with some degree of sentience. Trees felt denser and slower than grasses. Grasses felt denser than insects.

I could smell the animals all around us. Big cats. Tiny lizards. Spiders as large as my hand. And the birds—there were so many birds, making so much noise it was as if a riot were going on.

I sat up, bracing myself against the pain I expected to rip through my chest, but it did not come. And I didn't have to struggle to sit up. I sat up easily and bounced up onto my feet without hesitation. I looked down at my body, dressed in a long red kalasiris, and searched the length of each arm and leg. "What *is* this?"

"This is your new life, Rhianikki," said a soft voice. It was the vampire Violet. "You are a vampire now. My blood runs in your veins."

"And a little bit of mine," said Makeet, sitting nearby.

"And a lot of mine." Luca's deep voice was reassuring, and I spun to face him. "Luca!"

"And I'm not alone." He pulled his arm around from behind his back, and there, snuggled in the crook of his elbow, was a sleek black cat.

"Secret!" I took her from him and hugged her to my chin. "Oh, Secret, how I've missed you!"

She sniffed me, then she growled a little, and then sniffed again. "I seem different to her. Oh! Listen! Do you hear it?"

"We hear everything, but we'll teach you how to—"

"You needn't hear everything," I said. "Just focus on the things you wish to hear."

They looked at each other and laughed, and I understood that was what they had been about to teach me.

Luca and Violet came to either side of me. She put a friendly arm around my shoulder, and we walked. Secret jumped from my arms but kept pace beside us.

"Where are we?" I asked.

"A great jungle," Luca said. "I've heard it called a rain forest. There was a road, well, a worn track, at least, from where we found you, to here. It goes further."

"It's so alive. And so different from the desert."

He nodded. "I was made by the second vampire in existence, Rhianikki. And the older the vampire, the more powerful the blood."

"Yes, I know this." I loved the way my cat followed along at my side, her gait perfectly paced to mine, and so close her side rubbed my calf with each step.

"His blood runs in you," Violet said. "As it does in me. That makes you a very powerful fledgling vampire."

"Oh, I have a revelation for you, Violet. I would have been a very powerful vampire either way."

"I don't doubt it."

We walked a bit farther. "Will you tell me your real name?" I asked Violet.

"How do you know Violet is not my real name?" she asked with a look toward Luca.

"I don't know how I know, but I knew it the first time you said it was. Your true name is... important to you."

"It is a name of which I've never been worthy. It was my mother's name," she said. "Once I thought I would give it to my daughter, someday, but it wasn't to be."

"So why not use it yourself, then?"

"I have told you why." She cleared her throat. "Rhianikki, the queen has redoubled her efforts to hunt you down. Her guards are in pursuit, even now." Then she looked up. "Odd."

"What?" Luca asked.

She shook her head. "Nothing."

I lowered my head. "My father's funeral rites are long over. Now the queen can focus on what's most important to her. My end."

"You should change your name, as we all have," Luca said. "She will only stop pursuing you if she believes you are dead. Mine was Iskur, in my first life. Soon it will change again."

"I'll give it some thought."

"Your appearance," too," Violet said, and when I

scowled at the suggestion, she added, "She'll never stop hunting you, Rhianikki. And—"

"I already know what you are going to say. The queen's hunt for me, now that I am a vampire, puts all vampires at risk of discovery by someone other than those...owl sisters."

*The Sisterhood of Athena.* I heard those words whisper through my mind, and wondered who or what Athena was. I'd never heard the word before. Or was it a name?

It was a name. I saw a flash in my mind. I was standing in a room surrounded by people I loved, who wore faces I did not recognize. *He* was there. My beautiful vision. My someday love. He was there with me, and he might've been weak or injured, but I was... I was magnificent. The terrified women holding useless weapons around us were the same, somehow, as the women who'd tried to keep me in that place I'd only just escaped. And they called themselves The Sisterhood of Athena. And their symbol was still an owl.

"Rhianikki?"

I blinked out of the vision, back into my real present.

"We have not traveled far enough," Luca said. "We've never been this far south before. There are even more distant lands, where we could—"

"I'm going back," I said.

Luca closed his eyes. "I was afraid you would say that." Then he lifted his head, and looked up ahead of us. "It's so odd, I keep feeling..."

"You're right, Luca," I said. "She will never stop pursuing me, and it puts all of you at risk."

"All of *us*," Violet corrected. "You're one of us now."

"I must kill the queen. Then her sons can fight over the throne. One will die and the other will take it, and they'll forget all about me. It's the only way. I need to kill her. I need to rip her neck open and—" I stopped myself, my eyes widening at the direction my thoughts had taken just then.

"You are hungry," Luca said. "You must feed."

I made a face. "Drink blood, you mean."

"Not today, you won't!"

A woman barked the words as she stepped out of the shadows. It was Mathilde, and she held a child with a knife at his throat. There was something about the little boy that beckoned me, that compelled me.

*He's one of the Chosen*, Luca told me.

Men emerged from the foliage, and so did women of the sisterhood, all of them armed. There were swords and knives and spears and many crossbows with their bolts aimed at our chests. Violet moved nearer me, but stopped when the arrow turned her way.

"Do not move," Mathilde said. "We've no wish to kill you or the child."

"What is it you wish, then?" I asked. "For the deed you were so desperate to prevent has been done." I bared my fangs and hissed at her. I didn't know what made me do it. It felt instinctive. At my feet, my cat arched her back and did the same.

"This is wrong!" Betta stepped from the jungle. She held no weapon. Her face was a picture of devastation. "Our mandate is to observe. 'We shall observe and record. We shall intervene only to protect the supernatural order, which is entirely part of the natural order,'" she quoted. "So, say the scrolls of our way."

Mathilde lowered her eyes. "In this case, the supernatural order is a threat to the natural order. Rhianikki is too volatile a being to be entrusted with so much power. You heard her just now. She's been turned for mere hours, and already making plans to assassinate the Queen of Egypt."

Men came running to join them, but they were not my father's army. They were dressed randomly, some quite raggedly, and I searched their faces, I saw one that tugged at my memory. He had orange hair, like a baboon. I had seen him before—

At the camp of the child thieves!

*How did we not sense their presence?* Luca asked.

*The sisters know how to block,* I told him. *The merceneries stayed back and counted on us being distracted by their ambush. Then they ran to catch up. Look how they're sweating and panting.*

*You are nearest her,* Violet told me. *You can move faster than she can see. You must get the child while Luca and I get the weapons from the others, all right?*

*Yes.* And before I could blink, she was speeding one way, and Luca the other, moving so fast it was as if the wind whipped the weapons from the hands of the mortals who surrounded us. I flew into motion, seeing all around me as if the world was slowed down by my newborn vampire eyes. Blades and bows flew as if caught in a desert twister. I saw Luca running like a gazelle, each stride bringing him crashing into another of them. As they fell to the ground, Luca wrenched their weapons away and hurled them into the darkness with preternatural might.

Violet was his mirror on the opposite side, and as they approached the center at the speed of a hummingbird's wings, I saw Mathilde's eyes widen. And then I flashed forward and took hold of her arm, wrenched it away from the neck of the child. Then I flew with him back to a safe distance.

As soon as I stopped, I felt and then turned to see Mathilde raising her crossbow. She released its bolt at my chest.

Violet gave a bestial cry as she dove in front of the bolt, which went through her neck sideways, and still it sped toward me. My hand moved as if on its own and closed around the bolt, stopping it just as its tip touched my chest.

Violet was on the ground at my feet, her blood flowing like the most rapid parts of the river. Luca was on his knees beside her in an instant, pressing his hands to her neck on either side as if he could stop the flow. It would be like trying to stop the Nile.

"It's all right," she whispered. "It's already done."

"If we can stop the bleeding, you'll heal with the day sleep."

"But you can't," she said, "and the dawn is too many hours away."

I knew it was true, and I tipped my head back and roared as I turned my gaze to Mathilde, who was standing there, frozen, staring and trembling as her sisters and the soldiers all scattered in search of their weapons—or perhaps they were running away. It got very quiet, very quickly. Betta stood near a large tree, as if she too, were rooted there. She held the little boy in her arms.

Mathilde could've run away with the others, but she didn't move. Maybe she knew I would catch her anyway. Maybe she felt death's cold fingers reaching for her even before I did. I grabbed her by her hair, wrenched her head sideways. Then I sank my newborn fangs into her throat and I drank. And I liked it. The taste of the blood awakened something primal in me, and I opened my eyes and knew they were glowing. I saw everything through a luminous red haze, and tore her neck wider to increase the flow.

*Not after the final heartbeat, Rhianikki.* Luca's energy was soaked in grief.

I felt Mathilde's heartbeat as soon as I listened for it,

and I also felt her mind bleeding into mine. Everything she knew or thought she knew about the undead, about me, about Betta, I received all at once. I could not process it, but some parts stood out.

Betta had tried to stop this. She had tried.

Mathilde had decided to order Betta's execution once I'd been dealt with. She would never go along with the program.

The program... I drank deeper as her heartbeat skipped.

Vampires were propagating too quickly. But the sisterhood knew how to identify those who could become vampires, those called the Chosen. They just watched for their vampiric protectors to show up when the child was in trouble. Sometimes they even caused the trouble. And then they sent mercenaries to steal the child. They'd stopped when vampires had butchered most of their gang. But they had not given up the cause.

*Where are the children?* I drank still more, but the gaps between heartbeats had grown very long. *Tell me!* I tore deeper. I would swallow the last of her if it would help us find...

Luca came and pulled me off her, and her spent body fell to the ground.

I stood there, alive with the power of her life force thrumming through me, and I said, "They were behind the child-thieves. This path we've been following only exists because of them going back and forth to care for them. We'll find them at its end."

"Violet wants you," he said.

Nodding, I met Betta's eyes briefly, then turned and walked back to Violet, where she lay. Luca had tried to plug the holes in her neck with cloth, but blood leaked around it.

Not much, though. The trickle was slow, and growing slower.

I dropped to my knees and took her hand in mine. "We know where the children are. The stolen Chosen."

"I heard," she said.

"You saved my life."

"I did."

"I don't want you to die," I said.

"I'm ready. But I have something for you before I go."

"What is it?" I asked. There were tears streaming down my face. I was holding her hand in both of mine.

She leaned up and I leaned down, and she whispered into my ear. And then she laid back, and I felt her go. I felt her body empty itself of all that had been her.

V

We went on, following the path that wasn't a road, Luca and I, with Betta and the little boy following behind.

"I kept thinking I felt the Chosen," Luca said. "I would feel it briefly, just a flash. And yet... " He shook his head. "I think Violet felt it, too."

"The boy isn't very strong," I said. "And the others might've been too far away."

My sense of them grew stronger the further we went. It was like a force, pulling me onward. And as I went, a fierce sense of protectiveness rose up in me like it does in a mother lioness.

We came upon a long and narrow rectangular building with a thatched roof. And as we crept nearer, we knew the Chosen were inside. And not all of them were children.

After all, the child thieves had not been active for nearly eight years.

There were men, some of those mercenaries guarding the place. Two of them, one at each end. Luca looked at me. I nodded, knowing what needed to be done.

And then we swept in like death itself.

We freed the children and made it back to the headquarters of the sisterhood before nightfall. It had been abandoned. Not a sign of anyone remained. Now that vampires knew the location of the house, the Sisterhood of the Owl would not dare return.

There was plenty of mortal food left behind in the sprawling house. Betta got busy feeding the children, bathing and clothing them.

I sat with Luca, and watched the sky begin to pale. "It is the twentieth anniversary of my birth," I told him. "I made it."

"Well, you're not really alive. You're undead."

"Oh, you are mistaken, Luca. I am more alive than I have ever been."

Betta came outside where we were. "It will be light soon."

"I know." I hugged her and said, "I will not see you again, Betta. But as soon as the sun sets, know that help will be on its way for you and the children. The soldiers on our trail might as well make themselves good for something. We'll send them to rescue the children."

"I didn't know they were behind it," she said.

"I know you didn't." I kissed her cheek. She hugged me as hard as I thought her frail old arms could manage. "Go, back to the temple," I said. "You will be a hero now, bringing these children to their homes. And Elana needs you."

"I was thinking the same."

"Tell the world I was killed. Say that you witnessed it. Say my body was being transported to Luxor, per the queen's orders, and the boat capsized on the way. Make it real, Betta. Make it believable."

"But the merceneries, and the sisters, they all saw." Even as she said it, I heard the first cry. Betta couldn't hear it of course, not with her mortal ears. The sisters and the mercenaries had run as far away as they could. Miles by now. But still I heard the sounds when the vampires found them. Their short cries came from the darkness, one after the next, but only for a few minutes.

For vampires, though few in number, tend to care deeply for other vampires, and when one is in trouble, those others can feel and sense it.

And when one is murdered, as Violet had been, they take vengeance.

Luca's howls of grief had been heard and felt by every vampire nearby. And they'd likely passed it on to others.

"There are no more sisters or soldiers to say differently," I told Betta once the sounds had gone silent."

My cat jumped up onto my shoulder, crawled over into my arms, and I turned fully away from Betta and started walking.

I returned to Luca, who still knelt beside Violet's lifeless body where we had left her before. He had placed her in a cleared spot among, the deep grasses and huge, nodding buds that would bloom with the first touch of the sun.

I knelt beside her, too. I took her hands, and I said, "I hope there is an afterlife, and I hope your journey there is kind and easy and filled with blessings and helpful guides. I've asked Isis to make it just that way. And to honor your sacrifice, I accept the name you gave me. The name you felt unworthy to bear but hoped to pass on to your daughter. The name you whispered into my ear with your dying breath. I will take your name, and in that way, some of you will live on. Every time I hear this name, I will remember that I must embody your courage, your kindness, and your fierce loyalty."

I plucked a flower and laid it across her chest to burn with her when the sun rose. As I stood again, I turned to face Luca. "From now on I shall be known as Rhiannon."

# WINGS IN THE NIGHT

*Visit MaggieShayne.com/wings*

# STAY IN TOUCH!

**Follow Maggie Shayne on BOOKBUB!**
*Bookbub is a curated list (meaning only the good stuff) of free and deeply discounted ebooks in a daily email and on their website. No charge to readers and no upsells.*

Sign up here: Bookbub.com
Follow Maggie Shayne on Bookbub here:
Maggie-Shayne on Bookbub
*Never miss a freebie or discount again!*

**Sign up for Maggie's NEWSLETTER!**
Early looks at covers, new and upcoming releases, behind the scenes trivia, dog pictures, and sometimes a recipe!

MaggieShayne.com
*Sign up at the top of the page.*

**Join Maggie on SOCIAL!**

# STAY IN TOUCH!

Maggie on Facebook
Maggie Shayne Readers Group on Facebook
Maggie on Twitter
Maggie on Instagram

# About the Author

*New York Times* and *USA Today* bestselling novelist Maggie Shayne has published sixty-two novels and twenty-two novellas for five major publishers over the course of twenty-two years. She also spent a year writing for American daytime TV dramas *The Guiding Light* and *As the World Turns* and was offered the position of co-head writer of the former; a million-dollar offer she tearfully turned down. It was scary, turning down an offer that big. But her heart was in her books, and she'd found it impossible to do both.

In March 2014, she did something even scarier. She left the world's largest publisher and went "indie."

Now, she is embarking on an exciting new leg of her publishing journey with most of her titles moving to small press publisher, Oliver Heber Books.

Maggie's *Wings in the Night* series and her non-fiction spiritual self-help books continue to be published through Maggie's own company, Thunderfoot Publishing.

Maggie writes smalltown contemporary romances like the recent *McIntyre Men* series, which boasts "a miracle in every story." She cut her teeth on western-themed category romances like her classics *The Texas Brand* and *The Oklahoma Brands*.

Later, Maggie expanded into romantic suspense and thrillers like *The Mordecai Young series*, *The Secrets of Shadow Falls*, and her career-best, *The Brown and de Luca Novels*.

She is perhaps best known for her beloved paranormal

romances, perennial favorites *The Immortals*, the *By Magic series*, and one of the first vampire romance series ever published, (and still ongoing) *Wings in the Night*.

Now she's writing a series of page turning rom-com ghost mysteries, *The Fatal Series*.

Maggie is a fifteen-time RITA® Award nominee and one-time winner. She has received more than thirty other industry awards for her work, and has been nominated for many more.

She lives in the rolling green and forested hilltops of Cortland County NY, wine & dairy country, despite having sworn off both. She is a vegan Wiccan hippy living her best life with her beloved husband Lance, and usually at least two dogs.

Maggie also writes spiritual self-help books and runs an online magic shop, BlissBlog.org

For additional information, visit Maggie's website.
www.maggieshayne.com

Email Maggie @ maggie@maggieshayne.com